I Am Burt King

The King of Washington

BURT KING
WITH RANDY SIEGEL

Copyright © 2012 Randy Siegel
All rights reserved.

Email: theburtking@aol.com
Twitter: @theburtking

ISBN: 1466486422
ISBN 13: 9781466486423

To The Glory of My Greatness

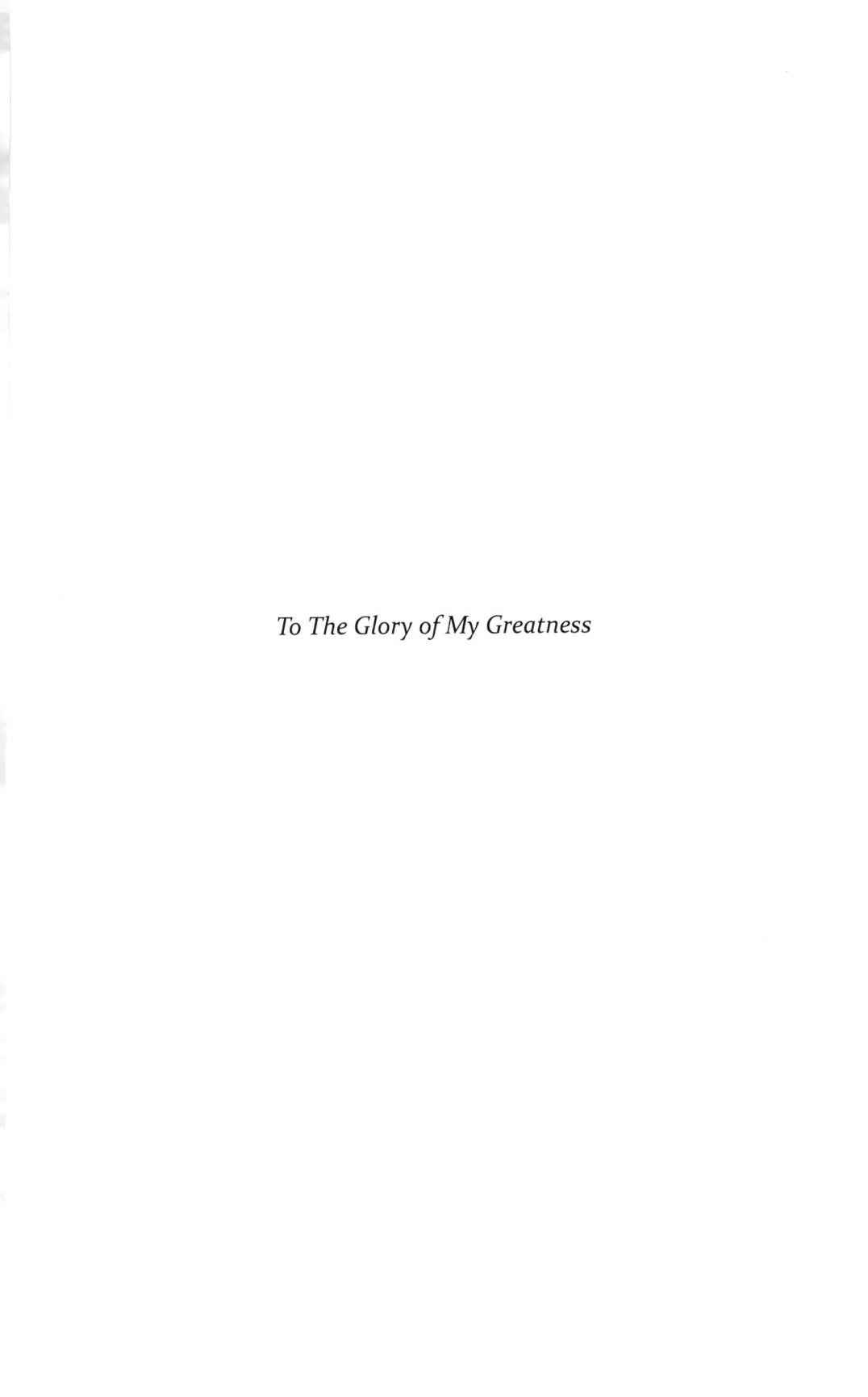

Author's Unconditional Release & Apology

On the advice of counsel, and to indemnify myself against fraudulent claims, liabilities and exposure to litigation, I hereby offer an unconditional, mostly heartfelt blanket apology to almost everyone I've ever hurt, lied to, misled or screwed, including family and former family members, friends and ex-friends, and the American people in its entirety – with only two exceptions: my intolerable mother and, of course, that rat bastard Einstein, who can go fuck himself. Nothing in this book you are reading should be construed as damaging or impugning the character of anyone or anything except perhaps, on minor occasions, myself.

To sum it all up, I unequivocally and categorically admit no wrongdoing whatsoever, for the most part. Damn. That was painful.

Obligatory Introduction

CALL ME "ASSHOLE."

To tell you the truth, which, since the shit hit the fan, I've taught myself to do as much as possible, I'm totally at peace with future historians describing me as an asshole. It's a notable mark of distinction and probably my singular defining characteristic. Just ask my ex-wives, competitors, adversaries, arch enemies, criminals and certainly my former clients, including Presidents, Vice-Presidents, Prime Ministers, Kings, Queens, Princes, Senators, Congressmen, Mayors and even a few fairly benevolent, not insidiously evil Dictators and corporate chieftains. Hey, I know I wouldn't be where I am today if I hadn't been such an asshole. And no one would know my name, let alone want to buy my book.

As I write about my life and humbly take stock of its singular significance, with the help of my unbelievably annoying, overpaid ghostwriter, I will admit that being reflective gives me tremendous headaches, along with occasional nausea and plenty of flatulence. I can also say, without boasting, that despite a few imperfections, I am incredibly proud to have dedicated my professional life to my country and, of course, to my bank account, not in that particular order. Yes, a few of my critics might be right. Maybe I am a little self-centered, self-absorbed and more than a little biased, but they can go shove it where the sun don't shine, because I believe I've done plenty of good for our country even if I am not necessarily a particularly good person, which I pretty much know by now I'm not. The bottom line here is that this may be the story of my life you're holding in your hands, but it's your book, which gives you the right to call me whatever you want, including "Jerk," "Bastard," "Prick," "Shithead," "Scumbag," "Ass," "Ass-Wipe," "A-Hole" and, last but not least, "Asshole." I've been called a lot worse. And I've done a lot worse.

Before I chronicle my extensive experiences and adventures, culminating in a brilliant, insightful retelling of my life and arguably the most important one-week period in our nation's history since all those dead Presidents signed the Declaration of Independence, I am compelled to set the stage. This book is a comprehensive no-holds-barred account of my erroneously reported, ridiculously exaggerated and grossly misjudged life. But since my most recent life experiences contain, by far, the most interesting and commercially viable moments of my time on Earth – especially if the movie studios come calling – allow me before I get going to quickly summarize in a few, mercifully short pages the first five and a half decades of Burt King. And what a five and a half decades it was.

I was born in New Rotica, New York, a now run-down and rotting, formerly semi-nice run-of-the mill overbuilt patch of suburbia just about 30 miles north of New York City. According to my perpetually vicious, suffocating, hypercritical mother, who haunts me to this day (more to come), I was a disappointment in every aspect of my existence soon after my emergence from her birth canal. I should let you know up front that over the course of my entire life, nothing I have ever done has come remotely close to pleasing her. *Author's Note*: I realize I shouldn't bias you from the beginning about how reprehensible my mother really is. And I know that I'm supposed to be showing you how bad she is rather than merely telling you how terrible she is. But why can't I cut to the chase in my own autobiography? I was the one who had to live through all the pain and suffering she caused me, so I've definitely earned the right to tell my story my way.

Back in the day, New Rotica was a typical middle-class suburb, full of typical middle-class families hyper aggressively striving to live their own idealized, unattainable version of the mythical American Dream. I realized early on that the people of New Rotica behaved just like rats, except the rats in our area were bigger, had tails and seemed much more content with their surroundings.

Our neighborhood on Nirvana Drive was like all the others in town, filled with little people in little houses, on little lots with little lawns and little trees and little garages, so kids like me, who suffered through intense family dysfunction and searing emotional pain, had someplace to hide.

Nowadays, downtown New Rotica is nothing but a dilapidated mess, except for a five-star, 50-story RitzLife luxury condo complex that rises above the empty storefronts and assorted societal rubble and every morning spews out well-dressed yuppies who speed walk to the nearby train station while looking back over their shoulders to make sure sneaky muggers are not sneaking up behind them. Adjacent to the RitzLife condo is its evil twin, the famous or infamous, depending on your vantage point, RitzJustice – a five-star, 50-story federal penitentiary for white-collar criminals, featuring a 100,000-square-foot Canyon Ranch spa facility inside. Not only are the two towers owned and operated by the Ritz International Luxury Living and Prison chain, but they also share the same machine-gun-toting security guards who patrol the perimeter and protect the inhabitants from the outside world and from each other. Best of all, residents of both complexes are able to share extensive amenities, including the spa and a high-end underground shopping mall that runs beneath both edifices. I distinctly remember going right after it opened to visit an old stockbroker of mine, Al Flagoli, who was imprisoned at RitzJustice for securities fraud as well as trafficking in animal porn. He took me on a tour of the joint -- it was beautiful back then, and unlike the rest of New Rotica, it seems to have held up well, despite the crappy urban rot just outside the security fence. Must be the 30-foot barbed-wire walls.

Pardon the digression. Back to my story. My parents were a disaster – to each other and to me. Can't say enough bad and sad things about them. In short, and to save time, pages, self-pity and the need for more invasive, overpriced psychotherapy, my father was an affable, obese, beaten-down, depressed patsy for my maniacal mother's reign of dominatrix terror, featuring her relentless, assaultive behavior, intimidating glares (and biceps) and, above all, her never-ending quest to neuter or, at a minimum, neutralize every single person within 100 yards. Even today, at my relatively advanced middle age, I can close my eyes and hear my mother ruthlessly screaming at my father as he sulked so dispiritedly at the dinner table, head down, shoulders hunched, accepting his emasculation while picking aimlessly at whatever overcooked turgid grub my mother had bothered to prepare.

"Why do you have to be so stupid?"

"You are such a moron."

"You're a ridiculous excuse for a man."

"I married the most pathetic pussy in the world."

"Do you want our dumbass son to grow up to be a fat fuck like you?"

And when it came to yours truly, my mother always had a laser-like nastiness that frankly should have been illegal under the Geneva Conventions. Her idea of motherhood was constantly haranguing me with cruel and inhumane cut-downs like:

"You're a loser."

"You're a failure."

"Why can't you be like [fill in the blank with any neighbor or friend]'s son?"

"I am completely ashamed to be your mother."

"When I look at you, I want to vomit."

"Why did I give birth to you?"

"You are the bane of my existence."

No wonder I was a prolific bed-wetter for such a long time. After being balled out all day, I would suffer through terror-filled, panic-attack-prone nightmares, starring my mother as the mother-of-all-evil, a hideous villain chasing after me until I was suddenly awakened by the warm then cold dampness of my pajamas and sheets, as well as the stench of urine wafting through the room.

I'll never forget what my first therapist, Dr. Carpinski, told my mother and me in his office when I was eight: "Your son's bed-wetting is a manifestation of his intense psychological desire to take refuge from his family stress and seek solace in the soothing waters of his own urine." I remember this vividly because my mother kept repeating the diagnosis in front of me, lambasting my father for being a horrible role model and then commiserating with all her friends about her "screwed-up son." A week later, at our next and ultimately final session, she terminated Dr. Carpinski after he politely suggested that she might be the root cause of my pervasive anxiety. At which point she slapped him across the face, accused him of "insubordination" and threw a chair across his desk before dragging me out to the car by my left ear.

From there, things became even more excruciating. My mother continued to berate me publicly for my bed-wetting, which created severe angst in me to the point where I began peeing on myself during the day whenever I was under maternal attack. Afterward, not missing a beat, my mother would rub my soiled underpants in my face, literally and figuratively.

"Need me to change your diaper, Mister Pisser?" It was as if she derived some perverse thrill from trying her damnedest to make me pee on myself.

But as bad as I had it – and I definitely had it bad – my father had it worse. Much worse. What my parents suffered through together was not a marriage. It was more like an ultimate cage fight, and given how vicious my mother could be, the match was over way before it ever started.

The good news was that there were no other victims in our house since I was an only child. And although I don't know this for sure, I am willing to bet that the last time my parents ever had sex was the day I was miraculously conceived.

Oops. I almost forgot one important thing about my youth. Of all the serious challenges I had to face during my seriously challenging childhood, my seriously ridiculous name ranked pretty high on the list. Although you know my name as the exceptionally distinguished Burt King, I'm taking this opportunity to go public and painstakingly admit – confirming previously unconfirmed Internet rumors that have dogged me for a long time – that I was actually born Albert Einstein Stein, thanks to an incomprehensible decision by Maude and Harold Stein, my incomprehensible parents. Yes, I had the privilege of growing up in New Rotica, New York, with the absolute worst name in the history of the United States, if not the world. Albert Einstein Stein. Pathetically sad but true!

"Why did you name me Albert Einstein Stein?" I bravely asked my mother on a particularly trying day in third grade when several of my bastard classmates tied me up and locked me in the gym equipment closet for five hours before my teacher, Mr. Cossack, even noticed I was missing.

My mother slapped me across the face with brutal force while giving me one of those looks that basically said: "Who gave you the fucking right to ask me such an idiotic question?" And then she just sat there, shaking her head, before deigning to answer my simple query.

"We hoped, Albert, you would grow up to be as successful as Einstein," she said. "You know, do well in school, become a genius, accomplish great things. Too bad you ended up being such a fucking disappointment."

"How do you know?" I protested. "I'm only in third grade."

"Trust me," she scoffed. "I can already tell. The handwriting is on the wall."

"I'm mad you gave me such a stupid name," I countered.

"I'm mad God gave me such a stupid son," she opined as she walked out of the room.

To this day, I still can't believe my mother had the gall to push my father into agreeing to name me after Einstein, perhaps the most brilliant human ever to live, who gave us the Theory of Relativity, E=MC squared, quantum physics and all sorts of other monumentally brilliant crap. Was that an insane amount of pressure on a kid to do well in school or what? From kindergarten on, every time I got a bad grade, which was more frequently than not, my mother would rant about how I wasn't doing justice to my namesake.

And it got worse in elementary school. If the bullies only beat the crap out of me before school and after school, I considered it to be a good day.

"Toughen up, you pussy wussie," my mother told me once when I came home from school with a new round of bruises. "Stop whining about being a victim. What do you expect? You're a Jew."

In case you're curious, I'm not really a true Jew (not that there's anything wrong with that), and Stein is not even our family's real name. Legend has it that when my father, Harold Pockrockski, married my mother, Martha Nicholson, she agreed to take Pockrockski as her married name. For about two months. Then she dropped Catholicism, rejected the idea of organized religion altogether and went through a brief but intense Fascist phase, which culminated in her convincing my father to legally change their last name to Mussolini. Until the following year, when she discovered Scientology, became a devotee of Diuretics and dragged my dad to court to change their name again, this time to Cruise. Until the following year, right before I was born, when she became enamored with the notion of giving Judaism a shot during New Rotica Community College's spring production of *Fiddler on the Roof*. "The Jews may be odd people," she allegedly declared on the car ride home, "but you have to admit they are impressive." The next day, she went to court to file paperwork to change the family name for the third time in three years, this time to Stein.

"Your mother thought it would be advantageous for our children – er, our child – to be Jewish," my dad confided in me the night before my Bar Mitzvah. "She had a theory that more often than not, Jewish kids worked their butts off to get better grades, get into better colleges and get better jobs." But then my dad whispered to me that he was very worried about all the baggage that came with being Jewish. "You know, the discrimination, the persecution, the pressures, not enjoying bacon with your eggs or pepperoni on your pizza without feeling a little guilty."

"Then why did you agree to becoming Jewish?" I asked, pretty much knowing the answer.

"It was her decision, not mine, so I got the fuck out of the way."

As I absorbed the magnitude of this Kodak moment with my dad, he lit up another cigarette, took another sip of his vodka tonic and stared out the window, probably fantasizing about all the different ways someone as depressed as he was could end his misery on a permanent basis.

By the way, my Bar Mitzvah was a spectacular affair – until I peed in my pants when I flubbed part of my Torah portion and my mother began balling me out, right there in temple, during the service, in front of a few hundred horrified family members and friends.

"Goddamn it!" she screamed, her shrill voice echoing throughout the temple. "Can't my do-nothing son do any fucking thing right?"

"Calm down, Mrs. Stein," said the rabbi, who risked his life by coming to my rescue. "Your son is doing just fine. Please show some compassion."

"Fuck compassion!" she said before walking out, as a wet spot spread slowly across my brand-new powder-blue suit pants.

My mother swears to this day that she has the whole mess on video somewhere and occasionally threatens to post it on the Internet. "I've never been able to find this alleged evidence, but I've vowed repeatedly to destroy it if I can get my hands on it. Unless she's bluffing, just to terrorize me a little more.

"You had the worst Bar Mitzvah in the 5,000-year history of the Jewish people!" she loves to remind me in front of others.

Somehow I survived these years of abuse and eventually made it out of New Rotica alive. Yes, despite the odds and all the dysfunctional forces trying to destroy me, I escaped. In one piece. With a small speck of sanity. And my self-confidence in tatters but still sort of intact.

The day after I graduated from New Rotica High, I took all the money I had made working after school and on weekends cutting lawns, shoveling snow and washing dishes at a local pizzeria, and ran to a RitzJustice legal clinic, where I hired a lawyer to get my first name shortened (and made more masculine) to Burt and my last name legally changed from Stein to King, which at the time was the WASPiest, most elite, most impressive-sounding last name I could think of. Who in their right mind wouldn't want to be a King? While I was at it, and for only $500 dollars more, I had my middle name changed from Einstein to Heinz, a more respectable version of the "Eins" in "Einstein." Plus, I've always loved the ketchup. It's my favorite condiment.

This long-overdue name change signified the end of a traumatic period in my life and marked my newfound sense of independence, giving me a much-needed break from my emasculating, repressive past. Being named Albert Einstein Stein never made me feel good about myself or helped me win over any women. And the ever-present Einstein comparison not only haunted me daily but had given me a textbook inferiority complex, a deep, dark place from which I would always be fighting to escape.

Yet even to this day, years after leaving home with an infinitely better name, I am still occasionally terrorized by horrific nightmares in which the ghost of Albert Einstein, my personal tormentor, invades my brain, disrupts my precious beauty sleep and assaults me with a barrage of hostile questions and venomous personal attacks. In fact, late last night, after falling asleep, Einstein returned with a vengeance. I dreamt I was walking alone naked in a dark subterranean tunnel between the Capitol and the Boeing Senate Office Building. There were no lights and I had only a flashlight to guide me. Its beam was starting to flicker and fade, which obviously meant the batteries were about to die. And there was no one around to provide any assistance, which felt especially scary because these tunnels were usually packed with Senators, staffers, police and assorted others who had access to the privileged halls of power.

The only sounds came from my footsteps. As the surrounding silence grew more disconcerting, I walked faster and faster, turning corner after corner in search of some better-lit hallway or room, or an open door that might lead to my escape. But I kept stumbling in the darkness, ramming into walls I couldn't see and tripping all over my naked self.

As I rounded one particularly sharp bend, I was suddenly blinded by a harsh spotlight. And I could hear my arch-nemesis Einstein cackle in his inimitably evil, threatening way.

"Oh my! What shameful shit-fuck do we have here today?" he asked, knowing full well the answer.

"What do you want now?" I asked.

"I want you to know how mad I am."

"About what?"

"About how you've disgraced my name, you scum-sucking loser. You've discredited everything I ever stood for. You've diminished everything I ever accomplished. Look at yourself! Not only are you a hopelessly pathetic specimen, you're an embarrassment to the human race."

"You sound like my mother," I pointed out.

"Well, she's right, you know."

OBLIGATORY INTRODUCTION

Last week's Einstein intrusion wrecked a wonderful porno dream I was having about enjoying myself on the steps of the Home Depot Jefferson Memorial with Sandra Ruiz, the bodacious anchorwoman on the Channel 7 news. Worst part was that it was a gorgeous spring evening, the cherry blossoms were in full bloom, and there I was about to do it with this exceptionally voluptuous woman, when goddamn Einstein had to appear out of nowhere and ruin everything. As is usually the case once he wakes me up in the middle of the night with his cruel vindictiveness, I was too rattled to fall back asleep, so I took too many sleeping pills, which left me even more tired and cranky than usual the next day. But there's nothing I can do about this debilitating condition. Whenever Einstein shows up, I'm screwed. Plain and simple.

One of my worst Einstein nightmares of all-time happened last month, when the bastard caused me to shriek repeatedly in my sleep (according to my wife) and wake up in a hot sweat after he crashed a bubble bath I was taking (in my dreams) with the former Miss Colorado and now distinguished Senator from the great state of Colorado, Mrs. Colleen Rubio.

"Move aside, you pussy, and I'll show you what a real man does," he bragged after jumping in the tub between us.

"Screw you," I said. "Can't you leave me alone right now? Can't you see we're busy?"

"You'll never please this woman," he scoffed. "You have nothing to offer her or the rest of humankind."

I find it frankly amazing that between my parents and my own personal Nobel Prize–winning genius ghost, I'm still a fairly functional human being and not addicted to alcohol, painkillers or both. Which isn't to say I don't have my issues. I do. But who doesn't?

I blew town as fast as I could after high school, moving to Boston for college (more on that later), then to Washington, where I've been ever since. Why Washington, you might ask? Excellent question.

Let me be perfectly clear. I wasn't interested in politics per se. I didn't give a shit about whatever the issues of the day happened to be. When it came to principles or policies, my ideology was nonexistent. I simply wanted to work in a place where I could get rich, powerful and famous fast. Because Burt King has always been a man in a hurry.

A career in high finance was out of the question because, despite my considerable strengths in other areas, I had consistently sucked in math. A movie career was not an option because I was admittedly ugly – plus, most of the entertainment companies had left Hollywood and moved to South Korea. I had zero interest in being a lawyer, because it was a dead-end profession, full of too many miserable schmucks who were underpaid, overworked and always fantasizing about doing other things with their abject lives.

But a career in Washington was intriguing on many levels. I loved the idea of so much raw, naked power concentrated in such a small slice of land. Thanks to the maternal abuse I endured at home, I knew I could be a great street fighter in politics without ever needing to use my fists. I enjoyed the idea of being engaged in constant hand-to-hand combat without having to join the Army or risk my life going to war. I also knew the corridors of power in our nation's capital were oozing with sex, which was as exceptionally alluring back then as it is today. At that time in my life, I knew Washington was the place for me, and I've never, for the most part, been disappointed.

I started my Capitol career as a lowly coffee-fetching, phone-answering intern for the Senate Department of Cafeteria and Catering Services, then worked my ass off on any campaign I could find, often as an unpaid volunteer, slaving away for days and nights and years, and working for dozens of dickwads and dolts, to become, as you undoubtedly know, the world's preeminent big bucks political consultant, bar none. I credit my success to learning as a young political hack how to run bruising, no-holds-barred campaigns, sparing nothing or no one that stood in my way. The goal was to dominate, obliterate, dismember and annihilate the opponent. Four easy steps, just like my mother's style of parenting. More symmetry than I ever realized.

The same year I moved to Washington, my feckless father – who did accounting for a regional restaurant chain until he was laid off when the owner went to jail for tax fraud as well as polygamy – decided he couldn't stand life with my mother anymore and left us for a much happier place. How did he escape? By eating and drinking and chain-smoking himself to death as fast as he possibly could. When his bloated 300-pound-plus carcass finally keeled over at the dinner table one night into a bucket of Kentucky Fried Chicken, I was initially very sad. But when I saw his face for the last time, right before they closed the casket, he looked as peaceful and content as I had ever seen him. I realized right then I had to give him props for taking control of his own destiny.

From that point on, I tried my best to never go home or look back. I went forth in life and conquered. And boy, did I conquer. Every which way I could to the point where I hit it big. Real big, achieving levels of fame and wealth and sheer, naked power I never even imagined, proving my mother wrong whenever I could. I became a King in Washington, literally and figuratively.

As I grew older, made more money, met more women and reached higher and higher levels of success, several self-anointed experts, including certain spouses, friends, therapists and TV pundits, went so far as to suggest that my fractious relationship with my mother propelled me to accomplish such greatness; that in some weird way, I was driven to do so well mainly to disprove my mother's long-standing belief that I would inevitably be an abysmal failure, not to mention a complete waste of oxygen.

Of course, that's fucking true. However, I don't feel I owe my mother a dime of gratitude for what she did to me. I still resent all the pain, all the insults, all the pissing in my pants, which not coincidentally stopped when I finally escaped from the house of hell where I grew up.

Until recently, my mother has been living out her misery in relatively decent albeit angst-ridden health in Our Valley of the Saints Nursing Home for Overbearing, Cantankerous, Man-Hating Mothers, or someplace with a name like that, outside Trenton, New Jersey. She claims to whoever will listen that she has changed her faith for the last time and joined the ever-popular WalMartian MegaChurch, which offers all members 10 percent off any item at WalMart, as well as free shipping at WalMart.com. But I doubt my mother, even at her advanced age, is done changing religions. If some better belief system comes along that makes her feel better about her limitless anger and self-righteous self-loathing – or offers her even bigger storewide savings on stuff she never buys – I'm sure she'll give it a shot.

I never used to visit her more than once (or twice if absolutely necessary) a year, usually capitulating when the irrepressible pangs of guilt (a consequence of my only-child status) become overwhelming despite our mutual contempt, causing me to break down, head to New Jersey and brace myself for what is always a more exasperating visit than the one before it.

Well, that's a quick primer on my past. But that's ancient history, just a setup for the story I need to tell about everything that happened and how it happened and why it happened and what it all means for you and me and our country. Because, as you know, in one brief, mind-blowing, cataclysmic week, America changed forever. And so did I. Or at least I think I did.

So this is how it all went down. If you're wondering, I took copious notes on a daily basis because I knew I had a front seat to it all and was well aware that someday, my personal account, along with my treasure trove of documents, videos, tapes, emails and transcripts, would come in handy and be great fodder for a potentially lucrative book, which essentially is my autobiography – actually, my unauthorized autobiography, since the U.S. government is highly pissed I wrote such a revealing, tell-all masterpiece. Big thank-you's to my high-level contacts at the FBI, CIA, Google, Microsoft, Verizon and AT&T, who gave me as a favor, after much persuasion, access to most of my personal data, private communications, online storage files and surveillance records.

One final note: I have reconstructed all the conversations recounted herein to the best of my ability, so they should be 65–95 percent accurate given my outstanding recall skills, which can be, as you will see, both a blessing and a curse. I also relied on the recollections, recordings and tell-all tabloid accounts of other figures named on these pages to verify what I thought I said at any given time to them, as well as what they recall saying back to me, if, for some reason, I wasn't listening. Finally, the intermittent flashbacks to various traumas in my youth – which I use to round out the historical context of my profound existence on Earth – are essentially accurate too, since so many of these memories are indelibly seared in my psyche.

Okay, enough navel-gazing blather for now. Here is the real story of the week that wrecked my world.

Monday

I was luxuriating on my luxury toilet in my luxury bathroom in my luxury penthouse condo in Georgetown, well inside Washington's super-fortified green zone, where military might kept us wealthy *One Percenters* safe from the dregs and drivel of societal scum. There on the pot I sat, staring intently at my new built-in flat-screen tablet-ready tricked-out toilet-paper holder, perusing a leaked copy of the new *Washingtonian* magazine, which featured the one-and-only me on the back page "Naked Power" profile. I couldn't help but admire the exquisite photo spread, which was practically perfect except for my extra layers of facial flab. Still, I looked exceptionally distinguished standing just behind the President – but in front of the Secret Service agents – as our leader (and my most lucrative client) gave a speech I probably scripted in the White House Rose Garden. Even my rapidly evaporating hair, or what remained of it, looked halfway decent, an amazing feat that required extensive airbrushing and other digital effects the magazine's editors utilized (on my insistence) to keep me from looking like what I look like in real life.

Name: Burt King
Age: 55-Plus
Net Worth: Exceptionally high but richly deserved
Address: Versailles, Georgetown's ultimate luxury,
high-voltage gated condominium complex

Occupation: Political Consultant, Presidential Adviser, Campaign Strategist, Universally-Respected Genius
Car: Hummer MoFo3 [8.7 MPG on highway]
Favorite Drink: Whatever it takes
Favorite Sport: Rumor, Innuendo, Negativity, Hardball
Hobbies: Fighting, In-Fighting, Street-Fighting, Bare-Knuckle Politics
Last Book Read: I don't read books; I write them.
Last Vacation: When my wife left town to visit her parents
Next Vacation: No plans; waste of time
Heroes: Moses, Richard Nixon, Mick Jagger
Where I Plan to Retire: If I don't go to Hell, maybe Vegas
Words to Live By: "My candidate's victory is the other candidate's miserable defeat."

But as usual, this joyful, peaceful, pure moment of solitude, brought on by some well-deserved ego-gratification, did not last long.

While I was doing my business, the phone rang. It was the White House operator. She immediately put me through to the President, who was flying back from France on Wells Fargo Air Force One, after attending some global economic bullshit summit.

"For Christ's sake. What in God's name were you thinking?"

"Please, Mr. President, you gotta stop the religious references. They hurt your poll numbers among atheists."

"Cut the crap, Burt."

"What did I do wrong now, Mr. President?"

"C'mon, you know what you did!" he said.

"No, I do not."

"Have you seen your ridiculous *Washingtonian* interview? It's all over the Web. You're being eviscerated by our critics, and I'm pissed."

"That's strange. I was just reading it. I thought it came out exceptionally well."

"Well, it didn't. Your ego is completely out of control," he whined. "This is not the image one of my closest advisers should be projecting."

"Hey!" I shot back. "What do you mean *one of* your closest advisers? You know as well as I do that I am your closest, second to none. Now you've really hurt my feelings."

"Just shut up and listen to me," said the President. "You drive me crazy."

"C'est la vie!" I responded. But he did not find the French reference amusing.

MONDAY

"Don't delude yourself," he said. "This magazine profile is embarrassing. For both of us. You come across like an arrogant, self-absorbed asshole."

"I am," I reminded him.

"How can you be so shameless?" he asked.

"How can you be so ungrateful?"

"How can I be so stupid to put up with all your shit?"

"Oh, I am soooo very sorry, Mr. President," I said facetiously. "Have you forgotten your margin of victory when I got you elected?"

"You didn't get me elected!" he yelled. "I did it myself."

"Don't be delusional!" I yelled back.

"Fuck you, King."

And with that, the President of the Free World hung up, leaving me smiling on the toilet. I tried to reflect on what had just occurred. After a half-second of superficial analysis, I concluded that everything was going to be fine. The President would surely calm down. He'd quickly forget about this matter. And he would be calling me for advice on some critically important matter by the end of the week, if not the end of the day.

That unbelievably rich bitch needed me even more than I needed him. Sure, Antonio Strump IV may have been worth a few trillion dollars thanks to the businesses and real estate and all sorts of other shit he and his family had owned for generations. His net worth may have exceeded the Gross National Product of most continents. He may have paid me more money than any other political consultant had ever dreamed of earning in the history of politics. But I can tell you this: Without me, Antonio Strump was nothing. And deep down inside, he knew the truth as much as I did.

I moseyed on over to the other side of my super-sized bathroom. It was time to take a bubble bath. And not just any ordinary start-the-day-right bubble bath. I was in dire need of an extra-special spiritual and physical cleansing in my $50,000 gold-plated tub, where I soaked every morning, eyes shut tight, trying to relax, trying to escape the banality of my life, trying to repress memories of my dysfunctional mother, my dysfunctional marriages and my dysfunctional clients. As I began to revel in the warm, soothing glory of thousands of itty-bitty super-soapy bubbles, my solitude was shattered by a scream. I snapped out of my blissful state and jumped to my feet buck-naked, grabbing the nearest towel to cover myself as the bathroom door flew open and banged harshly against the wall.

Juanita, my wife at this moment in history, was visibly upset, shaking her head while glaring, as only a highly agitated, perpetually aggrieved wife can. A roll of unused condoms dangled from her hand.

"Do these belong to you, Burt?" she asked, expecting the worst. "I found them in a pair of your pants."

Note to brain: Bath time was officially over. Time to utilize delay tactics while preparing to run for cover. This was going to get ugly fast.

"And what were you doing looking in my pants?" I complained with too much indignation.

"I was looking for condoms," she said matter-of-factly.

"Well, they're not mine," I lied.

"Yeah, right," she said sarcastically. "Then whose are they? The President's? Or the First Lady's?"

I was officially under attack. I had no choice now but to start spinning.

"I bought them for us, Juanita. I thought we could be together again, you know, in the Biblical sense."

"Fat chance. We haven't had sex in ages."

"Actually, 5 months and 16 days, to be exact."

"Whatever. We're not having sex again anytime soon. I don't want it and you don't deserve it. You have no one to blame for what happened but yourself."

"I told you a thousand times she was just an office temp giving me a back rub after a particularly stressful conference call. I know it looked bad when you walked in, but it wasn't really that bad. You completely overreacted. It was nothing more than an in-office massage to release all my tension."

"I saw what I saw and that's that."

"So when will you finally forgive me?"

"None of your goddamn business, you pig. Now tell me right this second: Why are there condoms in your pants? And don't tell me you were doing focus group research for condom manufacturers, okay?"

This was deteriorating rapidly. I tried another approach, having nothing left to lose. Let the bullshit flow.

"Okay, okay, Juanita, I'll tell you what happened. Senator Kamisaki gave me the condoms as a gift. He picked them up on his recent trip to China. He said all the Communist Party officials swear by this brand. Check them out; they're triple-ribbed and they glow in the dark."

"Shut up. You're drowning in your own bullshit."

"C'mon, Juanita, would I lie to you?" As soon as I uttered that line, I knew I was toast. She said nothing in response, but her watery eyes said everything. I was already tried and convicted.

I toweled off, reached over for my robe and started to walk out, because I knew, based on past experience, that Juanita and I were now seconds away from a major quake on the marital meltdown Richter scale. Definitely a 7.0, enough force to do serious damage to what little remained of our marriage.

"Why do you insist on being such an incredible asshole?" she asked, blocking the door. "Do you enjoy it?"

"Excellent questions," I answered, more like a pretentious college professor than an overwrought political consultant. "But a more appropriate question might have been "Am I really an asshole or have you turned me into one?"

"Hold on a second!" she shrieked. "Are you now blaming me for making you who you are?"

"You certainly haven't helped things with your constant criticism and relentless attacks on my character, eating habits and alleged lack of hygiene. In fact, when you assess the facts and analyze all the available data on our marriage, when you look objectively at who's responsible for all the pain, misery, hurt and heartbreak we've endured, when you take stock of the abrupt cessation of regular, meaningful marital intercourse, physical as well as verbal, you have to admit that everything that is wrong with us is entirely your fault. You have failed me. You have betrayed me."

As always, in both my professional and personal lives, turning the tables by attacking my attacker felt intoxicatingly good. I felt a surge of adrenaline and the momentum shift back in my favor, buoyed by my innate ability to always assume the moral high ground, even when I was careening down the low road at too high a speed.

At this juncture, I knew I had to stay on the offensive, being as offensive as I could be: "So, are you willing, right here, right now, to accept responsibility for your actions? Are you prepared to apologize for your sins against me and the sacred institution of marriage?"

Juanita's face turned beet red, as if it were about to explode and splatter blood everywhere, which would have been a bitch to clean off the $1500-per-square-foot ceramic floor tiles. "Can you tell me why you enjoy making me so miserable?" she uttered with a high level of hostility.

"I was about to ask you the exact same question."

"You're killing me!"

"Ain't my problem," I said dismissively. "It's a dog-eat-dog world out there."

"So are you saying we're both dogs?" she cried.

"Speak for yourself," I answered.

At best, I was infuriating her much more than she was infuriating me. I took solace in the fact that I was now winning this particular battle, this daily test of wills, due to my masterful debate skills, super-quick response times and unrestrained, relentless aggression. Thanks to these God-given talents, I was on the verge of a hard-fought victory after a substantial week-long losing streak in our seemingly endless competition to drive each other insane.

"I can't take this anymore," she declared with a definitive wince as she turned around, walked out and slammed the bathroom door behind her.

As I was prone to do, I prematurely celebrated my victory without contemplating Juanita's next move. Seconds later, the bathroom door swung open and she barged back in, clutching my $50,000 BrainBerry Platinum watch, my sacred BrainBerry, the stylish phone and full-featured voice-activated communications ultra limited-edition watch you could sync directly to your brain via a pea-sized transmitter implanted in your ear canal. This revolutionary Web-ready dynamo was the be-all, end-all of my collection of material possessions– my most vital organ, the undeniable 24 carat gold and diamond -encrusted engine of my professional essence.

I knew instantly that my inflamed wife had returned to mete out my punishment. And I was most unprepared for its severity. I watched in horror as she marched over to the toilet, lifted the cover and let my BrainBerry dangle perilously over the bowl.

"You deserve this in so many ways," she said with more venom than usual, reveling in her effective attempt at revenge.

"Oh, my God," I yelped. "Don't do it, Juanita. Please don't. Not my BrainBerry! Anything else but that. I can't live without it. I'll be cut off from the world. I'll be completely screwed."

"What a shame then," she said in the most clinical, unemotional way. "Looks like you're completely screwed."

Just then, the BrainBerry buzzed. Juanita checked the screen to see who was calling. "Looks like the Secretary of State is looking for you," she said with no sympathy. "Should I tell her we're in the middle of another domestic dispute?"

"Give me a minute. I need to speak with her. I have to tell her something real important."

"I bet," she said coldly. "You're probably sleeping with her, too."

That was ages ago, I thought to myself.

The buzzing finally stopped as the call went to voicemail.

I took a step toward Juanita. "Now, calm down, honey, and give me back my BrainBerry. I need it."

"Then tell me the truth about the condoms."

"I did. I'm telling you the truth. I swear on a stack of bibles."

"You're such a liar. You've probably never even read the Bible."

"That's none of your business."

"Do you even have a conscience?"

"Nope. Been there. Done that."

"Is this your definition of a healthy relationship?"

"I wouldn't know one if I saw one."

"That's your problem, Burt."

" No, *you* are my problem."

"You're being unbelievably offensive."

"Ask me if I care."

The BrainBerry buzzed again. Juanita checked the caller ID as I inched closer. "It's someone from the Jordanian Embassy."

"Must be Ambassador Whossein calling about war or peace. The future of the Middle East may be hanging in the balance."

"So is our marriage. Your fifth. My first. And last."

I raced toward my venomous wife and lunged for the BrainBerry. But it was too late. With a psychotic smile worthy of the Wicked Witch of the West, she dropped my most prized possession into the recently soiled toilet and flushed.

I winced in pain as she laughed cruelly at my expense.

"Goddamn you, Burt King!" she added for good measure. "You are despicable!"

"For the last time," I howled, "ask me if I care."

"Shame on me for marrying you."

"Glad you figured out that it's all your fault," I chided her.

At that, Juanita double-slapped me good and hard, right across both cheeks. In my experience, American women slap you once. But Latin women, when they're really pissed, slap you twice. And not to sound like a pussy, but this time it really hurt.

I reacted maturely, with grace and fortitude. I grabbed her high-end designer hair dryer and fired it across the room, where it crashed against the bathroom mirror, smashing the dryer into several pieces and leaving the mirror a splintered mess of glass, which rained down into our $72,000 his-and-her sinks, purchased ages ago in a long-forgotten, romantic nanosecond of marital bliss.

Juanita broke down and began sobbing uncontrollably. I don't know why, and in retrospect I wish I hadn't done it, but I cracked a smile. I will admit, after the fact, this was inappropriate, given that my wife was in serious pain.

"You're an insensitive son-of-a-bitch," she reminded me as she continued to cry.

"But other than that, you still love me, right?" I asked, rubbing it in.

"You're pushing me over the edge," she said. "I'm warning you."

"Bring it on, baby," I snarled, invoking my favorite cut-down line from elementary-school recess.

In a confrontation like this, at home or at work, I often pictured myself starring in my own reality TV show or documentary film, giving a brilliant, Emmy- or Oscar-winning performance deserving of rave reviews from all the critics. Today's altercation was shaping up to be one of my best ever, executed with exemplary deftness. A little dig here, a little poke there, a gradual escalation in tension and tone, punctuated with a more aggressive assault of each other's character, leading to a violent crescendo featuring the explosive, simultaneous shattering of her hair dryer and the mirror. All told a strong, dramatic, yet justified response to her cruel and inhumane drowning of my BrainBerry watch. War is never pretty, even when the battleground is an oversized, opulent master bathroom.

I was so incredibly proud of myself in that moment that it took me awhile to notice that Juanita had pulled a pair of frighteningly long metal scissors out of one of the bathroom drawers. I wasn't sure if she was about to stab me in the heart, cut off one of my irreplaceable body parts or merely scare me.

Juanita held the scissors high in the air as if to punctuate an important point.

I stepped back to protect my groin area – just to be safe.

"What are you so afraid of, you coward?" she said.

"Oh, nothing in particular," I lied.

She stared at me with a double shot of contempt. "You are beyond pathetic," she said. "How can you even look at yourself in the mirror?"

"Here, watch," I said mockingly, bending over the bathroom counter for a close-up shot of myself in the broken mirror. "I may be beyond pathetic, but I do enjoy admiring the essence of my pathetic persona whenever I can."

In slow motion, as if to make a point, I reached deep into my nostril and yanked out an errant, unjustifiably long nose hair.

"You disgust me," she announced for probably the millionth time since we'd met, as she calmly fired the scissors at my head, missing, intentionally, I would like to believe, by a foot.

"So what else is new?" I asked while bending over to pick the scissors off the glass-covered floor for safekeeping. "I am who I am and we are who we are and life is what it is, and there is nothing you or I or anyone else can do to improve the situation. So if, in fact, I do disgust you, all I ask is that you try to ignore my disgusting demeanor and look the other way. Just pretend I do not exist and I am not here, living with you in the capital of our great albeit overly stressed nation."

"I can't do this anymore!" she said as she stormed out of the bathroom.

Unsure exactly what to do next, I lathered up for a badly needed shave and proceeded as usual to nick and cut my face all over the place. Must have been all that tension oozing out of my body, just like the blood now oozing out of my face. A short while later, I heard the front door slam. Juanita was gone, on her way down in the elevator to the garage, where she would soon find solace behind the wheel of her $250,000 silver Corvette, a "Will You Forgive Me for Being a Jerk?" present from me after our last all-out screamfest, which erupted in the underground parking garage at the Kennedy Center during some stupid rap version of *Richard III*. I insisted on leaving at intermission, and Juanita, of course, insisted on staying, because the place was crawling with A-list celebrities and paparazzi, and she felt important being present at such an elite event. Let's just say I hated the play even more than I hated the thought of spending the night sleeping alone and very uncomfortably on my office couch, with no intern around to rub away the stress.

Ah, Juanita. The one and only Juanita Ortega King, my 50 percent Venezuelan, 50 percent spoiled, 100 percent pain-in-the-ass wife, a match made in hell for her 100 percent pain-in-the-ass husband. Yet I'll be the first to admit that, despite our extreme dysfunction and all the blood-pressure spikes we inflicted on each other, I still had feelings for her. I just didn't always know what to do with them. Juanita was as spicy hot now as the day I met her, nearly a decade ago, at a Baltimore campaign rally for Luzinski, the only gubernatorial candidate I ever worked for who was arrested for murder after he won the general election but before he was sworn into office. How was I supposed to know he was going to kill his wife the day after she filed for divorce?

Based on my extensive experience, under five different regimes, I had learned the hard way that the institution of marriage was not for everyone. But maybe I was one of those weak, delusional, hopelessly romantic souls who were too lazy, unconfident or chicken-shit to face the ups and downs of life without a partner. Maybe I was afraid to live out my life of misery alone. Who knows? Who cares?

As I finished getting ready to leave for work, I listened to my conscience and decided to face up to my adult responsibilities by taking Populace, our annoyingly neurotic poodle – or should I say Juanita's annoyingly neurotic poodle – for as brief a walk as possible. It was my token humanitarian deed of the day. I grabbed Populace's leash and took him down in the elevator to our parking garage for what would hopefully be a quick piss, because going for a walk outside was out of the question. Too hot and humid and not enough time. I had places to go, clients to bill.

But Populace was in no hurry to do his business so I could head out and do mine. It was as if the dog was messing with me just so he could make me late. When he realized I was expecting him to pee in the garage under someone's rear tire instead of under his favorite tree, he growled at me as if to protest. So I growled back. Maybe he had to poop. But I couldn't care less. I'd forgotten to bring a shit bag with me, so any defecation was out of the question. I had to get my ass down to the Capitol for an urgent appointment. The fate of our nation's democracy was more important than Populace's bodily functions.

My crappy old backup BrainBerry device, the banged-up handheld one I kept around the house for emergencies like this, began to vibrate uncontrollably. It was the Speaker's secretary, as whiny as ever:

"The Speaker is anxiously waiting for you, Mr. King. Where are you?"

"I'm on my way," I lied. "I'm just stuck in a little traffic."

At that moment, right in the middle of my little white lie, Populace peed all over my sensational Italian calfskin shoes. So I kicked him in the butt, not too gently, causing him to howl. I realized Populace probably hated me now as much as Juanita did. But this didn't bother me in the least. I was fed up with this devious dog.

Populace had always been a thorn in my side. I knew as soon as we got him, from some stupid breeder, that he was not your typical dog. He had special powers. I'd always known dogs had a sixth sense. Or a seventh, if you included their ability to admire their own excrement with awe and pride. But Populace had an eighth sense, something extra, something almost supernatural: My mutt from hell had the innate ability to tell when I was lying to someone over the phone and the dexterity to pee on cue all over me, as if to punish me for my dishonesty. Which explains why I hated to speak on the phone in his presence, why he'd just unloaded on me and why most rooms in our home and most of my shoes had the faint yet distinct stench of dog urine.

As I rode back up in the elevator with my canine tormentor, I debated whether or not to drop Populace off at the dog pound, on a permanent basis, thereby putting an end to this misery. But Juanita would never in a million years forgive me. Especially after our conflagration this morning, there was no way making a unilateral decision to do away with the dog was worth the risk, no matter how much those shoes cost me ($1,850).

A few minutes later, I was heading down Massachusetts Avenue toward Capitol Hill in typically bottle-necked stop-and-go traffic, surrounded by proud-to-be gas-guzzling town cars, SUVs and oh-so-self-righteous politically correct electric cars, and dreaming about having a big, badass, screaming police siren on top of my Hummer. I pictured myself blowing past every car on the road, leaving other drivers in the dust to marvel at the blur of my indestructible combat armor and pulsating red lights. I'd speed at will, sailing through traffic lights at 100 miles per hour, then parking wherever the hell I wanted. All because of who I was and what I did for a living.

When you consider the essence of what I do professionally, helping the hapless and hopelessly insecure politicians who try in vain to manage our largely unmanageable nation, it's apparent that I am as much in the emergency-response business as any policeman, fireman or EMT professional. Like them, I get frantic 911 calls all the time and have no choice but to drop what I am doing and spring into action, saving my clients from danger, rushing them to safety, stitching up their wounds and protecting them from everyone and everything that is trying to damage them. Which is why I deserved a siren. Hell, yes.

I flipped on the radio and listened to the news. The government of Qatar had finally closed on its purchase of Texas, which the U.S. was forced to sell in bankruptcy court to help pay off the national debt. The coast-to-coast heat wave continued to shatter records, although I believed, contrary to the politically correct whiners, the culprit wasn't global warming but excessive human flatulence due to too many people eating too many gas-producing foods. And Vice-President Doltish was giving a speech in Nashville, commemorating Middle Class Appreciation Day (my idea) and attending a groundbreaking ceremony for the 500th Marriott Middle Class Temporary Housing Facility to be built in the U.S. since banks stopped offering mortgages to people making less than $500,000 a year because the repayment risks were understandably too great.

Despite the radio announcer droning on about this or that, there was nothing really new going on in Washington. A few more murders. A few more stabbings. A teacher hurt during a student brawl at a local nursery school. Another City Hall moron indicted on embezzlement charges after he bought his daughter a Picasso. Another prominent business executive arrested for DUI with a prostitute who, despite his protestations, was not his wife. Another demonstration outside a local McDonalds over the skyrocketing price of fries due to the potato shortage. And another young man, this time from Northern Virginia, killed in the war against Canada during a guerilla attack on our troops inside a Toronto shopping mall.

"We loved our son and he loved our country," said his father on the radio. "He made the ultimate sacrifice."

He sure did. Those rat bastard Canadians needed to be taught a lesson. Ungrateful hockey-loving louts. For centuries, we protected them, subsidized them, traded with them, vacationed with them – and then when we needed help two years ago, when we needed their oil after the Arabs cut us off, they refused to give us a price break and instead tried to gouge us.

In the final analysis, the crazy Canadian government left us no choice but to take unilateral action and seize their oil fields. We had to go in on a preemptive basis and protect our national-security interests before the U.S. economy got even more screwed up and gas costs rose to over $6 a gallon. What were we supposed to do in that situation? Just bend over and take it up the butt? No way.

In the ultimate act of aggression, rather than accept our decision to invade, the Canadians decided to start a war over it. They ran like babies to the United Nations, and when we ignored the UN's condemnation of our actions, the Canadian government decided, rather unwisely, I might add, to declare war on us. I felt at the time like most Americans: If those weasely, war-mongering Canucks wanted to test the mettle of the United States, bring it on.

And bring it on we did. Not only did we invade Canada and launch major ground and air attacks against their largest cities, including Toronto, Montreal, Ottawa and Vancouver, but we deployed for the first time ever our $275 trillion Haliburton Solar System Sunshield, an orbiting mass of metallic magic that soars through space effectively blocking the sun from reaching any part of Canada. It's a brilliantly brutal weapon, but in Canada's case, the punishment fits the crime. Despite the world outcry and accusations of cruelty leveled against the U.S. government, I can say, without equivocation, that those wayward

Canadians deserved their descent into Ice Age hell after the profound lack of respect they showed us. It may have been summer in America, but it was brutally cold in Canada, and I would rather be too warm than too cold any day of the week.

As I write these words, our war against Canada continues with no end in sight. The casualties have been unfortunately high – over 15,000 Americans have died in battle – but the cause endures. If the United States of America, the beacon of light in a ludicrous world, won't fight for what is right, who the hell will? Belize?

The truth of the matter is that the USA will always be at war. It's the way things have been, and it's the way things will always be. A majority of the American people who vote have shown their willingness over the years to live in a perpetual state of war, fearing all foreigners while displaying the best characteristics of supreme jingoism, which is a wonderful thing in my line of work. By now it's obvious that wars abroad – or at home – help bring us together as a nation and distract those cynical mutts in the media from writing negative stories about societal problems we can't solve that reflect poorly on the leadership and confidence of those of us in charge. By fostering a siege-like mentality among the people and distracting them from things they need to be distracted from, these wars make unquestioned, unconditional patriotism the all-encompassing focus of the day. Which is why politicians who want to win must respect the tenor of the times and make war work to their advantage. Which is why I have been so brilliant and successful doing what I do for a living. Which is why I've made obscene amounts of money over my career.

As I've always urged my clients to stress in their speeches and commercials, "If the U.S. doesn't stand up for itself and kick some serious un-American ass, no one else will."

Like most highly influential decision-makers in Washington, I've never served a day of my life in the Armed Forces. Despite my complete lack of military experience, I have deep admiration for those brave souls who have known the evils of war. I am continually awed by their commitment and perseverance every time I read the newspaper or tune into the History Channel. Our country would not be what it is today without the sacrifices made during the Revolutionary War, the Civil War, World Wars I and II, the Korean War, the Vietnam War, the Iraq War, the Iran War and, most recently, the War Against Samoa and now the War Against Canada.

I do believe, however, that in some profound way, these veterans of the battlefield, who risked their lives in combat and shirked from nothing, would respect me for surviving the warlike conditions my evil-minded mother fostered throughout my childhood, as well as the attacks she has launched against me in adulthood. U.S. troops aren't the only ones who've fought hard in combat.

From my years of experience, I know that if politicians want to be taken seriously when it comes to world affairs, they have no choice but to stand tall, stay firm, trash talk the enemy whenever necessary and, last but not least, gesticulate forcefully against a backdrop overflowing with American flags. Because Americans want leaders who appear tough. Even if they are spineless cowards offstage. And it's a helluva lot easier for politicians to wrap themselves around the flag than to keep Social Security solvent or end poverty.

As I approached the Hill, the traffic flow down Independence Avenue improved to the point of being halfway decent, which meant my mood was halfway decent by the time I made it past Capitol security, parked in the underground garage and rode the elevator up to the Speaker's Capitol hideaway. Ramirez was on the phone when I entered. I saw the sprawling stress-induced red blotches on his face and could tell he had already been drinking and was quite upset. Luckily for him, I had arrived just in the nick of time. So I got right to work. I plopped into his overstuffed couch, put a pillow under my head for comfort and support, stretched my legs out and waited.

I said nothing and waited for him to hang up. I would make him speak first. He was the Speaker of the House, and he had summoned me there, so he should speak first, right? The worker bees buzzed in the other room, making calls, making copies, making coffee, completely oblivious to their boss's newest self-inflicted crisis that was more likely than not about to rear its ugly head.

The Speaker finally hung up, rubbed his forehead and started speaking to me in a quivering voice, too shaken to even look me in the eyes.

"I'm totally fucked, Burt. This time, more than any other time, I really screwed up," he moaned. "I'm in over my head. I did something bad again and I'm worried sick it's gonna get out."

"We'll get through this," I said, lying to both of us once again. "Whatever it is, we'll figure something out."

"What was I thinking?" he said in half-assed disbelief.

"With all due respect, Mr. Speaker, let's skip the drama. Remember, I charge by the hour."

Ramirez and I had been through so much repulsive and rancid crap together, I felt like I worked in the waste-management business. Better yet, the emergency-response sex-scandal-management business.

"So how we gonna clean up this fucking mess?" Ramirez asked in a panic.

"Shut up a second," I stopped him. "Catch your breath and tell me the story. The whole story."

"Same story as usual."

"Same story or new same story."

"New same story."

"Female or male?"

"How dare you insinuate such a thing!"

"You heard me. Female or male?"

"Female."

"Girl or woman?"

He paused to contemplate the complexity of such a simple question. "Not exactly sure."

"What do you mean 'not exactly sure'?" How can you not know the difference?"

"Depends on how old you mean by 'woman.'"

"Jeez. Is she 21 or younger?"

"Not sure. She's a college intern for one of my committees. Judiciary committee, I think."

"How old is she exactly?"

"How am I supposed to know? Like I said, all I know is she's in college."

"I guess we should be thankful she's not in high school."

"Stop insulting me. That affair was a long time ago."

"So, did you have sex with this college girl?"

"Not exactly."

"Which means what?"

"We had intimate physical contact, but we stopped short of actual consummation."

"What?"

"I swear, on a stack of bibles, we did not do the actual deed."

"Huh?"

"I can tell you, unequivocally, I did not have an inappropriate relationship with that woman."

"Okay, spare me your Bill Clinton bullshit," I shot back, losing my patience at his parsing. "No one gives a crap if you had or didn't have a relationship. What's the definition of a relationship?"

"I really don't know," he said meekly.

"Tell me then, Mr. Speaker, how would you explain your relationship with this youngster to the media, or to your wife and kids?"

"We were interrupted last night. The damn buzzer went off. I had to go vote. And she had to go back to her dorm."

I bit my tongue, not knowing whether to congratulate him for his self-restraint or criticize him for his warped, misguided priorities. Instead, I continued on with my inane interrogation.

"Did you leave any evidence behind?"

"What do you mean?"

"Could an FBI forensic squad find any physical evidence from you of anything unethical that may have happened? Did you leave a stain on her dress?"

"No," he said, with a momentary flash of relief. "But she did snap a few quick pictures of us naked, sitting on my desk and posing in front of the Congressional Seal. She said she wanted proof of such a magnificent moment."

"Great," I said without meaning it. "This is significantly worse than the cheerleader. Exponentially worse then Miss Tanzania. Infinitely worse than Congressman Hayes. If those photos get out, Mr. Speaker, you're finished. Your political career will be over. Your marriage will be over. Your life as you know it will be over. For all I know, you'll end up in jail, where you'll be posing naked with the other inmates."

"I'm sorry. I promise you I will stop screwing around right now. No more naughtiness for me."

"Fine." It was all I could say, because I knew there was no chance he'd keep that promise. Enough of this nonsense. My mind was overloaded and had left the room, floating way back in time to my own overpowering, oversexed memories of when I was last young and crazy in love, nearly 40 years ago.

I was a sophomore in college, a rank amateur at the game of Life, despite my age-appropriate overconfidence. First day of English class at the South Boston campus of Bangalore University, sitting in a lecture titled "Lesbians in Modern Latvian Literature," which I thought (accurately) had the potential to be a good magnet for members of the opposite sex. She strolled in, appearing like a heavenly vision on a clear blue day, introduced by the pompous Indian professor on the large video screen as our on-site in-person teaching assistant, there to help us with whatever we needed for an additional fee. I knew right then I would need a lot of help, no matter the price.

Sitting in that classroom on that crisp, hormones-raging autumn day, I was, for the first time in my life, beyond speechless as I watched unadulterated perfection in action, all natural with no artificial ingredients or artifice of any kind. Stunning drop-dead looks, infectious personality, off-the-chart levels of confidence, poise and class. In other words, she was totally unattainable for a gawky, geeky New Rotica boy of my vintage. Yet for some strange reason I still don't completely understand, the 100,000 to 1 odds against me did nothing to deter me. Rather, I was inspired to see if I could somehow get her attention, and then eventually win her affection.

It was, pure and simple, lust at first sight. For me and every other male in the room. I knew every one of us would be competing against one another to get face time with her at those prescheduled weekly extra help sessions. But I had my own ideas of how to separate myself from the pack. I realized I had to do exceptionally poorly in class, whatever it took, so I could request and receive some private extra help sessions from this once-in-a-lifetime T.A.

I intentionally tanked on the first two papers, flunking as planned. After one month, I was summoned to a video chat with the professor, live from Bangalore, exactly as I had hoped.

"Mr. King, did you have trouble with the English language in high school?" he asked while sucking on an unlit pipe for what I assumed was either a major tobacco addiction or excessive dramatic effect.

"No, sir. My teachers led me to believe that I was an excellent writer."

"And this was a high school for normal kids?"

"Yes."

"Accredited by which state, may I ask?"

"New York."

"And if we can be honest with each other, how did you in a million years get into Bangalore University? From the look of things, you appear to be neither a good student nor an outstanding athlete. In all my years of dealing with Americans, I have rarely seen someone with so little potential."

"You sound like my mother," I remarked.

"I hope I don't look like her," he said nastily.

"So what exactly is your problem with my writing?" I asked.

"Banal. Sophomoric. Trite. Overwritten. Completely lacking in originality and substance. Totally devoid of meaning."

"But other than that, you respect my work," I said with plenty of well-deserved snot in my attitude.

"It had no redeeming value," he said, giving me the perfect setup shot. Point, game, match.

"Maybe if I got some extra help," I pleaded, "I might have a better chance of impressing you."

"Okay, King," he said, with the slightest hint of sympathy. "I can tell you're floundering. Here's what I want you to do. Make an appointment to see my on-site teaching assistant. As you know, and according to the binding terms and conditions in the fine print on the contract you signed to take this course, any and all extra help provided by my T.A. will be billed to your credit card at the flat rate of $799 per hour. But it should be worth it, even though Bangalore U. will not guarantee any level of derived value or quantifiable academic improvement in writing. Maybe my T.A. – I think her name is Zoey – can help salvage you as a student, if it's at all humanly possible."

He wrote out the appropriate paperwork to prescribe this well-deserved intervention and emailed it to me right away. I happily raced back to my dorm, filled out the forms, entered my credit-card information and sent in my desperate pitch for private extra help sessions. "I can't open up about my personal issues if there are other students around," I pleaded.

And that's exactly how, in a streak of genius, I negotiated quality time with the inimitable Zoey Edwards.

"Didn't you learn to write in high school?" she said in the most patronizing way possible, when we met alone for the first time in an otherwise empty classroom.

"I most certainly did," I answered, my defensiveness diminishing by the second as I took comfort in the fact that she and I were breathing the same air in the same room together.

"You could have fooled me," she sneered. "The good news is that Hemingway and Faulkner didn't learn to write in a day, so I can probably teach you to write a little better in a semester."

"Who are Hemingway and Faulkner?" I asked.

She gave me a dirty look, which I found sexually riveting. "Oh, just two dead writers from long ago."

"Were they talented?"

"Never mind," she said. "Look. I can help you become a decent writer, but only if you give me a chance."

"I will give you a chance," I said, starting to melt.

And sure enough, little by little, steadily but not too quickly, I showed gradual improvement in my writing. More vivid imagery, less ponderous prose, not so much flowery, overwritten, self-absorbed drivel.

As we discussed the lesbian-infused texts we were reading in class, I can recite Zoey's witticisms, which were way over my head, like I heard them yesterday.

"I think Tolstoy, in particular, would have been appalled by this story's inexcusable stylistic failings."

"A dialectic fissure is clearly at the root of what ails this protagonist's anal retentive relationship with her pathologically manipulative mother-in-law...."

"No credible cabal of Latvian lesbian heroines would ever accept the oppressive edicts of the ruling class without taking to the streets with Vuvuzelas and then machine-gunning their enemies...."

I did everything I could to impress Zoey while also demonstrating acute symptoms of severe T.A. dependency. As my grades improved and my classroom participation became laudable, I made sure she knew I gave her all the credit. Over time, I worked diligently to position myself in classroom discussions as the thoughtful, oh-so-sensitive male in a roomful of angry, dispossessed women and sadly silent, overly intimidated men. In a way, it was my first political campaign, trying to win a vote I desperately needed. And ultimately, I was kind of victorious.

"Much better, Burt," she said one night after reviewing my latest paper on "Why 20th Century Latvian Lesbians Could Help American Men Confront Their Self-Loathing." "You can do this now. You really can write."

"That's so nice of you to say," I replied, skyrocketing up to Cloud 9, full of pride, full of myself and ready to take a big risk.

"Can I take you out some night to thank you for what you've done for me?"

To my surprise, and I'm sure to my mother's, this supremely beautiful young woman, the object of my fantastical desires, did not say no.

"You certainly are unique," she told me the night of our quasi-date, which consisted of a shared pizza, beers, deep conversation and lots of laughter at a local dive bar in South Boston. "I don't think I've ever met someone like you."

I took that as a giant compliment, and my overactive imagination kicked into gear. I pictured Zoey and me, a few years into the future, decked out in full wedding regalia, walking down the aisle, rejoicing in holy matrimony. I knew she would be the one, my ultimate mate for life.

After pizza, I took the plunge and asked her to join me for ice cream. My treat. I even remember what flavors we ordered: Mint Chocolate Chip (hers) and Rocky Road (mine).

Our first date together was picture perfect. Except for the tragic fact that it was also our last.

"I'll be your friend but that's it," she said, dismembering my self-esteem as we walked back to campus and I tried shamelessly yet unsuccessfully to give her a kiss. "You're a nice guy," she added after wiping my saliva off her cheek, "but I need you to know that I don't do relationships. They're not for me. They make no sense."

"Say what?" was my witty rejoinder.

"I said I don't do relationships. They are unnatural...too complicated and ultimately damaging to the personal growth of each individual. Always end up being a waste of time and energy."

"Do you really believe that?" I asked.

"Yes. Anything more than being casual, inconsequential friends is basically not in the cards. You need to know that now so you won't get your hopes up and eventually be disappointed. I've already disappointed a lot of men like you."

"Really?" I gurgled as my pure, blissful moment of happiness turned to complete crap.

"Really," she said, fully aware that her message was starting to sink in.

"So that's that?" I asked as I began drowning in dejection. "We're finished."

"C'mon, you nut," she laughed. "We can't be finished. We never started. We've got our entire lives in front of us. Big plans. Big goals. I can't be tied down. By anyone or anything."

"Earth to Burt!" screamed the Speaker. "Stop daydreaming on my couch. Can't you see I'm in crisis here?"

Regrettably, my focus left the past and returned to the present. I scratched my head to give the appearance that I was thinking deep, profound thoughts, trying to find a fail-safe strategy to save this pathetic fuck's sorry ass.

"Okay, Mr. Speaker," I said. "I may have a solution."

"Yes," he replied with an unwarranted surfeit of excitement and respect.

"Is your new young female friend ambitious?"

"Isn't everyone in this miserable swamp of a city?"

"I suppose," I said. "But that's not really the point. The point here is that we need to end this potential embarrassment before it becomes an extreme embarrassment. Which is why you have to buy this young woman's silence. And you need to stay away from her. Forever!"

"Well, then, what do we need to do?"

"I will meet with your love intern right away and remind her of the rules of engagement around here."

"What rules? I thought there were no rules."

MONDAY

"Precisely. And she better realize that. If she's going to make trouble for us, we will make twice as much trouble for her, her family and her friends. If she loves her loved ones, she will do everything we say."

"Got it," the Speaker said, sounding relieved. "So you'll handle it. I don't need to do anything at this point?"

"The only thing you have to do is keep paying my bills as promptly as possible."

"What happens next?"

"I'll make a call and get this young woman a very lucrative job far, far away, provided she signs our iron-clad confidentiality agreement. Full-time, good salary, nice benefits and a monthly hush-money allowance, all in exchange for her acknowledgment that if she ever, in a million years, goes public or causes you one iota of trouble, she will be fired immediately, dragged through the mud, run out of town and then shipped back to whatever hellhole she came from. Got it?"

"What if she refuses to leave?"

"Trust me. When I get done with her, she won't have a choice."

"Thanks a lot, Burt. I could never survive without you."

"That, Mr. Speaker, is a searing indictment of us both." I got up to walk out. "Enjoy the rest of the afternoon. Happy New Year! And try to stay out of trouble for a month or two. Keep your zipper zipped!"

"I'll give it my best shot," he said in a most unconvincing way. "By the way, if you want to meet my girlfriend, I'm throwing a coming out party for her this Saturday to celebrate the launch of her new political blog. Mildred is going to be out of town all weekend visiting her brother in Tampa."

I collapsed back on the couch, dejected but not defeated. "You are never seeing her again."

"I'm not?" he asked, appearing shocked. "Why?"

"Did you hear a fucking thing I just said, Mr. Speaker? This insane affair is over. Finished. Kaput. Unless you want your career to be."

He hesitated, slowly nodding to himself as if considering the remnants of his conscience, which Capitol Hill had clearly eviscerated by the time he reached the pinnacle of his career. "But she's so exquisite. She completes me."

"I thought I completed you," I pointed out. "We've won a lot of elections together. And I've done more than my fair share to keep you out of jail."

"I know. But this is different. This girl makes me come alive. She makes me feel really powerful, more powerful than even I know I am."

"You gotta break it off," I said. "Or I'm going to have to fire you as a client." This tactic usually rebooted the deliberative calculations of even the most thick-headed pols.

"Fine, I'll cancel the party. I just want one more night with her. A romantic dinner, followed by a night of uninhibited fornication."

"No fucking way!" I howled, amazed at his brazen stupidity. "Here's the deal, Mr. Speaker: Stop thinking about this woman. Start worrying about the rest of your life."

"Okay, sounds like a good plan," he shrugged, giving me lip service. "You're always one step ahead, Burt."

"You're lucky one of us is, Mr. Speaker," I said, as I stood up and prepared to escape.

As I drove to the office, I tried to find something somewhat humorous about the Speaker's latest installment of Penile Peccadilloes. But I couldn't. I just kept thinking that the Secret Service better do a great job protecting the President and Vice-President, because if this particular Speaker of the House ever had to assume the Presidency, our country would be kaput.

The irony was that Ramirez was a likable fellow, an accomplished, not too lightweight of a legislator and a good-hearted, thoughtful Democrat. Which didn't mean much these days, as all political parties had devolved into meaningless, malleable entities, silly caricatures of their former selves. Which, by the way, is why I never had a problem working for Democrats or Republicans or Independents or Communists, Fascists or plain old Dictators, for that matter, as long as their cash was green. When you stripped them down to their bare essentials, it was basically impossible to tell any of these candidates apart, despite their party labels and platforms. In reality, the only things they cared about were gaining more power and advancing the special interests of their biggest campaign donors. But that's the way it's always been. And always will be. Cynical? Yes. The brutal truth? Unquestionably.

My head was still hurting from my morning overdose of inanity when I drove up to my office. I pulled around to the valet station, as I always do. Jones was waiting for me right in front, as he always does. Dapper as usual in his neatly pressed black pants, white dress shirt and food-stained tie. Not sure why I liked this kid, but I did. Sure, he was a disrespectful smart-ass. But he was also a solid car-parking professional who worked his butt off from 6 a.m. until 8 p.m. every day so he could afford to take college classes at night. At least, that's what he'd tell me around the holidays when he would remind me incessantly that it was end-of-the-year tip time.

The other thing I used to like about Jones was his raw intelligence. He was intensely interested in politics and followed current events closely, which was odd these days for someone his age. Or someone any age in our Age of Ignorance, when 95 percent of the population would be hard-pressed to name the President, Vice-President or any foreign country with the possible exception of Canada or Mexico and maybe the one they emigrated from. Moreover, Jones was highly entertaining: a cocky, humorous clown who liked to egg me on and tease me about who I was and what I did for a living. Even though he had no idea what I did for a living.

"Hey, good morning, Mr. Politics!" he hollered. "Whose blood you got on your hands today?"

"No blood on my hands today, Jones," I fired back. "I promise."

"You always have blood on your hands," he scoffed. "You're a serial killer."

"Says who?"

"Says me and every other man, woman and child in this screwed-up country. You think you're the almighty King and we ain't nothing but your peasants."

"Whatever, Jones. Look, I need my car back at noon. And I need it washed and waxed. Got a big lunch today."

"Where you going for lunch? The White House?" He was in a jealous mood.

"Nope. Guess again."

"Capitol Hill?"

"Nope. Already been there today."

He was getting miffed. "The Pentagon."

"Nope. My lunch is top secret, and you'll have to kill me to find out."

"Stop playing me for a fool, you fool," he chuckled, as he wound himself up and started in with his hyperkinetic hand gestures. "I really don't care where you're going. All I know is when you're done with your stupid meeting, the U.S. government machine will still be crushing the common man, and you and all your evil rich friends will still be blowing dollar bills out your asses. But someday, I swear, the oppressed will rise up, and you'll be a dead man."

"Have a good morning, Jones," I said, walking away. "And don't forget to clean the floor mats this time. Lots of crap all over them."

"Because you're full of crap," he laughed before mumbling a string of profanities under his breath. Usually, I would duke it out with him long enough to win the last word, but there was no time for that today. It was time to start dialing for dollars, and my morning stream of conference calls with clients was about to begin.

My wildly successful, insanely lucrative political-consulting firm (or "Strategic Advisory Firm," as we say in the trade) was called SDI, which I had originally incorporated as Slice and Dice Inc. before more than a few clients convinced me that was a tad over the top. Our opulent offices were located in a royally-appointed, distinguished-looking two-floor suite high atop the K Street power corridor just above Connecticut Avenue. This was the official home of my hackery. Way in the back of our 12,750-square-foot, $195-per-square-foot shop was my own office, my inner sanctum, where I would go to think and scheme and write and yap on the phone and hide. Most importantly of all, it's where I reveled in all the money and fame I'd made for myself by masterminding lethal, take-no-prisoners campaigns of all kinds The white walls with gold trim were covered from floor to ceiling with memorabilia from all the political wars I'd waged, all the elections I'd won, all the controversial companies whose stock price I'd saved, all the exceptionally good things I'd done for the sake of mankind.

As you might expect, there was not a shard of evidence on display from any of the losing campaigns I'd worked on, which, thankfully, was still a rather infrequent occurrence. Where I sat and worked was my own hall of fame, my own private version of Cooperstown or Canton or Graceland. Sometimes, when I was in the middle of something mindless or stupid or I was simply bored to tears, which happened often in my line of work, I'd gaze up from my oversized desk, which was a real life-size replica of the President's desk in the Oval Office (screw Freud – I don't care what he'd think), and stared lovingly at my surroundings, taking it all in, trying to absorb the magnitude and magnificence of everything I've accomplished.

On this morning, as I was ripping up a hideously insipid speech the Korzinski campaign had sent me before their erratic, emotionally unstable, pill-popping candidate addressed the City Club of Cleveland to defend his indefensible record as a do-nothing Senator, my solitude was interrupted by a loud smash against the large plate-glass window behind my desk. Then came a second bang, followed quickly by a third. I jumped up, wheeled around and looked out the window, trying to ascertain what was unfolding. Staring directly at me, perched on a large tree branch, overhanging a long thread of electrical wires probably belonging to the phone company or cable company or some CIA surveillance unit that was paranoid enough to keep an eye on someone as paranoid as me, was the ugliest, scrawniest, meanest-looking and most likely rabid black squirrel I'd ever seen.

As I pressed my face against the window, the rodent smiled, leapt off the branch while swinging from the wire and slammed head-first into the glass, making another big bang before bouncing back to the branch. I immediately recognized that I was under attack from a crazy kamikaze squirrel. In an act of retaliation, I whacked the window with my fist as hard as I could, trying to scare him away. All he did in response was flash me a contemptuous look. So I gave one right back to him, which inspired him to reciprocate by lifting up his paw and giving me what must have been the squirrel equivalent of the "go fuck yourself" middle-finger gesture. This greatly offended me, so I hit the window again, this time much harder – too much harder, hard enough to shatter it, sending glass flying everywhere. The squirrel looked at me in shock as if I were truly a nut job, then finally fled the scene.

Okay, maybe I was being too thin-skinned. Maybe I had overreacted. Nonetheless, this unexpected, unsettling confrontation, along with the shards of broken glass covering my floor and a couple of small cuts on my hands, ended up depressing me all morning. As the workmen arrived to board up the busted window, I sulked at my desk, too dispirited to get anything done. I had done nothing to provoke the little shit, but I had been victimized nonetheless. A goddamn squirrel had the audacity to give me, Burt Heinz King, the preeminent political consultant in the country, if not the world, the finger. Was this some cosmic foreshadowing of Armageddon?

It wasn't until noon that I calmed down enough to head downstairs into the Bat Cave, my affectionate name for my editing studio, my workshop, my dungeon of doom, where I used my indisputable brilliance to produce the most brutally effective political ads ever created for television and the Internet. I had no equal when it came to my talent for driving poll numbers up and down with a precision that would have made even the most famous artists in history gag with jealousy.

"Where the fuck have you been?" was Big Al's friendly greeting when I found him hunched over a row of video monitors and computers, where he had presumably spent the night. "I need a life too," he groaned.

"What are you doing, bad boy?" I asked.

"Nothing out of the ordinary. Just digitally inserting Congressman Schwartz's opponent into perverted porn videos we can spread online, anonymously, of course, and then use in our new TV ads."

"What's that poor sap's name?" I couldn't remember.

"Korn," said Big Al. "Rhymes with porn. As in, 'Say No to Porn, Say No to Korn.' See where I'm going with this?"

"Good idea. The press will eat this up. And our paid bloggers will inflict unimaginable damage. We'll burn this poor bastard to a crisp."

Big Al wheeled around from the computer bank and slapped me five, a joint affirmation of our cutthroat creativity.

Al Frum, all 6 feet 5, 275 pounds of him (hence the name Big Al), was my editor, writer, alter ego and co-conspirator. A former college football player turned FBI agent who made adult films on the side, he was a kindred spirit who knew better than anyone I'd ever met how to make my insidious ideas come to life. I may have been the one who flew the plane, but without his editing and technical skills, I'd have been just another run-of-the-mill consultant with two-bit clients and enough half-baked ideas to fill the Atlantic Ocean.

With Big Al at my side, and a small, dedicated staff of young, underpaid, overworked glorified interns with excessive ambition and delusions of grandeur, I rocketed SDI to the top of our highly competitive field. Big Al and I worked seamlessly together to define and consistently refine state-of-the-art negative campaigning, perfecting our ever-expanding playbook along the way. And in one of my more magnanimous, altruistic moments, I bit the bullet and made Big Al an equity partner in SDI. I gave him a 3 percent stake as an act of good faith, leaving the other 97 percent for myself. It's been worth it on every level.

Just like great NFL quarterbacks, Big Al and I always knew which plays to call to win the game. We knew how to exploit every weakness in our opponent's defense. We knew how to anticipate and neutralize every offensive weapon that our opponent might deploy. And we were always relentless. Unbelievably relentless.

Here's our patented, foolproof, fail-safe, five-step guide to winning a political campaign under any circumstances:

1. Paint your opponent as a proponent of massive tax hikes, regardless of his record.
2. Tie your opponent to criminal activity, regardless of the truth.
3. Raise questions about your opponent's American heritage, regardless of his lineage.
4. Raise questions about your opponent's marital state, sexual proclivities or possible perversions, regardless of reality.
5. Bombard the fucker with all sorts of outrageous, unsubstantiated allegations 24 hours before Election Day, throwing him on the defensive and giving him no time to get on the air or online to set the record straight.

MONDAY

I reviewed a rough cut of Big Al's latest edit on the Korn Porn spot and gave my approval. "This kinda reminds me of the time we digitally inserted Governor Bartz's opponent into Muslim attire, gave him a starring role in a terrorist propaganda video and then plastered it all over the Web," I said.

"I'll never forget that!" howled Al. "The lousy fuck was hauled off by the FBI on Suspicion of Insurrection charges with one month left in the campaign."

"And can you recall exactly how much his poll numbers dropped?"

"Oh, about 43 points in 12 hours, if I remember correctly," Al answered. "The Governor won re-election in a romp."

"You are correct," I replied, offering my congratulations. "Best part was, by the time all charges were dropped against Bartz's opponent, the election was over – and so was that loser's political career."

"I wonder whatever happened to him," Big Al mused. "What was his name? Hamas or Hummus or something like that?"

"Can't even remember," I replied. "He's probably sweeping floors somewhere in Seattle or teaching political science at some shitty high school."

Big Al started laughing again.

"What's so funny?" I wondered.

"I was just thinking about that time, must have been 15 years ago, when you got those five death-row inmates in Tennessee to endorse Senator Carrolton's opponent."

"Ah, yes, the "Death Row Inmates for Davidson" spot. I remember it like it was yesterday. We may have had to pay their families thousands of dollars, but that particular stunt did millions of dollars in damage to the schmuck's short-lived campaign."

I first met Big Al at a book party at the Georgetown mansion of some State Department official whose name I now cannot remember. Must have been 25 years ago. I was just starting to make my name, slowly but surely, in the political-consulting business.

At the time, I had just turned 30 and was a lowly gofer for one of the top Democratic campaign consultants in the country, an egomaniacal, wheezing, obese nutcase, Ed Foster, who smoked cigars, drank like a fish (until he inevitably puked) and unsuccessfully chased young women and men like they were going out of style. A genius on one level, a miserable slob on every other.

During these inglorious days, I was Foster's chauffeur, errand boy and condom-carrying barf-bag assistant, who occasionally did a little research, scriptwriting and commercial-editing on the side. It was a classic case of paying one's dues while holding one's nose. One night, Foster asked me to attend some high-society reception at some former ambassador's mansion – or, more likely, to drive him to it so he could get drunk out of his mind, make passes at anyone within reach and not worry about how he would get home.

Anyway, there I was at this stuffy, super-boring event, and all the blowhards were ignoring me because I was a peon and they erroneously thought they weren't and the party was starting to break up, I was dead tired and I couldn't find Foster and I really wanted to go home to my ratty apartment in Adams Morgan because a really cute girl had just moved in that day and I wanted to see if she needed any assistance unpacking. So I was looking everywhere for fuckhead Foster, inside and outside, upstairs and downstairs. I even checked the garage and the bottom of the pool to see if, in his inebriated state, he had fallen in. But he was nowhere to be found.

"Who you looking for?" said a rather large, tuxedoed waiter who was outside packing up the catering truck.

"Ed Foster," I said with clear desperation.

"And who are you?" he asked in a decidedly unfriendly manner.

"His slave."

"Okay, hold on a second," he said, as he climbed inside the back of the catering truck.

Two minutes later, he returned to tell me that Foster had left the premises an hour before in a silver Lexus with Congressman Prout, one of the more aggressive female swingers on the Hill.

"And how do you know that?" I asked.

"None of your damn business," he said before walking back into the house, leaving me more than a little perplexed.

I left immediately and raced back to my apartment, just in time to run into that cute girl's hulking boyfriend, who apparently was moving in too. So I went straight to bed, another wasted Washington evening.

A week later, I was running an errand for Foster at a Tyson Corner mall when who should I run into but that waiter from the Georgetown book party. Except this time, he was wearing a running suit and walking very fast.

"Hey, remember me?" I asked.

"No, now get your ass out of my way."

"C'mon, don't act like we never met," I said, catching up to him.

"You're confusing me with someone else. Now, so long and farewell forever."

Off he went down the concourse, until he was tackled from behind by some equally large guy in a trench coat. As they wrestled on the floor, yelling obscenities at each other and attracting a substantial crowd, his assailant pulled out a knife, triggering a shot of adrenaline in my body that instantly transformed me instant superhero. I swooped in and kicked the knifeman in the back of the head as hard as I could with a blow that would have made my mom proud (for no more than a nanosecond), right as a posse of mall security guards came running over to break up the altercation.

"Thanks, man," said the mysterious waiter turned brawler.

"No sweat," I responded. "Just doing my job as a public citizen. You know, upholding the law, protecting the peace."

Before the security guards hauled the knife man away, one of them asked me a couple of questions for the report he had to file. I gave my name and address and a quick description of what I saw, and then I left. That was that, until a week later, when the waiter guy called me out of the blue, thanked me for my assistance at the mall and invited me out for a beer.

"How'd you get my number?" I asked.

"I don't know. I just got it."

By now, I was curious and broke enough to accept his invitation, so three days later, we met at the Heinous Anus, and he told me his story.

He had recently started working at the FBI as a trainee in their high-tech surveillance unit, and he hated his job. "Too much paperwork, too many rules and the pay sucks," he said.

"So what do you want to do?" I asked.

"I want to do what you do. Fight the fight. Right the wrongs. Serve my country. And make shitloads of money."

"How do you know what I do?"

"I know everything about you."

"And how is that?"

"I read your file this morning at the office. I want to get into political consulting in a major way. And I know you're ready to make your move, too."

Too many beers later, Al had convinced me to resign from my job with Foster, start my own firm and hire him on as an associate on a trial basis.

"I hope you're as good as you say you are," I remember telling him.

"Likewise," he said.

And the rest, as they say, is history.

After brainstorming with Al about the right music for the "No Porn, No Korn" spot, I strolled back to my office to return a couple of calls before my second most profitable clients, those crazy Russian Pavlov brothers, picked me up in their stretch limo. I was supposed to be their family's guest for lunch at Decadence, the restaurant in the Gazprom-HayAdams Hotel, their favorite Washington establishment.

"Hello, Burt!" shouted Alexi, as the uniformed driver opened my door and I climbed inside.

"Does the King want to eat or fuck?" said Josef, who appeared at first glance to be getting it on with one, if not two, of the buxom, barely dressed hookers in the back seat.

This was a surprisingly tough choice: Between my morning blowout with Juanita and then having to rush to the Hill to bail out the sexually compromised Speaker, I hadn't had the chance to eat breakfast or grab a snack, and now I was sufficiently famished. An empty, growling stomach made me more irritable than usual; I recognized that it was time to feed my inner beast. Plus, the ladies in back looked over-the-top skanky. A definite disease risk. Even I had standards.

"Would you mind if we ate lunch?" I said wearily. "I'm famished."

"Whatever you say, Burt," Alexi said. "We can meet my father, have lunch and then fuck later."

If you've never heard of them, which is hard to believe, the Pavlov family was perhaps the wealthiest family in the world, even after their terrible setback in Alaska a few years ago, when, in the space of six months, their nuclear power plant outside Anchorage had a catastrophic meltdown – mortally nuking nearly 10,000 residents and rendering a 600-square-mile region uninhabitable – and one of their offshore oil rigs exploded in the Gulf of Alaska, spilling more crude oil than there was water in both the Gulf and most of the Bering Sea. They basically eradicated all the area commerce and tourism-- not to mention a few thousand species of wildlife.

Despite these record-breaking environmental debacles, the Pavlovs survived and eventually thrived, thanks to some inspiringly brilliant crisis-management expertise and high-wire political/regulatory/judicial machinations devised by none other than me. College marketing classes still teach a case study based on my "Sorry we fucked up but shit happens now let's forget about it and move on!" corporate ad campaign.

In the years since, the Pavlovs had bounced back in a big way. Their Moscow-based energy company, UWind, controlled nearly 90 percent of the wind rights around the world. Chances are, if you had wind where you lived, the Pavlovs owned the rights to buy it and sell it, thanks to a series of bold supply-side corner-the-market deals they did to ensure that anyone who owned a wind-powered anything was utterly dependent on them. Alexi and Josef, barely in their 30s, were now running UWind under the watchful eye of their father, Bo (who was born Boris IV but officially became Bo after spending his sex-crazed college years partying in Athens, Georgia, while ostensibly attending the University of Georgia, during which time his oil-rich parents endowed a new medical school and built a $125 million I.M. Pei-inspired DKE fraternity mansion for their Bo and his buddies). The Pavlov clan was the first trillion-dollar family in Russia, even though Alexi and Josef spent more time in New York, Santa Barbara and Monaco than in Moscow.

For the last few years, ever since those dual oil accidents, I had done what I call "strategic threat-based consulting" for the Pavlovs, for a sweet $1 million-a-month retainer – plus $10 million a year in political donations I could direct to candidates of my choosing, i.e., candidates who hired Slice & Dice. Pretty sweet, eh?

My Russian friends were in town today to celebrate my latest victory defending their turf. A group of wayward Congressmen had moronically introduced legislation that would have effectively outlawed the family's ability to control the wind market in the U.S. Let's just say that bill never made it out of committee, and every single one of those Congressmen was impeached from office and is doing something else for a living, like flipping burgers, cleaning up pigeon shit or greeting customers at their friendly neighborhood KoreaMart Superstore.

Whenever the Pavlovs needed something done in our nation's capital, I was, as I deserved to be, their go-to guy. And as our limo pulled into the hotel driveway, I was feeling even more important and loved than ususal.

"All rise for the King," laughed Boris, giving me a bear hug as his sons and I entered their supersized presidential suite. "Wonderful to see you again."

"Great to see you too, Boris," I responded, scanning the room for any sign of his most recent wife. "Is Electra joining us today?"

"No, she's back in Moscow with her family," Boris said, as he escorted me down the hallway toward the private elevator, which would take us up to the rooftop restaurant for what I knew from experience would be a scrumptious, overpriced lunch.

"Please give Electra my regards," I said, not really meaning it. I snuck a peek at my watch, calculating that I had 90 minutes max to eat and run before my next appointment, a very important speech I had to give to a very important audience.

"Where the fuck are you going, Boris?" yelled a woman's voice from the back bedroom, a voice I did not recognize.

"Are we waiting for someone else?" I asked, as the elevator doors opened.

"We most certainly are not," said Boris.

"I want my damn money!" wailed the unhappy voice. "You owe me $15,000."

"Are you sure, Boris?" I asked again.

"Absolutely sure, Burt," Boris said with certainty as he stepped into the elevator. "We need to get going. As you know, time is money."

"I know. I know," I laughed, as the elevator doors shut. "How is the mighty Pavlov family doing?"

"We need help with Congress," said Josef.

"With what?" I asked. "Has something gone awry in one of the committees? I usually hear about that stuff before you do."

"Not really," said Boris. "We just need to know for sure that nothing bad will happen to UWind in the future. You see, our business is good – actually, very good, actually, exceptionally good – and we must ensure it stays that way. No problems. No regulations. No surprises."

"How can I be of assistance?" I asked, as the maître d' seated us at our oversized booth looking out on the White House, with the Capitol and Pentagon off in the distance.

"Our family has no faith in Congress," said Alexi. "After everything we've been through, we can't trust them anymore. We know they think we're too big. They've tried to break our wind monopoly before, and we know it's only a matter of time before they try again."

"Those dirty bastards!" I said in my most sycophantic voice.

"They won't mind their own fucking business," said Boris.

"Tell me what the esteemed Pavlovs are thinking," I said as I munched on some bread.

"Look," said Josef, "we can't afford to have something go wrong again. We need to protect UWind – and ourselves – from their crazy bullshit."

"What exactly did you have in mind?" I wondered.

"So, Burt," said Boris, "we've assessed the situation, and we'd like, with your assistance, to make a strategic investment. We want to buy a majority interest in the House and Senate, which works out to exactly 218 Representatives and 51 Senators."

"You want to buy what?" I sputtered, not sure if they proposed what I think they proposed.

"You heard us right," said Alexi. "The Pavlov family wants to purchase a controlling interest in the House and Senate. To protect UWind's best interests. Ideally, we'd buy an equal number of Republicans and Democrats so we can be proactively bipartisan in our approach."

"Yeah," echoed Boris. "We ran the numbers and concluded it's a deal worth doing. Not exactly cheap, but the best insurance money can buy."

"Oh my, you're serious, aren't you?"

The Pavlovs nodded in unison, not exhibiting even the faintest sign of a smile.

"Tell me again why you want to buy a controlling share of Congress?" I asked deferentially. "You already make big campaign contributions to nearly every one in Congress, even when they don't have serious opponents. These legislators already owe you."

"In theory, yes, but in reality, that's just not good enough," Boris said firmly. "You can't trust these bastards. They'll fuck over their friends in a heartbeat if a better deal comes along. Have you forgotten we almost got ambushed by that legislation last time around? It taught us a real lesson: Campaign contributions buy you consideration; ownership buys you absolute control."

"You can't just buy a member of Congress like you buy a car or an airplane," I reminded them.

"Says who?" asked Alexi. "Who says it can't be done?"

"Says me," I replied. "I would do anything to help your family, but this is impossible. Trust me."

"You're wrong, Burt," said Josef. "Everything is for sale, if you're willing to pay enough for it. And according to our intelligence operatives, most members of Congress are more than willing to consider an outright acquisition if the money is right."

Boris dangled a handwritten list of names in front of my face. "We are prepared to offer each of these legislators $10 million a year," he said matter-of-factly. "All we ask is that they vote our way a few times a year when we need them."

"It couldn't be any more straightforward," added Bo.

"It's impossible," I said. "Not only is this scheme impractical and unethical, but it's illegal."

"We've never heard you use words like 'impossible,' 'impractical,' 'unethical' and 'illegal,'" Boris said. "You've always told us that in this town, you've got to pay to play. So here we are, offering to pay in a big way to play in a big way, and you're telling us it can't be done?"

"That's right. I'm telling you it can't be done."

"If that's the case," huffed Alexi, "I guess our family will have to find another Washington adviser who believes it *can* be done."

The three Pavlovs stood up and prepared to stomp out in unison, leaving me sitting there all alone, embarrassed and fired, suddenly without my dearly beloved UWind retainer.

I recalibrated the imminent reality of the situation and concluded it was time for a U-turn to save my UWind account.

"Okay, okay, sit down and relax," I said. "I'm sure we can figure something out."

And they sat back down. And we talked. And we agreed to the following plan of action, because I, Burt King, am a man of action.

The Pavlovs would endow a new UWind Foundation think tank, housed in magnificent office space on K Street and run by a high-powered, exceptionally well-paid, well-heeled board of advisers comprised of Congressional spouses, offspring and other influential, related parties that could guarantee the votes we needed whenever necessary. Different approach, same outcome. As easy as 1-2-3. Congress would never cross the Pavlovs again. Big smiles around the table. A delectable lunchtime meal after all. Close call averted.

As I walked triumphantly out of the Gazprom-HayAdams and waited for a cab, I was hit with a liquid splat of something smack in the middle of my head. While I recoiled from the blow, the foreign substance dripped slowly down my neck onto my shirt collar, oozing onto my $12,000 Moldavian suit, I had a dreadful epiphany: I was the innocent victim of a random bird-shit drive-by. "Christ almighty!" I screamed to the unforgiving heavens, as another load of shit hit the bridge of my nose, sending me into a full-fledged tantrum.

First I was assaulted by a lunatic squirrel. Now this mockery of justice, officially ruining my already hideous day. Sadly, I was scheduled to give a speech at the Hyundai Hilton that afternoon, for an insanely high honorarium, to the annual convention for the American Society of Seminal Political Consultants, or ASSPAC, as it is known in the trade. The organizers of ASSPAC had invited me, as they undeniably should have, to spread my nuggets of brilliance for a half hour without even having to take dumb questions from the peons. Just speak and cash the check. Doesn't get more simple than that. Total time commitment: 60 minutes (30 minutes at the hotel, plus 15 minutes travel time each way). Total payday: $150,000, or $2,500 dollars per minute, or $42 per second. Not bad for an honest hour's work.

I used to look forward to attending this massive gabfest every year when I was an up-and-coming political consultant, well before I became the runaway hit of my chosen profession. I would network my tail off, shaking every hand, kissing every ass, doing everything I could at every session, reception, exhibit hall booth wherever – anything to impress my more experienced colleagues with my novel ideas and innovative, insidious strategies and tactics. The goal was to get noticed, to catch the eye of the bigwig consultants at that time and make it known that I was available to co-consult or scoop up their crappy campaign scraps if they were too busy running multiple campaigns, producing too many attack ads and stage-managing hordes of unstable, neurotic politicians.

But nowadays, ASSPAC had little sentimental value. I may have been Jesus or Moses to those conventioneers paying big bucks to see me but I had zero interest in my flock. Another crappy analogy, but hopefully you get my point.

I snapped out of my self-pitying stupor, ran back inside the hotel, hit the bathroom and wiped off as much shit as I could with every cloth towel available. But it didn't do the trick. The stain and stench were way too visible. Still, there was no cause for panic. I knew I didn't have enough time to run home and change, but I had plenty of time to call Felix Futz, the effete but highly effective, obsequiously loyal manager of the Men's Department at ShanghaiSak's, and have him pull a nice-ass suit off the rack for me, which he dutifully did for $7,500 including tax. The suit was pressed and bagged and waiting for me by the loading dock when I drove up. In a town as treacherous as Washington, that's what true friends were for – even if Futz wasn't technically a friend. I mean, I would never have a meal with him or respect him or anything like that.

A few short minutes later, I was standing tall, resplendent in my new attire, towering over the ASSPAC podium (thanks to a conveniently placed step stool), lighting the room on fire with my exceptional wit and wisdom, sailing through my trademark motivational speech, which I had perfected over the years:

"You and I and every consultant in this room are masters of the universe, masters of our domain, masters of the masses or, at a minimum, masters of manipulating the masses. We are the glue that keeps democracy functional. We are the oil that greases the outcome of each election. We are the K-Y Jelly that keeps the right voters lubricated the right way to ensure that our candidate will emerge victorious. Yes, we may wreak havoc over the course of a bruising campaign, but we promise to uphold the United States Constitution and honor our professional code of ethics.

Come hell or high water, we make a holy commitment to our high-priced clients that, above all, we will do whatever it takes to win. And in fulfilling our pledge, we will spare no expense in eviscerating the opposition, flogging the carcass of the dying media and, last but not least cynically increasing or decreasing voter turnout by the exact percentage needed to achieve the desired electoral results."

On and on I went, the undulating crowd caught up in an orgy of worship.

"Most people don't give a shit about voting. The few who do vote are like Play-doh: They are there to be molded in any way, shape or form we deem appropriate. They are lost and confused without us. It is our moral responsibility to lead them to where we need them to go. For we are their shepherds and they are the sheep."

More thunderous applause with each stem-winding, crowd-pleasing oratorical thrust.

"What is truth? Truth is an illusion, a pathetic, pitiful crutch for losers and whiners and self-righteous sons of bitches who can't deal with reality."

As usual, I had the crowd right where I wanted them.

"I am here today to tell you that I, Burt King, do not care about the truth. I don't care about the facts. If you want to be a success in our profession, you have to fuck the facts. If you don't, the facts are going to end up fucking you."

The frenzy began to build. "Never ever forget that our clients pay us to win. And whatever it takes, baby, I will win. Unless, of course, my candidate stinks or commits an indefensible felony within a year of Election Day, and then, 99 times out of 100, even with my inestimable brilliance, there is nothing I can do to overcome this suckability quotient and get my loser elected.

"The inalienable truth in our profession is this: When we do our jobs right, no one can stop us. No one. Not even those scumbags in the media. Those biased whining jerks whose newspapers are dying, whose magazines are dying, whose tv stations are dying and whose websites are full of shit that no one, and I mean no one, gives a shit about. Which is why every one of us in this room should rise up and join together and tell the media to go fuck itself."

My disciples jumped to their feet, giving me the standing ovation that I so deservedly deserved as I launched into my close:

"Give me an F!" I challenged the crowd.

"F!" they yelled back.

"Fuck the media!" I shouted, before rolling on. "Give me a U!"

"U!" they shot back.

"Unleash everything you got. Give me a C!"

"C!" they squealed.

"Give me a K!"

"K!" they hollered back.

"Kick some fucking ass! Whatta we got?"

"Fuck the media!" the adoring audience began chanting rhythmically as I strutted across the stage, waving and saluting and even bowing a few times for good measure.

I, Burt King, was unstoppable, unbeatable and worth every dollar I was being paid to address ASSPAC. At least, in theory, until I got hit in the face with the first of several tomatoes, followed by a barrage of eggs, water balloons and two flying dead fish launched by a deranged gang of protesters who simultaneously rushed the stage, targeting me with their venom. As I tried to flee the bedlam, a riot ensued. I knew my speech was over. I worried my life might be as well.

"Power to the people!" the mob shouted as they chased after me. "Death to the consultants, death to the politicians!" Not exactly a novel approach, but they made their point. The worst part was that instead of coming to my defense, the audience full of my admiring political hacks ran for their lives, leaving me all alone to fend for myself while these criminals splattered me with their foodstuffs. In the space of a minute, I had gone from über-adulation at the height of my profession to target practice for the unwashed, misinformed and maniacal masses.

As I bolted backstage, amidst a sea of shrieks and whistles and the hissing of exploding canisters filled with what I could tell was tear gas, some asshole tackled me to the ground, slapping me on the ass until a security guard miraculously appeared out of nowhere and clubbed the jerk in the back of the head with the butt of his gun. I looked at the protester's bloodied, dizzy, soon-to-be unconscious face as he was dragged away in cuffs. Somehow, before his eyes closed, he mustered enough energy to flip me off and whisper hoarsely, "We'll be back, Burt."

I didn't stop to ponder the meaning of his menacing taunt. I just kept right on running, escaping through an exit door that led to a loading dock that led to L Street and my freedom.

Convinced there was now a sufficient police presence on the scene to safeguard my safety, I walked around to the front of the Hyundai Hilton on 16th Street to watch with glee as the police dragged all of the detained, deranged protesters out the door and into the waiting police van for their all-expenses-paid, all-amenities-included first-class trip to jail.

"Get a fucking life," I yelled at one of the cuffed fools who tried to spit on me and missed.

"You stink, King! You stink!" he yelled back at the top of his lungs, until two beefy security guards kicked him to the ground, taped his mouth shut with plastic tape and tossed him in the van with the rest of his nutty brethren.

"Enjoy your jail time," I threw in for good measure.

I decided not to go back to my office as a disheveled, hopelessly soiled mess to do stupid things for stupid clients at stupid rates. The progression of events on this particular day had put me in a funk again. I was feeling particularly negative about basically everything I could think of at this juncture of my life. Which is why I decided I had earned the right to end my work day early and go to the movies.

I decompressed for the next couple of hours by sitting alone in an air-conditioned theater in Upper NW, thoroughly enjoying two new, highly recommended X-rated films: *Poontang on the Potomac* and *American Idols Gone Wild*. My mood was much, much better by the time I walked out. I felt recharged and refreshed.

My day got even better when I arrived home to discover that despite my best, most pessimistic guess, Juanita had not moved out or changed the locks or filed a temporary restraining order against me. Hallelujah. She was in the living room, sitting on our handmade Italian-leather couch, holding a class of white wine and watching *Celebrity Death Match*, the popular reality show on which two over-the-hill celebrities tried to kill each other with machetes. As bloody as it would invariably get, it was the number one series in America, brilliantly capitalizing on our lust for celebrities and thirst for blood. Hence, a perennial prime-time ratings juggernaut.

I tried my absolute best to give Juanita a sweet "I'm so sorry" look when she glanced up and saw me walking toward the couch. She didn't exactly smile back, but she didn't pull out a high-powered rifle and shoot me dead, either. Not sure why she always came back after we fought, but I was always glad she did, no matter how screwed up things were between us or how bad I'd been behaving. I was hoping that after a few minutes of awkward, tentative interaction, we'd settle back down into our married routine, ignoring our latest blowout as if nothing that bad had ever happened.

"How was the rest of your day, honey?" I asked sheepishly.

"It's been a walk in the park compared to what you put me through this morning," she said without taking her eyes off the TV, where a show-stopping, extra-gory decapitation had just taken place.

"Sorry about that," I said. "I hope it won't happen again."

"Who are you kidding?" she replied icily. "Of course it will."

"Yeah, you're probably right." I shrugged.

"Why in God's name did I ever marry you?" Juanita asked during the next commercial, her voice dripping with sarcasm as we sat together on the couch, trying unsuccessfully to bring closure to another ridiculously trying day.

"Because I floored you with my genius, good looks, greatness and animal magnetism."

"Hardly."

"Because I blew you away with my kindness, sensitivity, brilliance and inner beauty."

"Fat chance."

"Because I'm the most famous political consultant in America and you get off on your proximity to power?"

"Wrong. You know I don't respect what you do for a living."

"Okay, then, let me ask you: Why *did* you marry me?"

"Because I was temporarily insane."

"Didn't you admire any of my fabulous attributes?"

"Who are you fooling, Burt?"

"Good question," I said. "It's clear you were the one I fooled. Because you married me. So, in a court of law, any judge would rule that you have no one to blame but yourself."

"Don't worry," Juanita said, as she rolled over on the couch and thrust her bare feet in my face. "I blame myself every day."

A few hours later, thanks to my infinite gifts of gab and repentance, I somehow convinced Juanita to consent to having makeup sex with me. It took all my persuasive abilities, including repeatedly apologizing for that morning's transgressions while whining about feeling "lonely, insecure and terribly depressed." Yet despite my luck in seducing her and ending our prolonged sexual drought, things did not go well in bed. She clearly wasn't into it. It was like she was going through the motions. Like she'd have rather been watching TV. Or doing the dishes. Or paying the bills. No emotion, no passion, not much of anything. Except for an infuriating amount of yawns.

The worst part of our love-making attempt was that Juanita insisted on listening to her music while we were having sex. At least, I assumed she was listening to music. But for all I knew, she was listening to the weather or a Spanish-language talk show. At one point, when I got my left knee tangled up in the wires from her ear buds and accidentally pulled them out, she shoved me aside with a sharp elbow as if I were intentionally interrupting her listening pleasure.

After we were done, or, more accurately, after I was done, I couldn't fall asleep. My mind kept racing about stupid things like random polling numbers, past-due invoices, prior cases of sexually transmitted diseases and my ultimate legacy in life. Adding to my insomnia was a longer-than-normal air-raid siren, which rattled me because I had been led to believe by high-ranking Pentagon officials that we had successfully destroyed the entire Canadian Air Force. They were obviously wrong. Unless some other country had decided to bomb us and start a war.

By now, it was nearly 2 a.m., and I was getting really pissed that I couldn't fall asleep. Sadly, the angrier I got, the more wide awake I became. I was stuck in a vicious cycle, like when I'm incredibly mad and incredibly hungry and I keep getting madder and hungrier because I don't know whether to scream before I eat or eat before I scream.

To get my mind off my problems, I decided to pass the time by calibrating the rhythm of Juanita's snoring with the help of my trusty alarm clock. And for the next half hour, that's what I did – timed her nasal expulsions, which were hitting, on average, 20 snorts a minute. While this exercise was distracting enough to a certain extent, it didn't help put me to sleep. Switching gears, I opened the drawer on my nightstand and pulled out my radio and headphones. It was time to check in with real America on the radio dial, courtesy of my favorite talk-show demigod, the one and only Max Morrison, broadcasting live from midnight until 5 a.m. on 150 stations in all 50 states, which is why he lovingly called himself, in a burst of characteristic bravado, the Voice of America.

"Welcome back, America," he started in after a commercial break for a new FDA-approved hemorrhoid cream containing wd-50 and bark from a cedar tree. "This is Max Morrison, broadcasting live from the land of the free and the home of the brave – and tonight, more than any other night, I want to know if you're as fed up as I am about the sewage that plagues our great country: the liberals, the liars, the gays, the lesbos, the immigrants, the bloodsucking minorities and the criminals. If we don't work together to protect America from these evildoers, derelicts and pussy politicians –, if we don't stop our enemies now, if we don't get this country back on track before we become just another run-of-the-mill nation of nitwits, if we don't stop kissing the butts of these butthole countries that are nothing more than communist, socialist, terrorist fronts – then we are doomed, and our country is doomed, and are future is doomed. You got it? We're in a fight to the death for our lives and our liberties. Okay, then, let's open up the phone lines and start talking about what the fuck we're going to do to save the U.S.A."

Boy, Max was on a roll tonight. He seemed to be in a particularly toxic mood. Like me. Which made for some highly entertaining talk radio.

"Let's go to Brad in Buffalo. Hi, Brad, how are you tonight?"

"Not so good, Max. I got problems at work."

"And what are your problems, Brad?"

"Let's just say I am a victim of bullshit discrimination."

"And how are you being discriminated against?"

"Here's the deal. I'm white and my boss ain't, and he hates my guts because I'm white and he's black."

"I see," said Max. "When you say he hates you, how do you know for sure?"

"He's always calling me names," Brad said.

"Like what?"

"Lazy ass, dumb-ass, white trash, honkey, crap like that."

"And how do you respond when he calls you names?"

"I give it back right to him, calling him things that make him real mad."

"Such as?"

"The usual. The N-word, Jungle Bunny, Sambo, Spic-lover – you know, names like that."

"Spic-lover?"

"Yeah, there are a lot of Spanish-speaking dudes that work in the warehouse with us, and my boss seems to treat them a lot better than me. As if he thinks us whites are the worst."

"Okay, Brad," Max said. "I get the picture. Let's dig a little deeper into your situation, and then I can give you some advice on how to respond."

"Sounds good," said the engaged caller.

"Are you willing to die for your beliefs?" asked Max.

"What do you mean?"

"If I asked you to take part in a revolution to take our country back from those who are trying to take it over, would you be willing to fight and risk your life in battle?"

"Hmmm," Brad said, unsure how to respond.

"Do you own a gun, Brad?"

"Of course. Doesn't everyone?"

"If I asked you to assassinate one of our enemies, would you agree, even if you might get killed or wounded or locked up in jail for the rest of your life?"

"To be honest," Brad sputtered, "I don't think so. As much as I hate my boss and my job, I would miss my friends and my family and my freedom."

"Well then, Brad, what you're saying is that you are a pathetic wimp of the first degree: a two-bit shit parading around as an oppressed white man. No wonder white people are on the verge of losing their rights. They're too cowardly to fight for them."

And with that, Max hung up on Brad from Buffalo.

"Our next caller is Nora from Dallas. Go ahead, Nora."

"Hi, Max."

"How can I help you, Nora?"

"I'm calling to say I think you're real sexy when you get all hot and dirty with your callers. Are you ever available for phone sex?"

"For you, Nora, and for everyone else out there who finds me sexy, you can satisfy your sexual urges anytime, day or night, by calling my 24-hour sex line, 1-900-MAX-SMUT. That's 1-900-629-7688. And I swear, from the bottom of my groin, we'll get down to business. For only $7.99 per minute, plus all applicable taxes and service charges.

"Time for Cindy from San Diego," Max continued. "Welcome to the show, Cindy."

"Thanks for taking my call, Max," she said with over-the-top giddiness. "Can you tell me where it's legal to hunt immigrants?"

"Sure, Cindy. Twenty-two states currently allow the legal hunting of immigrants during all or part of the year. Your best bet is to go to www.immigrant-hunting.com, a featured advertiser on this show, for complete rules and regulations searchable by state, city, even zip code."

The last caller I heard that night was Adam from Ft. Wayne. He sounded like a pimply teenager, seemingly unable to keep a straight face while asking his loaded question:

"Max, do you think the President deserves to die?"

I sat up in bed, bracing for the response. I knew Morrison hated pretty much everyone, but I had little sense of where Strump ranked on his hit list.

"No, I do not," Morrison said with great conviction. "President Strump may be misguided, he may be incompetent, he may be grossly negligent and delusional about the threats we face from within, but he does not deserve to die. He should, however, be impeached and bitch-slapped on national TV for being a quintessential all-American idiot."

That hurt. I made a mental note to make sure Morrison was on the White House enemies list, the IRS's mandatory audit list and the Transportation

Security Administration's "no-fly list" for the foreseeable future. And with that, I flipped off the radio and somehow finally fell asleep.

Right before 4 a.m., I was awakened again by what I thought was a small explosion. But after looking out of our floor-to-ceiling windows, I concluded it was just a summer thunderstorm passing through town, temporarily dissipating the hideous humidity that made Washington such a steamy, suffocating place this time of year.

Tuesday

When my alarm clock finally buzzed and it was lamentably time to get up, I found myself alone in bed. After doing my business, I discovered Juanita sitting by herself at the kitchen table, visibly distressed. She was slumped over in her chair, gazing out the window, weeping, completely oblivious to my presence in the room. I assumed she was deep in thought, trying to figure out which would be easier: jumping out the window to her death or throwing me out the window to mine.

"What's wrong with you now?" I asked.

"Everything. I woke up this morning and realized that every single thing in my life is wrong. With me, with us, with this world."

Not exactly sure how to respond, I grabbed a half-frozen bagel off of our $175,000 granite and solid-gold kitchen island and shoved it into my mouth without even trying to properly chew.

Yes, I am much too fast an eater, one of my many faults. As I devoured the bagel, I could swear I heard my mother yelling at me: "Albert Einstein Stein! Slow down and eat your food properly or you'll get a stomachache – or worse, diarrhea."

Juanita gave me a brutally dismissive look as I tried unsuccessfully to swallow the hunk of bagel. It was time for me to speak, but I couldn't without fear of choking, so in the interest of time, and for the sake of calming her down and avoiding another unpleasant marital conflict to start my day, I walked over to the sink and spit out the bagel, freeing me to respond.

"Do you regret the sex we had last night?" I asked sheepishly.

"I can't believe you treated me that way," Juanita said.

"What way? What did I do?"

"You cried out for another woman in your sleep," she whined. "You called out for Tyra."

"I did?" I said, speedily trying to decipher what was unfolding.

"You must have been having some X-rated sex dream about Tyra, who I assume is someone you know intimately. You were ooohing and ahhing and moaning and groaning like you were doing it with her. And some other guy named Einstein. Some sick, perverted three-way, right in the middle of our bed."

Not good, Burt. Not good at all.

I reached into the deep recesses of my mind and tried to recover from my egregious error.

"I'm sure, honey, that it was just a harmless and completely fictional dream, er, nightmare."

"Didn't sound like fiction," said my unconvinced spouse. "You and Tyra sure seemed to be on a first-name basis."

"I didn't mean any offense. I swear. I've been having these wicked nightmares about Albert Einstein and getting kidnapped by illegal aliens on spaceships, and I must have had a particularly bad one last night. My anti-dream pills must not be working anymore."

"And do you usually have sex with your captors in these dreams?"

"Look, I do whatever I have to do in order to stay alive. Even if it's against my will."

"Bullshit, Burt. Bullshit."

Time to change the subject.

"I have a big surprise for you today," I said, with all the sugar I could summon.

"You do?" she asked, suddenly exhibiting a tiny ray of hope that maybe I wasn't such an impossible jerk.

"Yes, I do. I've been thinking long and hard for some time now about what is the most wonderful thing I can do for you - to help make your life easier, to give you more freedom, to give you more support - and, drum roll please...I have decided that we should get you an au pair."

"An au pair?" she said, wincing. "To live with us? In our condo?"

TUESDAY

"Yes. An au pair, from Sweden, just like our neighbors down the hall, Secretary Winslow and his wife, have. Imagine having someone here 24/7, living with us, cooking, cleaning, running errands, making the bed, dusting, mopping, making us cocktails – whatever we need, whenever we need it. Wouldn't that be wonderful?"

"But we don't have any kids," Juanita shot back. "We already have a housecleaning service five days a week. We hardly ever cook. Why in heaven's name do you think we need an au pair from Sweden?"

"I sincerely believe it would be nice to have a young au pair from Sweden around the house – you know, just to do stuff for us. Shop for groceries, walk the dog, vacuum, cut the lawn, whatever."

"We don't have a lawn."

"True, but we could buy some plants for our balcony. And enjoy full-service Swedish massages whenever we wanted."

"Screw you and all your stupid ideas," Juanita shouted, loud enough for our downstairs neighbors to hear. No doubt they would momentarily be calling building security on us once again. She stood up, flipped me the bird and stormed out of the kitchen.

Despite her aggressive and unexpectedly nasty response, I decided to exercise tremendous restraint by choosing not to react to her anger. Instead, I walked over to the kitchen sink, grabbed the soggy remnants of my insufficiently defrosted bagel, plopped it into my mouth and headed for the bathroom, where I knew I could always take refuge and avoid getting into another altercation with my increasingly high-strung, high-maintenance wife. I had just enough time to take a bath before before escaping to the office where I could make some serious money monetizing my unparalleled political acumen. Enough marital dysfunction for now.

The rest of my morning was uneventful, just how I like it, filled with meaningless calls to frantic candidates, gossip-hungry reporters and a brief, unsatisfying phone-sex session with some chick from 1-900-GOP-SLUT – although I was half tempted to call 1-900-MAX-SMUT to check out what arousing services Morrison was offering his listeners.

What else did I do? I came up with a new campaign ad for Governor Krause in North Carolina, linking his opponent's cousin to a fourth-generation descendant of Hitler. All I can say is that the family tree genealogy software available on the Internet is amazing. Later, Secretary of Interior Frankovic called me up to discuss his exciting new initiative to build the world's largest casino in Yosemite

National Park, in partnership with some Slovenian Underworld conglomerate that I had introduced him to a while back. I also wrote a fundraising speech for Congressman Schultz from Oklahoma to give to the Arab League of Oil Producing Nations. "Oil fuels the human race" was the catchy coda I added to bring his pitch to a hearty conclusion. Then I had a boring but brief videoconference with the schmoes at the Republican Campaign Committee, who had hired me to develop talking points for their Congressional candidates, even though the Democratic Congressional Campaign Committee had hired me to do the exact same thing. Only in Washington, kids. Only in Washington.

Right before lunch, I was summoned to the White House for a consultation with you-know-who. Strump seemed unusually agitated when I walked in to brief him on his latest poll numbers, which were dropping precipitously.

"What's wrong with you?" I asked. "Did you wake up on the wrong side of the bed this morning, or does Congress want to impeach you?"

"Shut up, Burt," he said. "So you haven't heard the latest?"

"About what?"

"FBI and ATF broke up another assassination attempt against me."

"No shit," I said. "Who was behind it? The Canadians?"

"Those assholes at Dunkin' Donuts."

"No way."

"They apparently wanted me dead because I refused to have the FDA reclassify donuts as vegetables so they could be eligible for government school-lunch programs. They must take me for a fool."

"That's nuts," I said. "You took the right stand on that issue, Mr. President. It's good to be bold every once in awhile."

"Those dicks gave me $250 million in SuperPac money for my Presidential campaign. And now they want to kill me. What gives?"

"They must feel they're not getting their money's worth."

"What a crock!" he said. "We helped them win all those airport and turnpike contracts, and this is how they show their gratitude? By hiring a gang of Costa Rican mercenaries to come after me?"

"Doesn't make much sense. Unless the Donut geniuses think your Vice-President may treat them better if he takes office upon your death."

"Doltish may look like a donut, but I doubt he's in their pocket. Other special interests might own him, but not Big Donut."

"And who owns you?" I had to ask.

"Who do you think?"

"Big Potato? Big Computer? The Pentagon? Please tell me. I'm dying to know."

"Everyone owns me," he answered sarcastically. "I am an equal-opportunity advocate for every special-interest group out there."

"Moving right along," I continued, "can we review your newest less-than-stellar poll numbers? Even the Aborigines hate your guts."

"Get out of here, Burt," the President said, ushering me out of the Oval Office. "I have more important things to do than talk to you."

"Like what?"

"Like anything else but listening to you talk about my poll numbers."

"Whatever you say, sir," I replied in the most sarcastic tone of voice I could muster. "What do you want to talk about?"

"What am I going to say in my nationally televised address for Quadrillion Day? It's next week."

"No worries, sir. I'm almost finished." That wasn't true, but who cared? I would get it done. I always did.

"When can I see what you've written?"

"I don't have the new text with me," I said. I hadn't even started. But I knew I could fake my way through this potentially awkward situation with ease.

For those of you who are too young to appreciate the essence of Quadrillion Day, let me take a second to explain.

To help burnish our tattered image around the globe, the White House and Congress created Quadrillion Day, an idiotic yet insidiously effective holiday on which our country gave thanks to China, Russia, India, South Africa, Luxembourg and the other foreign countries who loyally bought our Treasury Notes and helped finance our debt, which had doubled in the previous 12 months to more than two quadrillion dollars, as all but the super-rich (like *moi*) continued to binge on credit cards they would never pay off, housing they could never afford and other wasteful things they didn't even need. Counting the multiple wars we'd been fighting on every continent and the budget-busting military spending required to maintain the superiority of our armed forces, we'd been bathing in an ocean of red ink for an eternity.

The good news was that if America was drowning in debt, the American people never seemed to care, because Quadrillion Day had become a popular holiday, celebrated with parades, picnics and other pomp. It was a welcome day off from work or school for nearly everyone in the country except me.

The White House speechwriters had actually sent me a halfway-decent first draft of the President's Quadrillion Day pontification. In recent months, the young wordsmiths in the West Wing had been pumping out too much "Blah! Blah! Blah!" and not enough "Rah! Rah! Rah!" This draft, conversely, was decently mediocre, but there was no persuasive rhetoric to stir emotions as we, the people, celebrated on Quadrillion Day our global superiority as the biggest consumers on earth. Standing in the Oval Office with the President that day, I chose to improvise an appropriate climax that I knew he would appreciate enough to actually thank me for.

"And as we go forth from this day, spending so nobly on our dreams and desires, accumulating possessions like there's no tomorrow, let no one hold back – let no one one say to themselves or to their loved ones: 'I can't afford to buy what I want.' Because without buying, we are nothing. And we are something. Damnit, yes, we are. We are what we buy. It's the American way, the American dream and our God-given right to shop freely and frequently with fortitude. So go forth and spend, people, and God bless America."

"Awesome close, Burt," the President chuckled. "I hope I don't choke up when I read it."

"A guaranteed home run, sir."

"Promise?" he teased.

"Have I ever misled you?"

"All the time."

"You're right!" I cackled, before we shook hands and I headed out.

After that fun interlude, I drove over to the fabulously overpriced Capitol Hill eatery De Toqueville's, located in the lobby of NRA Hyatt Hotel and Rifle Range, for my hastily arranged lunch with one Muffy Huffington, the collegiate paramour of the Speaker of the House. Not only was I ready to have a direct discussion with her about the need to terminate her inappropriate relationship with the Speaker, but I would personally give her the great news about her wonderful new job opportunity, all requisite strings attached. The only thing she needed to do was leave Washington immediately and never ever come back until the Speaker was retired or dead. If she refused to leave town, her promising career would be over before it began. And she and her family would find themselves under siege from a private goon squad I would (indirectly) hire to make their lives excruciatingly miserable.

Huffington was already waiting in my reserved VIP power booth in the back when I arrived. Gorgeous, young, blonde and exceptionally buxom – a quadruple

TUESDAY

threat in our nation's capital. A woman like her, even without the way-too-tight dress and significant cleavage leakage, was at once intoxicating and highly flammable. I had to admit that, as stupid as the Speaker was, he sure had good taste when it came to risking his reputation for self-indulgent carnal enjoyment.

She came after me as soon as I sat down..

"What's this all about?" she asked. "The Speaker said you wanted to meet me and that he would be joining us. Where is he?"

"He's not coming," I said. "Not tonight, not tomorrow, not ever again. You two are through. Your fling is finished."

"Says who?" she shot back.

"Says him and says me."

"Who are you to tell me who I can screw?"

"I'm a close friend and adviser of the Speaker – and if you don't listen to me, I will be your worst nightmare."

"Is that a threat?"

"Nope," I lied. "Consider it a friendly reminder."

"Okay. Fine, Mr. King."

"So you know who I am," I responded with glee, my ego relishing the recognition.

"Who doesn't?"

"Good point," I said, with a low dose of mock humility. "Now, tell me, how old are you?"

"Old enough to know what you're all about."

"What year are you in college?"

"I just graduated last month."

"That's a relief. Do you have a job lined up yet?"

"Not yet. But I have big plans."

"I bet you do."

"Look." She paused, stroking her long hair as if to make a point. "Let's skip the stupid talk about the Speaker and me. Our relationship is none of your business."

"Oh, yes, it is," I interrupted. "When the Speaker has a problem, he pays me to make it my problem, and I solve the problem. But luckily for you, honey, I have a $100,000-a-year solution. All you have to do is stop seeing the Speaker and you're the winner of a dream job working smack dab in the middle of the Capitol building."

"Are you kidding me?" she asked, suddenly intrigued.

"Nope," I said assuredly.

"Wow! You're offering me a job in the Capitol?"

"That's what I said."

"Really?" she asked again.

"Really," I replied. "The Capitol building in Sacramento, California, home of the California State Assembly. It will be heaven on earth for you there. You can rub shoulders with legislators and lobbyists as you learn the ins and outs of democracy, California-style, just a two-hour drive from glorious San Francisco to the south and stunningly beautiful Lake Tahoe to the east. Life doesn't get much better than that."

"Whoa!" she stammered. "But I'm from Boston. All my family lives on the East Coast."

"Ask me if I care," I said, making it evident that I didn't.

She chortled with laughter, shaking her head. And then she shot back.

"Did the Speaker tell you about the wild sex romp we had last night in his office? Not only did we rearrange his office furniture, if you get my drift, but I bet we broke two lamps, maybe three. We made so much noise, I'm surprised the Capitol police didn't investigate."

"You did what?" I asked, incapable of believing what I had just heard.

"We did everything, every which way."

"No way!" I bellowed.

"Yes, way! And it's all on tape."

"What do you mean it's all on tape?"

"Henry, or should I say Mr. Speaker, allowed me to shoot some terrific live-action video. You see, Mr. King, I told him I'm making a documentary film about all of his legislative accomplishments. I'm gonna enter it in the Sundance Film Festival next year."

Fuck him, I thought. He swears to me he's going to take my advice and shut down this ticking time bomb of a relationship, and all he does is *lie* right to my face and make a dangerous situation a million times worse.

"Frankly, it doesn't matter what happened last night," I sighed, relieved that Populace was not present to pee all over my shoes. "All I need to know is: Will you take this job offer, move to California and cut off all contact with the Speaker? Yes or no?"

She paused, buying enough time to calculate all the different angles and potential outcomes. Finally, she spoke, with more certitude than was warranted, given the power dynamics of this particular situation.

TUESDAY

"Okay, but I want an iron-clad contract for the job. Five years."

"And why is that?"

"Because I'm not about to move my ass all the way to California and then have you make one phone call and get me fired."

"I would never let that happen."

"Five years, $100,000 a year with a 10 percent annual raise, a private health insurance policy and the maximum 401(k) employer match. That's my final offer, so take it or leave it."

"Okay, done," I said, not really caring much about the details, since I wasn't going to be paying the freight. The tools on the Speaker's campaign committee could worry about that.

"Thank you, Mr. King. It's a privilege doing business with you."

"The privilege is mine," I said, realizing that since the deal was done, I could get up and leave without wasting time on lunch.

"Oh," she blurted out, "I forgot one other thing."

"And what is that?" I asked, preparing for her to hondle me for something else.

"Do you find me attractive?" she asked.

"What sort of question is that?"

"Do you find me attractive, Mr. King? Or should I call you Burt?"

"Given our significant age difference and the wide disparity in our social standing, Mr. King is fine," I said.

Huffington sighed deeply as her eyes darted around the room. She was up to no good. "Okay, okay, Mr. King," she said wryly, "I'll make you one more deal."

"I'm not here to make another deal," I said. "One deal with you is one too many."

"Every single thing in this town is a deal," she replied, grabbing my hand. "And the negotiating never ends. You should know that as well as anybody."

"Whatever you say," I said, more than amused but still confused about where this was heading. "What's your deal?"

"I will accept your proposal and take this job in California and stop seeing the Speaker immediately – but only if we get together."

"What do you mean 'get together'? We're together right here in this restaurant."

"What I mean is that you and I get together and go do it, right now, upstairs, right here at this hotel. I realize the rooms are expensive, and I know from prior experience they don't rent them by the hour, but I assure you it will be well worth your while, an experience you'll never forget."

This turn of events certainly took me by surprise. "Whuh?" I asked, displaying an uncharacteristic disorientation.

"You heard me. I will agree to everything and sign right on the dotted line – if we go upstairs and have consensual, no-strings-attached, one-time-only sexual relations."

"What?" I asked, pleading for clarity.

I read your *Washingtonian* interview. I want to add you to my list."

"Your list?"

"My list of high-powered lovers. I want to conquer, sexually speaking, the most important men in politics. It's my calling. It's what I do. It's my thing."

I felt more than a slight twinge in *my* thing and pondered this predicament. My brain said no. My thing said yes. I made a feeble attempt to deliberate for a few seconds as she stared at me, waiting for my decision. But in this case, no compromise was possible, and once again, my thing prevailed.

I grabbed her thigh under the table and she grabbed mine back. Things escalated rapidly. Ninety minutes later, after a raucous interlude during which I discovered that the young, nubile Huffington was quite the young dominatrix ("I am your Majority Whip!" she shrieked, spanking me as I lay handcuffed to a bed post), I was feeling eternally grateful, excessively dirty – and a tiny bit guilty, because I was running late to meet Juanita for our weekly attempt at marriage therapy. Nonetheless, I had no regrets. I had not been the aggressor. I was not out looking for trouble. Huffington wanted me, and I was unselfish enough to fulfill her request.

As I raced crosstown through thick traffic, I tried to regain my focus, reposition my hair (so I didn't look more disheveled than usual) and brace for the latest high-priced bullshit from our wacked-out New Age therapist, who must have believed in miracles.

When I finally hustled into Dr. Rabinowitz's waiting room, Juanita gave me a low-level evil eye, maybe a 4 out of 10, which I found odd.

"You're late again, Burt," she moaned. "Why are you always late?"

"Sorry, but I was tied up," I said, silently congratulating myself on the double entendre.

"Just so you know, Dr. Rabinowitz wants us to try something new today."

"What? Get drunk and pass out?"

"No," said Juanita. "She wants us to join two other couples for a six-way group-therapy session."

"Over my dead body," I said. "Sharing our issues with her is bad enough. Sharing our issues with complete strangers would be cruel and unusual punishment. For us *and* for them."

"I know it sounds different and perhaps intimidating," said Dr. Rabinowitz, who had slipped into the waiting room without me noticing, "but sharing your marital issues with similarly challenged strangers in the friendly confines of my office, and with my professional direction, could very well be an important first step toward a successful and ultimately satisfying resolution."

Whatever that crap means, I thought, as I rolled my eyes.

"Please, Burt," said the good doctor, reacting to my uncomfortable body language. "Just trust me on this."

"For $750 an hour," I whined, "I really don't have a choice, do I?" Juanita elbowed me in the ribs.

"Scratch that – sounds like a wonderful idea," I said, in complete mockery of my manliness.

When I was much younger, I often fantasized about having a foursome or a sixsome or maybe a twelvesome, sexually speaking. This sixsome talking session would likely be as close as I would ever get. Might sound titillating for you, but it definitely wasn't for me.

The first couple was Thomas and Gina, both probably in their late thirties, from suburban Virginia. Thomas, as I discovered when he slipped me a business card right after we met, was a landscaper and reeked like any serious pothead; Gina, as I discovered when she slipped me a business card right after Thomas had, was a high-strung real estate lawyer who seemed bitter about her husband cutting grass and smoking grass all day while she was suing and defending and parsing and negotiating the hours away and billing every five-minute increment of her day to ungrateful clients she held in contempt.

"I hate my life and I hate my wife," Thomas whispered in my ear as we sat down in our cute little circle. "She's way too judgmental. Nothing I do is ever close to being good enough for that bitch."

"Sometimes I feel like killing myself, but I have too much work to do," Gina had written on the back of her business card, in a shameless effort to generate some pity from me before we started spilling our guts to the strangers surrounding us. "Any chance you could hook me up with a job interview at the Justice Department?" This was an exceedingly inappropriate request at a most inappropriate time, which I chose not to acknowledge. I've always despised people in D.C. who have the audacity to ask for big favors without offering anything of value in return. Burt King wasn't born yesterday, though as my body continues to sag and ache, I often wish I was.

The other couple, Tony and Indira, a mismatched Italian-Indian cross-cultural pair in their forties, was a bloody mess. I don't really know why they were even still trying to stay together. Anyone within 500 feet of them could tell this would be impossible, a gravity-defying feat that had zero chance of success. They didn't even walk into the room together. Indira slunk in well behind Tony, as if he were farting up a storm. And it wasn't just their body language that was radioactive. Their intense contempt for each other was palpable as soon as they opened their mouths

"We are dead to each other," Indira began during Dr. Rabinowitz's around-the-circle introductions. "My husband, and I use that term loosely, is sadly incapable of loving anyone but himself. I've been emotionally abandoned."

"Is that why you fucked the garbage man last year?" said Tony the sap.

"At least he treated me with dignity and respect," Indira protested. "About time someone did."

"What about the Jehovah's Witness last month?"

"He showed up at our front door and touched me spiritually."

I glanced over at Juanita, who looked appalled by this, giving me hope that we were both feeling much better – for at least a millisecond or two – about the highs and lows of our tenuous marital status. I was just glad that neither Tony nor Gina appeared to be packing a gun, because we might all have been killed in the crossfire.

$1,500 later, we had let the other couples do nearly all the venting, save for Juanita calling me out on "being more invested in my professional life than in my personal life."

I chose not to respond to that accusation for three reasons. First, I wasn't really paying attention, because I was too busy replying to a never-ending stream of emails. Second, the less I said in front of these people, the better. Who knew what Rabinowitz or these four strangers might be conspiring to do to embarrass me or violate the confidentiality of this conversation? Maybe they were surreptitiously recording this session so they could sell my personal dirt to my enemies or competitors, who were plentiful. Or so they could auction it off on e-Bay to a fan or a stalker. Last but not least, Juanita's attack on me was categorically true: I *was* more invested in my professional life than in my personal life. The record was what it was.

"Please, Burt," Rabinowitz begged, "you have to open up and be honest with us so we can feel your pain and help you."

"No, thanks," I uttered, deeply absorbed in a series of exceptionally meaningless emails.

"You heard me, Burt," said Rabinowitz. "You gotta open up here and show us some emotion."

Juanita elbowed me in the ribs again.

"Emotion?" I whined. "Emotion? What's emotion? It's nothing but diarrhea of the brain. I've got no use for it. It's a waste of time and, in this case, money."

"For God's sake, Burt," said Juanita. "Act your age."

"No disrespect to anyone here tonight," I said somberly, "but my feelings are too profound and too overwhelming to put into words right now. Plus, I need to take a dump." I rose from my chair to walk out, making a beeline for the bathroom, where I took refuge for a good 20 minutes before returning for the final portion of group inanity.

When I finally ushered Juanita out the door and into the parking lot, all I could think of was why so many dysfunctional couples were stupid enough to pay exorbitant amounts of money to have highly trained professionals waste time trying to fix what rarely could be fixed: the congenitally mismatched personalities of the two people involved.

I once read an article in *The New York Times*, when it was still a newspaper and not just a website, which claimed that intensive marriage counseling could save a troubled marriage in three out of four cases. But I think that's nuts. Those respondents were either self-delusional or just duping the pollster so they didn't come across as deviants who had just wasted boatloads of money. No way does this stuff work three-quarters of the time. I could maybe believe three-quarters of one percent, but 75 percent? No way.

"When will you be home tonight for dinner?" Juanita asked as she got into her car. "My parents' flight arrives at 7 p.m. I know they're looking forward to seeing you."

Fuck me, I thought, recoiling in agony. I had completely forgotten that Juanita's parents, the inimitable Jorge and Maria Sanchez, were flying in from Miami to visit us, wreak havoc on my life and – worst of all – stay with us, for what promised to be 24 hours of sheer torture. I would rather be dead than have to subject myself to her parents staying even one night with us, but jumping off a tall building was out of the question (too messy), and fleeing to another country and applying for political asylum would wreck my U.S. consulting business. I was hosed. There was no way to avoid this inevitable mess, unless I faked being called out of town on an urgent, unanticipated and top-secret assignment for one of my clients. Which was absolutely worth considering.

As I snaked through annoyingly thick traffic on my way back to the office, I wracked my brain on how I could avoid seeing my in-laws this evening without blowing a hole through my marriage. But to no avail. There was no credible way out.

Speaking of misfits, Povich, my own crazy blogger-stalker and the self-appointed Chairman and CEO of the Burt King fan club, was hiding out by the entrance to the parking garage, lying in wait behind Jones' booth. No matter how many times I implored Jones and building security to keep Povich away from me, the nutty bugger always found a way to slip inside so he could either harangue me about whatever stupid thing was on his obnoxious mind or pepper me with accusatory questions until I coughed up a quote he could use on his moronic blog: "PovichPower," which sadly enjoyed a large, loyal following on Capitol Hill.

"I couldn't stop him today," Jones said, as if he didn't care and wasn't sorry. "He said it was an emergency. As you know, when Povich makes up his mind to see you, he's unstoppable."

"You suck at your job, Jones," I reminded him.

"You suck at your job, King," he reminded me.

"Okay, Povich, do I need to call the cops today?" I asked, as I hurried to get out of my car and into the building, feeling hassled by this violation of my personal space. In the not-too-distant past, I seriously considered pressing "stalking" charges against Povich or even hiring a hit man to rough him up a little. But this plan didn't make sense on two levels: One, the hit man that was recommended to me by a contact at the Ugandan Embassy wanted way too much money; and two, Povich, despite being a royal pain in the ass, had always seemed, in my calculation, to be nothing more than another dependably harmless oddball with another stupid blog.

"Hi, Mr. King," Povich said. "I'm medicated and on my best behavior today."

"Great. That makes my day," I fibbed.

"That was a bad ruckus at the ASSPAC convention," said Povich. "You're damn lucky those protesters didn't kill you."

"I'm sure glad they didn't," I said, speeding away from him.

"So am I," said Povich. "If they had killed you yesterday, we wouldn't be with each other today."

"How right you are, my friend," I said with above-average insincerity.

Povich followed closely behind, breathlessly trying to keep up with my rapid pace. I noticed he had pulled out his video camera.

"Hey, Mr. King," he said tentatively. "I need to ask you something very personal."

"And what might that be?"

"I just heard a rumor from a well-placed, confidential, anonymous source that you misbehaved badly at your marital-counseling session this afternoon and admitted to your therapist that you're ready to come out of the closet and confirm you're bisexual."

"Get the fuck out of my face," I said.

"Is that on the record or off?" he said with a nervous giggle.

"I am not bisexual or trisexual, and even if I were, who gives a shit?

"I assume this is all on the record?" Povich said, still filming and getting increasingly excited about where this idiotic conversation was headed.

"It sure is," I said, before grabbing his video recorder and heaving it across the lobby, smashing it to pieces. The last thing I saw before sliding into the elevator was Povich crying like a baby, clutching his permanently damaged device. Screw him.

The rest of my afternoon and, for that matter, the rest of my day, sucked big-time. Overflowing with too much anger and stress, even for someone as angry and stressed out as me.

First, Governor Cox's wife made him scuttle our new TV spot, because she didn't like the way the film crew lit her face. He said she was complaining that both her forehead and nose looked too shiny. Truth be told, it was hard enough to light her face even before she had her first of three face-lifts. Her old facial features sadly weren't built for primetime viewing, and her new ones were a big step backward for a woman so obsessed with her looks. Even more troubling, I have no doubt she knew it. She wouldn't admit it, of course, but she knew it. Her new and improved face was over-the-top overdone, it looked perpetually icy, as if her last plastic surgeon had driven a Zamboni machine around and around her neck and cheeks while freezing shut her mouth, nose and eyes.

Then Congresswoman O'Grady called to say she was separating from her husband. "Can't you digitally excise him from all my ads?" she begged. "I caught him with the babysitter again, and this time we're through."

I didn't remind her, but she had told me the exact same thing during her last campaign, when she caught her husband in bed with her primary opponent's wife. Fortunately, in a rare display of mutual restraint and embarrassment, both campaigns covered up the whole messy affair, and somehow the press never found out.

"Sorry to be the bearer of bad news, Eileen, but you can't digitally remove your husband from all your ads without leaving a big gaping hole. And people would notice if yesterday he was in the ads with your kids, and today, suddenly, your kids are fatherless."

"Then what the fuck am I supposed to do?"

"We have only one choice," I said. "We need to pull the ads off the air immediately and film new ones."

"Won't that cost a fortune?"

"Only about $2 million, give or take $1 million."

"Forget about it, Burt. Couldn't you cover up his face with someone else's? Or blur it out so no one recognizes him?"

"That would still cost $150,000 for our retouching services alone."

"Whatever. Keep the asshole in the ads then. I'll deal with the fallout after the campaign."

The day got progressively worse from there. Next, I saw the rough cut of the Kleinhart spot. It was as boring and uninspiring as humanly possible. I expressed my displeasure to Big Al, and he got all defensive. The ad sucked, whether he grasped it or not.

Then Katie quit, marking the sixth time in two years that my assistant, or whatever you call your personal peon, was fired or walked out on me. She even had the audacity to let me know on her way out the door that she was going to work for Stinson, that two-timing fuck-face consultant who loves to tell potential clients behind my back that I am an arrogant, corrupt pussy, not to mention a hack. Stinson is too stupid to understand that Washington is too small a town to trash me like that. If only he knew what I'd been doing to him. When I heard recently he was bad-mouthing me to reporters about giving the President such piss-poor advice, I went viral with a barrage of anonymous online allegations that my rival had a thing for young boys and cross-dressing, which was false but made a big dent in his reputation anyway, thanks to search-engine optimization. Whoever Googled him would have little doubt that this shit was both a pervert and a pedophile. All's fair in love and war, right?

"You're dead to me," I told Katie, who didn't seem to care.

"Thanks for all the experience you gave me, Mr. King," she said, nonplussed.

"What experience?" I said. "I didn't give you any experience."

TUESDAY

"You taught me more than I ever learned at George Mason."

"You went to college? I never would have guessed."

"I discussed my education when you interviewed me for this job last month," she said matter-of-factly. "Graduated *Cum Laude*, year before last. Don't you remember?"

"You know, Stinson is a lech," I pointed out.

"But I bet he's a nicer one than you," she fired back as she stormed out, leaving me to ponder the notion that maybe Katie was smarter and sassier than I ever gave her credit for being. I used to think her legs were a far greater asset than her brain. But after this conversation, the longest one we'd ever shared, I was convinced she was a big enough smartass to have a wide variety of career options in this town.

Some time after Katie left for good, I must have dozed off at my desk, because the phone abruptly woke me up from a nightmare, this one involving Miriam, wife No. 3, and, of course, Einstein teaming up to cut my body in half with a hacksaw. Back in the day, Miriam was a good wife – a loyal, attentive wife. I'd always had a soft spot in my heart for her. And I know she had similar feelings for me. Until I screwed things up by screwing our cleaning lady. Yes, with one wickedly bad decision on one wickedly hot afternoon, I lost a good wife and a great cleaning lady.

It's pathetic I still have nightmares about Miriam and for that matter, most of my other ex-wives. Like the other night, I had a terrible dream in which in which Victoria, wife No. 2 poisoned me to death by putting cyanide in my martini. Ah, Victoria....That was, the first and last time I will ever marry a reporter, let alone the gossip columnist for the *Washington Dispatch*. We had so little in common aside from our insatiable thirst for power and hunger for gossip; we never should have gotten married. We were fools to walk down the aisle in that Georgetown bar. I've done a few of moronic things in my day, but that one would surely make my all-time top 10 list.

Then there was the dream the night before, which featured wife No. 1, Tara, cutting off my peewee with a carrot peeler while Einstein held me down. As you might imagine, it took Tara several minutes of scraping back and forth, peeling away my manhood little by little, while she and my namesake nemesis laughed uncontrollably. And to make a bad situation much worse, my mother made a cameo in this dream. She stood in the background, cheering them on, while I was being tortured. As you can imagine, the physical and emotional pain of this ordeal were intense. If only Dr. Rabinowitz knew how really agonizing my sleeping hours were, thanks in large part to the ghost of the cruelest genius ever to walk the face of this earth.

The weirdest thing of all is that I've never had a dream about Marlena, wife No. 4, a stewardess I married a week after I met her on a plane. And who divorced me right after she caught me in a compromising position with a stewardess from Air Moscow.

Back to the present. I awoke from my slumber in a hot sweat, face-down on my desk, drooling on my papers and seeing on the clock that I would now officially be late for dinner, which would put me right back in Juanita's doghouse and start the invasion of my in-laws on a sour note. For this transgression, I would undoubtedly pay a steep price.

I stumbled back down to the garage and grabbed my keys from Jones.

"Where are you going tonight, King of Kings?" Jones asked.

"I am going to hell."

"I knew it. I knew it all along," said Jones, full of glee. "Good to see that some fuckers get what they deserve."

I moped up Pennsylvania Avenue in the Hummer as slowly as I could without getting rear-ended by the ocean of impatient bastards behind me. I crawled along at 10 miles under the speed limit, decelerating to miss as many lights as possible so that I would be late to dinner without missing it entirely. In this situation, my bottom line was simple: Better late than never, better late than on time, and better real late, like toward the end of dessert, than never.

Juanita, my angel of fire (not exactly sure about that metaphor – maybe the fire evokes her fiery passion – but I was taught in college, by Zoey, among others, to indiscriminately use metaphors to spice up my prose), was from Venezuela, raised in a big-ass mansion with boatloads of servants. These days, her parents, Jorge and Maria, lived in a big-ass mansion with boatloads of servants in Miami, in a gated community on Biscayne Bay, with heavily armed guards who patrolled the grounds in souped-up Army jeeps, just waiting for the chance to shoot and kill trespassers or unruly landscapers. In this compound, even the pelicans were strip-searched by security.

To say my in-laws were wealthy was an understatement; they were way wealthier than me, and I was awesomely wealthy. Juanita had more cash hidden away in offshore accounts than half the world's dictators combined. Her folks had recently bought her two brothers, Uno and Juno, a gigantic five-star hotel/casino/dog track/ultimate cage-fighting complex near Ft. Lauderdale, even though the two of them, as best as I could tell, had never worked an honest day in their lives.

Jorge, as he told anyone who would listen, had been a high-ranking general in the (U.S.-financed) Venezuelan junta, before he stepped down to run a large construction company that was controlled by the junta and received billions in no-bid government contracts to build hotel, offices and jails all over the country. "I was the boss of all bosses," he liked to remind everyone. "And I still am."

In a classic stroke of good luck and great timing, Jorge and Maria took their gazillions and their young daughter and sons and bolted from Venezuela days before the last revolution, which came to be known as "The Tehran Smackdown." It pitted the lowly peasants against the overpowering military, but guess what, the people won in a shocker, thanks to the massive weaponry and financial support they surreptitiously received courtesy of the Iranian government -- in exchange for profit participation on every Venezuelan oil-drilling deal moving forward.

Although Jorge, who was in his late 60s, claimed to be retired, Juanita and I never believed it for a second. He still spent a ton of time working on the boards of two shadowy not-for-profit groups, which no one seemed to have even heard of: "The International Fund for Truth and Justice" and "Torturers Anonymous," both of which I was convinced were nothing more than storefronts for some international spy ring made of junta alumni and other nefarious forces.

Jorge's modus operandi was clear to everyone who crossed his path: "Once a general, always a general," he liked to say, showing that he was still in charge, pulling rank and doing whatever he needed to win whatever battle he was waging.

"Humans crave authority – in life and in business," he would spout. "And I like to give it to them. Whether they like it or not."

My mother-in-law, Maria, used to be kind and docile, happy in her homemaker role and playing the foil for her showboating husband. But in recent years, she had turned dour, almost to the point of being perpetually moody and bitter. Maybe she was finding it harder to cope with Jorge and his junta-esque behavior – which might also explain her continuous consumption of alcohol at all hours of the day and night. I could only hope Maria's sadness wasn't because she knew her daughter, the love of her life and my current wife, was unhappy in her marriage.

On the way up in the elevator, I braced myself. I hadn't seen Juanita's parents for several months, though any amount of time between visits with them seemed to fly by too quickly.

For a fleeting second, I fantasized that after I slogged my way through what remained of this interminably long meal, full of constipated conversation, Jorge and

Maria would say goodnight and head out to their hotel, where they would spend the night. But that would not be the case. They always insisted – actually, Juanita always insisted – that they stay with us whenever they were in town. So the torture never stopped until I went to work or, better yet, faked another trip out of town.

As soon as I walked through the door, I could see that I was not nearly late enough.

"Hello," Jorge said coldly without looking at me or getting up from our living room couch, where he was splayed out, transfixed by whatever inane investment tip they were foaming at the mouth about on CNBC, despite a stock market that had fallen 60 percent in the last year, a deep enough drop to spook me into taking most of my dough out of the Dubai Stock Exchange altogether.

"Hello, Jorge," I reciprocated without approaching him for a handshake. "How was your flight?"

"Fine," he said, barely acknowledging the question.

"Did you fly up private or commercial?"

"Believe it or not, we flew commercial," he said, finally looking up. "Both of our Miami friends with private planes are still under house arrest."

"Where's Maria?" I asked, looking for relief.

"In the kitchen with Juanita, making dinner. I hope it's ready soon, because I'm starving like a cannibal. We've been waiting for you. Do you realize how late you are?"

"Sorry," I said. "I had an urgent meeting that ran late. You should have started without me."

"I wanted to, but the women wanted to wait," he complained. "No one asked me what I wanted to do."

I fled into the kitchen, accidentally interrupting an intense mother-daughter conversation at the kitchen table.

Juanita and Maria stopped mid-sentence. An uncomfortable silence sucked the air out of the room.

"Hi, Burt," Maria said with palpable ambivalence as she gave me a half-hearted hug.

"Hi, honey," Juanita said with even less enthusiasm.

My antennae shot up.

"What's going on?" I asked. "I hope I didn't interrupt an important conversation."

"Oh, no, Burt," Maria said, in a voice that proved I did.

"We were catching up about family," Juanita added with a wobbly fake smile.

"Okay, then," I said, "I guess I'll go wash up for dinner. By the way, what are we having?"

"We're trying to decide what to make," said Maria.

"How about we grill some steaks?" said Juanita.

"Sounds good," I said. "Are the steaks already marinated?"

"Not yet," Juanita answered. "I haven't bought them yet."

"You gotta be kidding, Juanita," I said, in my pissiest voice. "Your father is starving and so am I."

"I'm doing the best I can, Burt," she said, raising her voice. "I'm sorry that isn't good enough for you."

"You don't get it. How can we have a steak dinner if you didn't buy any steaks?" I asked in too patronizing a voice, considering that Juanita's mom was in the kitchen giving me progressively dirtier looks as she witnessed this budding brouhaha. I pictured both women grabbing extra-long steak knives out of the drawer and chasing after me, pinning me to the ground with Jorge's help and slicing me into human filet mignon, which they would then grill for dinner and thoroughly enjoy at my expense.

"Calm down, Burt," said Juanita. "Lose the attitude. My mom and I can run out right now and buy some steaks at Georgio's. They come already marinated."

"Forget it," I said, as nicely as I could. "Let's go out for steaks at the Beltway Butcher."

Which we did, much to the chagrin of Jorge, who apparently wanted to spend the entire evening on the couch, flipping back and forth between channels to achieve maximum absorption of his TV news and talk shows. Trust me: Having appeared on more than my fair share of these shows, I can vouch that they are nothing more than mindless drivel produced for idiots by idiots.

Without going into great detail, because I'd prefer to forget about what happened and move on, our $949 dinner, including tip, at the Beltway Butcher was an unmitigated disaster. And there was no other way to spin it; I was a bad bad boy.

The problems started as soon as we sat down. The prick waiter never came to take our drink orders, and when I'm having dinner with the in-laws on my dime, I need a steady stream of alcohol to keep me sane during conversations like this:

"Burt thinks we should get an au pair," said Juanita. "From Sweden."

"Are you expecting?" Maria asked, instantly overcome with joy. "I'm gonna be a grandmama!"

"No, no," Juanita said dejectedly. "No baby on the way. Burt still thinks the world is too scary to bring another baby into it."

"Why would we be so self-centered as to bring an innocent child into this dysfunctional world?" I opined. "How can I, Burt King, be responsible for a child when I'm already responsible for our country?"

Silence. Only blank stares from around the table.

"And why ruin your daughter's insanely beautiful body?" I added with extra rhetorical juice. "I want an au pair, preferably from Sweden, because it would be nice to have someone around to help us cook and clean 24/7."

"And give Burt Swedish massages," Juanita added, trying to embarrass me in front of her parents.

"An au pair? That's the dumbest thing I've ever heard," said Jorge. "You don't have a family, so why do you need a servant?"

"Well," I countered, "if I remember correctly, you have multiple servants at your home in Miami, and you don't have any children still at home."

"That's none of your goddamn business," Jorge said, glaring at me as if I were about to be executed by one of his old Venezuelan firing squads. "I worked hard all my life and earned the right to have my servants. Not only do they serve at my pleasure, but it's their pleasure to serve me."

"Whatever you say, boss," I said submissively, with a thick-enough accent that even he got the point.

"Stop it, Burt," pleaded Juanita. "You and Daddy need to calm down right now. Please make this a nice night."

"Ain't gonna happen," I reminded her.

"Please, I beg you," said Maria. "This tension is enough to drive anyone to drink." No doubt she would demonstrate her point once the waiter finally arrived.

To make a long story short, 45 minutes later, I was hanging on by a thread, on the verge of passing out due to excessive banality mixed with excessive alcohol. I hadn't spoken in what felt like an eternity, and all I could think of to keep my eyes pried open was my insanely memorable, albeit exhausting romp that morning with Muffy Huffington.

"I need to go home and get some rest," I told Juanita, as I got up from the table (which seemed to be spinning), tossed her the keys to the Hummer and stumbled toward the exit.

"Don't worry about me," I added, knowing that the three of them wouldn't. "I'll grab a cab."

"But our steaks haven't arrived," said Juanita.

"Please give our steaks my regards," I said.

When I finally made it home, I barely had enough energy to get undressed and collapse into bed. What a long, strange day it had been. But even stranger days were yet to come.

Wednesday

Had to fly to NYC this morning for the grand opening of GangstaLand, our nation's newest urban theme park, brought to you by Disney and financed by the HUD (commonly known as the U.S. Department of Housing and Urban Development), to create jobs in the chronically depressed New York City area. New York's Mayor Hussein wanted me there for the kick-off event: a ribbon-cutting ceremony and VIP tour for a number of national and foreign officials, including half the United Nations and most of the Congressional delegation of New York, New Jersey and Connecticut.

Did I have much interest in seeing this over-budget, over-hyped theme park that simulated life in America's worst slums so that wealthy suburban families could pay $450 per adult and half price per kid to stroll around and experience how the other 99 percent of the population lived below the poverty line? Not really. But the CEO of Disney, Hector O'Brien, had offered me and all the other dignitaries in attendance the chance to invest early in their GangstaLand IPO, provided we supported their efforts to gain tax-exempt status for their enterprise, which they felt they wholeheartedly deserved, given that they were creating several hundred new jobs on the site of the old LaGuardia Airport, which was closed a decade ago and turned into a toxic waste landfill for the tri-state area before being reborn again as an amusement park. Assuming the stock market did not crash again, the GangstaLand IPO was tentatively scheduled for later this year, right after construction began on the second and third theme parks in Chicago and Los Angeles, respectively.

"This is like shooting fish in a barrel," O'Brien had told me over the phone the week before. "Your initial investment will be worth millions right after we take GangstaLand public."

In addition to the promise of making millions, I was curious to see some of the rides that were already generating tremendous buzz, especially the Liquor Store Shoot-Out – where you had 60 seconds to rob a real-life corner liquor store without getting shot by the trigger-happy cashier or police who'd been called to the scene – and the Escape From School Hell – where, posing as a teacher, you had to fight your way through the battle-scarred hallways and stairwells of an urban school, as scores of evil students on the loose tried to assault you with guns, knives and light explosives. I was also looking forward to the Riker's Island Splash Ride, where a high-tech motorized jet ski took you up and down, around and through the real Riker's Island, located right across the bay from GangstaLand, giving you an up-close and personal view of everything going on in New York's most infamous maximum-security prison.

The Disney designers were getting rave reviews for their state-of-the-art use of robotics, digital avatars and 3-D simulation in making the GangstaLand attractions as realistic and as scary as possible. As long as I didn't run into any former clients, I decided this wouldn't be such a bad break from my daily drudgery in D.C.

I also wanted to check out GangstaLand for nostalgic purposes. Back in the day, LaGuardia Airport was an iconic airfield where bigwigs like me would fly in and out of NYC. It was a time when Manhattan still mattered, when it was the center of the power grid, when Wall Street still controlled global financial markets before the big investment banks were burned to the ground during the Investor Uprisings – and then eclipsed by their bigger rivals in the Far East. I remembered when Broadway was filled with theatres and restaurants, before it was gobbled up by Chinatown, and when Central Park was open to the public, before it was privatized and converted into a walled-off gaming reserve for wealthy hunters who paid as much as $50,000 a year for the right to shoot elephants, deer, moose, squirrels, pigeons, rats and unarmed but still dangerous criminals who loitered in the park at their own risk.

New York was a much different place in those days, just like I was a much different person. We both were a lot nicer.

After my flight landed at the *National Bank of Abu Dhabi Kennedy Airport*, the mayor's greeters ushered me into a waiting helicopter. I landed in the

GangstaLand parking lot less than five minutes later. The place was a mob scene: thousands of people pushing up against the police barricades, trying to be the first ones let in; cars and limos gridlocked trying to find parking; more helicopters buzzing around overhead; sirens screaming everywhere, drowning out pronouncement and pleas from the overmatched police bullhorns and public-address system trying to keep some semblance of order amid the chaos.

What insanity! And to think that five years from now, if all went well, there could be GangstaLands all over the U.S. and around the world. I could taste the money I would be making.

My morning at GangstaLand went fairly well. I liked Liquor Store Shoot-Out a little more than Escape From School Hell, which required too much running for my hefty, out-of-shape, out-of-breath body, but both rides were frighteningly realistic. The urban fast-food concessions were surprisingly tasty. And there was only one brief hiccup the entire time I was there.

During my turn on the Riker's Island Splash Ride, wouldn't you know it, the ride broke down and left me and the South African Ambassador dangling 100 feet over the middle of the Riker's prison yard, where a group of highly amused inmates stopped their basketball game to watch gleefully as we stuck tourists squirmed nervously in mid-air.

"What you looking at, Honkey?" yelled one comedian.

"Come on down, bad boy, and bend over," shouted another.

Thankfully, a few long minutes later, the ride started back up and we were on our way.

"That was a close call," I laughed.

"But from a socioeconomic standpoint," said the Ambassador, "you have to admit, it was fascinating."

On my way back home from GangstaLand, I broke down in a barrage of guilt and hitched a ride on a U.S. Army helicopter to Fort Kraft Mac'N'Cheese, New Jersey's largest Army base, conveniently located 10 miles and a short 20-minute drive from my mother's nursing home, where I would spontaneously make one of those dreadful, unappreciated once-a-year (or every-other-year or every-third-year) visits to my biggest living tormentor (since Einstein was technically dead).

The goal was to catch my mother off guard, lest she had time to prepare for her inevitable attacks on my character, lifestyle and maternal negligence, which would definitely commence the moment I walked through her door.

"Look what the cat dragged in!" she snorted, as I entered her cramped, spartan room with that musty hospital smell.

"Good to see you too, Ma," I volleyed back.

"Why are you here?" she said. "I haven't seen you in such a long time, I figured you were in jail or maybe even dead, neither of which would have surprised me."

"Sorry to disappoint you, Ma. But look! I'm not in jail and, even better, I'm not dead yet."

"I know, I know," she sighed. "I saw you on TV twice this month, doing the devil's work, I assume. That President of yours is a putz. Who wears the pants in that White House?"

"That putz is my biggest client these days, Mom. You wouldn't believe the monthly retainer he pays me for my services."

"Then why don't you spend more on me? This place is a shithole, a chamber of horrors. You should be fucking ashamed of yourself."

"Thanks to you, I always used to be. But not so much anymore." Touché.

A half hour later, after the usual barrage of complaints and recriminations, my mother started to doze off for her pre-lunch nap, and I was free to go.

"See you soon, Ma!" I lied.

"I won't hold my breath waiting for you," she said, adding: "I would die if I did."

"That would be a shame," I said, lying once again.

I took a taxi back to Trenton, caught a ViagraAmerica speed train and, three hours later, pulled my Hummer back into the underground garage at Slice & Dice.

Oddly, Jones was nowhere in sight, which effectively meant there was no one around to park my car, which meant I would have to go deep into the bowels of the garage and actually park it myself. Which was completely beneath a man of my stature. So I honked and honked and honked, as if I possessed the magic power to make Jones suddenly appear by sheer force of will (and my insidiously loud and obnoxious horn).

Astoundingly, it worked. After a sustained barrage of ear-splitting honking, Jones came flying out of a fire-exit door down below, sprinting uphill toward me, carrying a laptop and swearing up a storm.

"What the fuck do you want, you motherfuckin' motherfucker?" he shouted at me.

"Good afternoon to you, too," I replied. "What's your damn problem?"

"You, King. You're my damn problem. Can't you see I'm on my break?"

"What are you doing right now that makes it so impossible for you to take a break from your break, be a good man and park my lovely vehicle?"

"None of your fuckin' business."

Whoooh! He was awfully fiery today.

"C'mon now, Jones, your business *is* my business," I egged him on. "You can tell me everything, including your deepest darkest secrets."

"Then why don't you tell me *your* deepest darkest secrets, Mr. King of Crap?"

"Because I don't like you and I don't trust you. But maybe that will change and our relationship will improve for the better – if you go ahead and disclose what you're doing at this moment that's so important that you can't park my vehicle. The mystery is killing me, my man."

"I'm studying," he said in a decidedly unfriendly tone.

I laughed, which upset him even more.

"What's so funny about me doing some studying, Mr. Condescending Cracker Ass?"

"Tell me," I said, trying to keep a straight face, "what are you studying?"

"I'm studying for law school. I'm almost halfway finished."

"You, of all people, are going to law school?"

"Why are you so surprised? Black people have brains just like everyone else, especially you white people."

"So, where are you going to law school? Georgetown, George Washington, American?"

"Hell, no. My people can't afford those schools. That's why I am going to law school on my damn computer."

"You're doing what?"

"You heard me. I'm going to law school online, at JewLawyer School of Law."

"Jewwhat?"

"JewLawyer School of Law. The best online law school available anywhere online. Every class is taught by a Jew."

"Never heard of it."

"That's your hang-up, not mine."

"Whatever you say, counselor."

"Don't patronize me, you patronizing pig."

"Calm down, Jones," I said, handing him my keys, my interest in prolonging this exchange quickly evaporating. "Sounds like a good program and a wonderful opportunity for you."

"Sure is. Great curriculum. Fantastic website. And I get to work at my own speed. It's everything I need for only $299 per month. I can attend classes whenever I have time, 24/7, even if I'm here at work or at my apartment hanging out with a girl."

"I'm glad to hear you have a girlfriend."

"That's plural, I don't have a girlfriend. I have girlfriends."

"I find that hard to believe," I teased.

"Fuck you, King. I'm one of the best online daters around. You wouldn't believe all the wild women I've met. You have no idea!"

"Congrats."

He mumbled another expletive, took my keys and got into my car. As he turned on the ignition, I tapped on the window, wanting to make sure he wasn't pissed at me and about to ram my Hummer into the nearest wall.

"I hope you have a fine day," I said.

"I bet you do," he snorted, as he rolled down the window.

I tried a different tactic.

"Seriously, Jones. I think it's great you're going to law school."

"Better late than never," he said, shrugging. "Shit, I'm almost 30. I need a future, too. You think I want to park cars the rest of my life? You think I want to live on tips from people like you? C'mon, King, be real. I want to get out there in the real world, like you, and do something meaningful."

"Then good luck, Jones," I said before turning around, walking up the garage ramp and heading back to the sanctuary of Slice & Dice.

Maybe it was the greasy ghetto food at Gangstaland or the hellacious visit with my mother, or maybe it was the shitty burger I wolfed down on the train back to D.C., but whatever it was, something had traumatized my bowels and given me an unusually bad case of diarrhea. For the next hour, I sped between my desk and the toilet, waiting for my bodily functions to stabilize, which they finally did just before 5 p.m. I remember the specific time because that's when I went downstairs to see what Big Al was up to in the Bat Cave.

Instead of slicing and dicing our clients' opponents, however, Big Al was staring at the TV with a mortified look on his face.

"I can't believe what happened to Chief Justice Adams," said Al, who was transfixed by multiple hyperkinetic, incomprehensible talking heads on CNN hyperventilating about something they deemed to be unusually urgent.

"What happened to him?" I asked.

For once, Big Al couldn't muster a response.

"U.S. Supreme Court Chief Justice Adams Abducted While Grocery Shopping," said the headline ticker scrolling across the bottom of the screen.

"Holy shit!" I stammered, trying to digest the magnitude of this shocking event.

Who could have done such a thing? Sure, Washington wasn't exactly the safest place when it came to crime, but it was still safer than Baghdad or Beirut or Vermont. Un-fucking-believable.... Just when you thought things were getting back to normal, just when these random acts of violence were supposed to be things of the past, just when the country was healing from the last heinous thing to happen – the suspension of major league baseball for an entire season after every single player flunked the drug test – this happened.

I assumed instantly, as everyone else probably did, that this kidnapping was the shameful act of a foreign terrorist – perhaps a vengeful Canadian pissed off about the war. But as I listened to the cacophony of craziness on CNN and pieced together more details, I was relieved to hear that the police had already apprehended a suspect, not of Middle Eastern or Canadian or liberal descent, but a 75 year-old grandmother from Syracuse, New York. According to eyewitnesses, she had unfurled a large banner outside the grocery store five minutes after the kidnapping, declaring "Justice for the Justice." The cops arriving on the scene cuffed her right away.

"The Lord ordered this kidnapping," she said, before being thrown into the back of a police car and hustled away from the swarming crowd. "He told us we must fight back and reclaim our country. And we will."

Big Al and I were dumbfounded, saying nothing to each other because there was nothing of consequence to say. After 20 minutes more of mind-numbing saturation coverage, I headed back upstairs to find some welcome distraction in my office.

But as hard as I tried to be productive and get some work done, I wasted the rest of the afternoon, completely transfixed by the Adams abduction. I surfed the Web intensely while flipping from one cable news channel to the next, discovering no new updates in the process but successfully avoiding the scripts, speeches, memos, surveillance videos, hate mail and other assorted crap piled up on my hopelessly cluttered desk.

I kept thinking back to the last time I had run into Justice Adams, coincidentally in the same Wisconsin Avenue shopping plaza where he was kidnapped.

It must have been four or five years earlier. I was picking up my shirts at the dry cleaners next to the grocery store, and who should be in front of me in line, decked out in a well-worn sweatshirt and sweatpants, but Chief Justice Keanu Adams, the diminutive head honcho of our Judiciary. I'd met him before, a long time ago, at a party at the Belarus Embassy thrown in honor of Chevan Chitsvinsky, the conductor of the National Symphony Orchestra. But at the dry cleaners that day, Adams had no idea I was standing there less than a foot behind him as he dropped of his dirty laundry, soiled from the wear and tear of dispensing justice for the masses, and picked up his sparkling clean, chemically-treated dark suits, white shirts and stately judicial robe.

"Good afternoon, Chief Justice Adams," I said in my most earnest voice, as he turned around to leave. "I almost didn't recognize you in sweats."

He gave me a sour look, which was warranted after my cheesy opening line.

"Do I know you?" he asked with mild irritation, as he grabbed his hangers off the hook and headed for the door.

"Maybe not," I said, moving closer. "But I certainly know who you are."

I smiled. He didn't.

"Yes, Justice Adams," I began, "I'm Burt King, esteemed political consultant and senior adviser to the President. We met at a party on Embassy Row a few years ago."

"Oh, yes," he said, with zero enthusiasm. "Nice to see you again," he added as he fled, letting the door slam behind him for emphasis.

Not very friendly. But I did get to talk with him, which meant I had now met him twice and was allowed to begin bragging to my clients and competitors that I was friends with the highest judicial figure in the land, enhancing my already-enhanced reputation for unrivaled, proximity to power.

As I sat at my desk, staring into oblivion, I was inconveniently interrupted by a call from Juanita.

"Are you picking us up tonight, or are we meeting you there?" she asked.

"Where are we going?" I said, still in a fog.

"We're taking my parents to the White House dinner!" she replied with glee. "Remember?"

"Shit, I forgot," I groaned, mad that I had forgotten but even madder that I had agreed to attend in the first place – and with my in-laws nonetheless.

"That's really terrible about Justice Adams," said Juanita.

"I'm sure the police will find him soon," I said. "I hope he'll be fine."

"I hope you're right."

"I usually am," I said, before hanging up and reentering my fog of nothingness.

Attending a fancy-schmancy black-tie dinner at the White House might sound to most people like a real honor, a vindication of one's superior Darwinian standing among the 384 million English-speaking (or Spanish-speaking) mammals in the United States of America. But I would rather enjoy wings and beer by myself at the bar at Humplebee's than dine with the

President and First Lady at the White House, surrounded by all those socialites and sycophants desperately trying to claw their way up Washington's slippery ladders of power, where I, and a few select others, sat in all our naked glory.

My problem was not with President Strump, who will go down in the annals of history as one of the most affable, albeit indecisive and pliable Presidents in recent memory.

My problem was with the First Lady. I didn't like to be around her. She made me uncomfortable. And gave me the willies. Want to know why? Hint: Her first name is Zoey. And, yes, we went to college together at Bangalore University in South Boston, where she was my tantalizing T.A. and the first, and possibly only, legitimately true love of my life. Until she shattered my heart.

To this day, Zoey Strump, *née* Edwards, remains my Achilles Heel. And everyone knows it: my wife, my ex-wives, my shrink, my mother, my masseuse, my barber, *The Bloomberg Times*, *The Washington Facebook Post*, *The EconoLodgemist*, etc. Even Jones liked to tease me about the big one who got away.

"So, you could have married the fucking First Lady?" he asked a few years back, after *The Post* ran the first of many long, overly detailed profiles of Zoey, blabbering about how our paths initially crossed in college, before we each became famous in our own right. "That's wild. With her love and support, maybe you could have been President," shrieked Jones. "Too bad you screwed it up, buddy. She seems like quite a lady. Sure would have brought your loser life to a much higher level."

Jones was such an asshole. Prescient, but nonetheless an asshole.

Zoey and I still ran into each other multiple times a year, usually when I was leaving the Oval Office after fixing something for her husband, or at some fancy White House dinner that I was morally obligated to attend – or at one of those high-society black-tie charity events around town where everybody who was anybody would show up just to be seen motoring around the ballroom, schmoozing and air-kissing all the high-powered people they spent the other 364 days of the year backstabbing.

Tonight just happened to be one of those awkward nights. A White House dinner honoring His Holy Highness Ed Rucinski, the newly elected President of Hexxonia, which, if you don't know, is a tiny, two-year old oil-rich African nation wholly owned by the fine folks at the Hexxon Oil Corporation. Rucinski used to be a soft-spoken Houston oil executive – until he moved to Hexxonia right after Hexxon bought Ghana, which happened to be weeks before hundreds of new oil wells were amazingly discovered. How's that for dumb luck? Now Hexonnia pumps more oil than Alaska and Texas combined, and Rucinski makes *Forbes*'s list of the World's Biggest Billionaires and *Dictators Life*'s list of the World's Richest Dictators year after year after year. He's also recognized around the globe as the U.S. State Department's favorite dictator, thanks to his unique brand of dictatorial democracy, which he established in Hexxonia, where there are open democratic elections every four years for every voter who commits in writing beforehand to support Rucinski and his hand-picked slate of candidates.

The way I saw it, Rucinski may have been plenty dirty, but running Hexxonia was a dirty job, and someone had to do it.

"Hello, Burt," the President said warmly, as I escorted Juanita and her star-struck parents through the receiving line.

"Any update on Justice Adams?" I asked.

"Nothing new to report," he whispered, ushering me along.

"Hello, Burt," said the First Lady, not so warmly.

"Hello, Zoey. How are you this evening?"

"Fine, thanks," she answered, shrugging, as I moved along.

"Damn! You have a hot wife," Rucinski whispered after shaking my hand, just before giving Juanita an unnecessarily long and highly inappropriate embrace, followed by a full-frontal kiss on the mouth – a serious violation of White House protocol.

Juanita and I brought her parents into the State Dining Room and were escorted to our seats. I could tell right away that our table was gonna suck. Maybe it was merely the bad luck of the draw – or maybe Zoey had instructed the White House Social Secretary to hide us in the far back corner of the room, as far the hell away from her as humanly possible. Joining us at Table 114 were a couple of lobbyists, the Ambassador from Iceland, who was as cold and distant as one might expect, and Hideki Hirsch, the first Japanese-Jewish All-Pro running-back in the NFL, who had no interest in anyone at our table except for Tiffany Motherwell, the newly minted Miss BodyBuilding USA, who sat to his right.

As I surveyed the scene, it was brutally obvious I would be forced to waste three precious hours of my life, primarily talking to Juanita's parents, making stupid small talk about inane matters so as not to look bored to death at a White House dinner. It would be a formidable challenge and a selfless humanitarian sacrifice, but given the suffocating mediocrity of my tablemates, there was basically no alternative.

There was, however, one empty seat to my right that held out some element of hope, or at least mystery. Whoever ended up taking that seat could theoretically be my salvation for the evening, emerging out of nowhere to instantaneously engage me in scintillating conversation, the likes of which I had never expected, especially at an elite gathering of Washington's most elite elitists. Or he could be another sleep-inducing windbag.

Unless, of course, the empty seat was a no-show due to traffic, a bad case of the flu or a 10-count indictment from earlier in the day.

"Good evening, my wealthy friends," said the President, welcoming everyone with his obligatory toast. "It is our great honor tonight to salute Ed Rucinski, the honorable President of Hexxonia. You, my friend, are a great friend of democracy, a great friend of America and a great friend of freedom, free enterprise and crude oil. Your nation's petroleum products power our nation's cars, trucks and lawnmowers. Your sweatshops make 71 percent of our T-shirts. Your army has stood shoulder to shoulder with us in the war against Canada. And I can never thank you enough for all the fun we've had playing golf together over the years. For all this, and for everything else you do for me, my supporters and, of course, the American people – we are eternally grateful."

"Thank you very much, Mr. President," said Rucinski. "It sure is an incredible honor to be at the White House this evening, among such distinguished people, and back in the country I used to call home. On behalf of all the citizens of Hexxonia, I bring you heartfelt thanks for your financial support, your military assistance, including your state-of-the-art weaponry, and, above all, your ever-increasing, everlasting consumption of market-priced oil."

As the two presidents embraced, flashbulbs flashed and wine glasses clinked, some knucklehead barreled into my chair from behind, groaning way too loudly, "I think I'm gonna puke!" I wheeled around, just as a morbidly obese tuxedoed body slammed into my right shoulder, knocking over the water glass I was holding.

I was soaked and pissed. "What the fuck?" I uttered as his oversized butt crash landed in the open seat next to me.

"Sorry, mate," said the big, blubbering, perspiring fool, who was now seated much too close to me for comfort. "Didn't see you there."

"What?"

"On second thought, I did see you there," he blubbered. "But there was nothing I could do to avoid the collision. Sorry about the spill. Thank goodness it's only water."

"Easy for you to say," I complained. "I'm wet and you're not."

"I may be dry, but I'm plenty drunk," he said proudly. "Too much gin in too short a time. Such is the sad yet epic story of my life."

"Yeah, whatever," I said, quickly losing interest in this loser.

"Pippin is the name," he said, sticking out his hand for a shake. "John Paul Pippin, to be exact."

Rather than be rude and make a scene in front of Juanita and her parents, who were watching my every move, probably to see if I went postal on the guy, I sucked it up and shook his hand. "Burt King," I said. "And this is my wife, Juanita, and her parents, Jorge and Maria, who are visiting us from Miami."

"An honor to meet all of you," he said, looking right into Juanita's eyes. "First or second?" he asked, now looking back at me. "Let me guess again – third?"

I shot him a confused look.

"Excuse me?" I said.

"First, second or third marriage?"

"Are you shitting me?" I responded. "What sort of question is that?"

"A good one, in my estimation," he cackled.

I chose not to explode. As unpleasant as this dope was, there was something about him I couldn't bring myself to despise. Something admirable about his audacity, something familiar about his no-holds-barred willingness to offend.

"My lovely Juanita is my fifth wife," I explained dispassionately. "And by far, without equal, my all-time best."

Juanita was not happy. Not even close. "Burt is my first husband," she said plaintively. "I've only made one mistake; he's made five."

"Ouch!" I said, feigning injury to my ego, which was feeling sufficiently bulletproof.

Pippin reached into his suit pocket and pulled out a small, silver flask, which he quickly unscrewed and took a swig from. "Anyone else need another drink before dinner?"

I watched with great admiration as Pippin took another swig, and then another in rapid succession. I was captivated by the unapologetic openness of his inebriation at, of all things, a White House dinner.

"Okay, Pippin," I began, "I gotta know. Who the hell are you, and why are you here at the White House tonight?"

"C'mon, chap," he said, putting his hand on my still-wet shoulder. "Don't you know who I am?"

"Nope," I said. "Don't you know who I am?"

WEDNESDAY

"I have no idea who you are, but that doesn't bother me as much as the apparent fact that you have no idea who I am."

"What about you?" he said, turning to Juanita. "Surely, you must know who John Paul Pippin is?"

"Can't say that I do," she said, still annoyed. "Did you used to be the Pope or something?"

"Not exactly, honey. So let me tell you who I am. I, John Paul Pippin III, the pride of Oklahoma City by way of Buffalo and San Diego, am the goddamn K-Mart Poet Laureate of our great country, as selected by the intellectually dishonest eggheads at the Library of Congress, authorized by Congress and approved by the President of the United Freakin' States of America."

"U-S-A, U-S-A," he chanted, loud enough for the surrounding tables to turn around and stare.

"Poet, my ass!" I said. "You're a drunk, not a poet."

"It's evident you know nothing about poetry," he sniffed. "Being a drunk and a poet are not mutually exclusive. They are complementary."

I still wasn't buying his bullshit. "You're as much a poet as I am."

"So, Mr. King, you're a poet, too? We should do a reading or rap together sometime."

"Cut the crap, Pippin. I know you're no poet."

"Fine then, my dear sir," he said, his voice turning defensive. "Why don't you take a look at this before I shove it up your ass?" And with that flourish of poetic prose, he yanked off his tie, unsnapped his tuxedo collar, ripped open his white dress shirt and pulled out, for our entire table to see, a dazzling, jewel-encrusted gold medallion hanging from a gold chain around his neck, which, I will admit, confirmed his status as the preeminent poet in the nation.

"I'll be damned," I offered with ample respect. "I never would have guessed."

"That's what all you ignoramuses say," said Pippin, as he took another swig and belched loud enough to send the Secret Service agents inching closer. Either he didn't know that White House security cameras were recording his every move, or he didn't care. I bet on the latter.

"Can I touch your medal?" Juanita asked, offering her hand.

"If I can touch your breasts," he said without missing a beat.

"Knock it off," was my chivalrous response. "Are you out of your mind?"

"Yes, and proud of it," Pippin said with a sly grin.

"You're a disgusting pig," said Juanita's mother.

"Yes, and proud of it," repeated Pippin.

"You're a despicable piece of scum," Juanita's father added in a fury.

"Right again, and proud of it, in case you can't tell," Pippin said, before continuing undaunted. "As my legions of loyal fans can attest, my uniquely idiosyncratic character has a profound impact on my uniquely brilliant, bitter yet disturbing poetry. Speaking of which, would you like to hear my newest work of art? It's going to be published in *The New Yorker* next month."

"Why not?" I said, hoping to ease the tension and calm everyone down, as the waiters deposited a limp-looking salad in front of me. "What's your poem called?"

"Nice of you to ask," he said facetiously. "Nice of you to care."

"My pleasure," I said.

"My newest poem," he announced, "is titled 'Defecate.' And here's a free sample of my genius."

With that, Pippin rose to his feet, climbed up on his chair and yelled at the top of his lungs, "Attention, everyone! Attention! May I please have your attention?" The entire room fell silent. I could see that the President and Zoey were playing along, acting as though this interruption was a scheduled part of the evening's festivities, unwittingly giving the Poet Laureate a once-in-a-lifetime opportunity.

In the most affected, pretentiously solemn voice he could muster despite slurring his words, Pippin began reciting his artistry:

<u>Defecate!</u>
To defecate
Or not to defecate.
That is the question.
I face every morning.
To drink
Or not to drink.
That is the choice.
I face every day.
To be a tortured, self-righteous intellectual
Or not to be a tortured, self-righteous intellectual.
In a city of idiots,
In a county of fools,
In a world of perpetual woe,
That is the issue.

I face all the time.
So those are my answers.
So please buy my poetry anthologies on
whatever digital platform you prefer,
And leave me the fuck alone.

Pippin stopped, took a long bow and stared around the room, reveling in the extreme discomfort confronting everyone – everyone except the President, who clapped weakly until Zoey grabbed his hands, cutting him off.

Honestly, I was mesmerized by this shocking performance. It was so beyond ridiculously hideous that it was inspiring. How brave! How daring! How ingeniously irreverent! I glanced over at Juanita, who looked like she was about to shriek, which would not have been an appropriate response at a State Dinner.

In a burst of unbridled glee, I leapt to my feet, shouting, "Bravo! Bravo, Maestro!"

My tablemates looked at me like I was insane, which I didn't mind as long as I could protect my new best friend from being ridiculed.

"Encore!" I yelled.

"It would be my honor and your privilege," said Pippin, taking another bow. And without missing a beat, he launched into:

<u>Bitch and Ho</u>
Bitch and Ho,
Yo, yo, yo!
Bitch and Ho,
No, no, no!
Bitch and Ho,
Go To and Fro,
Stealing my dough,
So they can blow it on blow.

I believe that was the last line Pippin delivered, but I will never be sure, because at that moment, he was manhandled by a gang of Secret Service agents, who tackled him to the ground and tasered him, to the seeming delight of the gawking dignitaries. Then, poor Pippin, barely conscious, was lifted high in the air and removed from the premises. Throughout the disruption, I remained chillingly calm, standing tall in a room full of cowards, even as Juanita's mom fainted, sending her daughter into a panic.

As the paramedics revived my mother-in-law and restrained my highly agitated father-in-law, I concluded that it was time for me to leave the scene. I knew I had already experienced the high point of the evening and had zero interest in sticking around for whatever happened next, because it would be boring by comparison. I reached for my phone, pushed the magic button and made it ring loud enough for everyone around me to hear. I felt strongly at peace, for the first time that day.

"Gotta take this call," I muttered apologetically as I stood and stepped away.

"Oh my God! That's horrible!" I exclaimed, loud enough for Juanita and her father to hear. "Unbelievable. I'll be right there.

"I'm terribly sorry, Juanita," I said sheepishly after returning to the table, feigning agitation. "I have a client emergency with the Russians that I must attend to right away. I hope you understand," I added, my voice overflowing with overcooked sympathy as I prepared to scram.

"Are you seriously going to leave a White House dinner early?" asked Jorge, whose attention was laser-focused on the veracity of what I was saying since Maria had come to and was recuperating nicely in her chair.

"I can't tell you what's going on or disclose why or where I need to go," I lied, "but let's just say it's a matter of extreme international security, which I know, Jorge, you can appreciate. You know, top-secret confidential stuff. The CIA or KGB or NBA would shoot me if I told everyone where I went every day. I can only say publicly, on deep background, that I have to meet some unbelievably important people at an undisclosed location."

"I'm sure you wouldn't lie to us," said Maria, rolling her eyes.

"See you later, Burt," scoffed Juanita, who was not buying my story either. I could tell her brain was working in overdrive as she tried to decipher the true meaning of my departure. No sense hanging around to hear her conclusion. I was starting to feel claustrophobic, in dire need of freedom. My sanity clock was ticking down to meltdown.

"Call a car service to take you home," I said. "I'll take the Hummer."

"Gee, thanks," said Juanita. She stopped staring at me, turned her back and wrote me off for the rest of the evening.

"Buenos noches," I said as I rushed away.

The appallingly understaffed fleet of grossly incompetent car fetchers took what seemed like forever to bring my Hummer around front. As was usually the case in these agonizing situations, my already-depleted reservoir of patience had run completely dry.

"Where the fuck have you been?" I sneered at the flailing valet as I flipped him a rolled-up buck. "Did you take my Hummer on a joyride?"

"No speaka Englis," he said, unfurling the bill and looking dejectedly at what he considered to be a substandard tip.

"That's your fucking problem," I said. "If you're gonna come live in our country, you better learn the goddamn language. Which is English, you moron."

The poor sap grinned at me before flipping me the bird – and then flipping out.

"You, Burt King, think you big shit. But we all know truth. You rich scumbag who screws USA up for hard-working people like me. You one more big fat fuck with big car and small penis." And with that, he marched right back toward the friendly confines of his valet booth.

"Do you want me to get you fired, you wackjob?" I shouted after him. "And in case you're wondering, I bet my penis is bigger than your penis."

That only prompted him to wheel around, walk back toward me in an ultra-menacing manner, drop his pants and urinate on the front of my car while repeating: "No speaka Englis, you cocksucker."

Instead of killing the bastard, which would have been an inconvenient, drawn-out process, replete with unflattering publicity, a long investigation and the distinct possibility of endless trials and appeals, I drove off in a huff with my already-too-high blood pressure pounding. Between this dispute with the valet and the turbulent White House dinner, I needed to blow off some steam. Stopping for a quick drink seemed like the most expedient solution. But where, o' where should I go?

Minutes later, I was racing up Connecticut Avenue, cutting over to Massachusetts and passing block after block of those stately, beautifully-manicured embassies filled with swashbuckling diplomats who shopped and partied and screwed their way through our nation's capital, where life was infinitely better for them than it ever would be in their own countries.

Then it hit me – the dreaded pang. The pang that, whenever it reared its ugly head, which was usually once or twice a day, sapped my strength, vanquished my spirit and filled my fragile, existential soul with insurmountable angst. Yes, I needed more than alcohol. I was in dire need of some immediate, consequential action, commonly referred to as "sex." And getting some at home this evening would be impossible. Juanita wouldn't do a single thing with me when her parents were staying in our guest bedroom – no matter what I said or did or offered as compensation. No way. Nothing. Nada. Been there, tried that.

"It's not appropriate," she would declare, despite my best attempts at begging. "They might hear us."

"We're not teenagers," I would counter. "We're a legally married couple. They should be happy if they hear us doing it after all the years we've been together."

"Sorry, Burt. No sexual contact permitted when my parents are here," she would say, rolling over and sliding to the far reaches of our bed, officially terminating the discussion.

On this night, I recognized the sad fact that going home was not going to get me what I knew I needed and felt I deserved, given the excessive angst in my life. I had no choice but to do my damnedest to satisfy my natural urges. Going hunting was the only solution.

Okay, time out for a second. At this point in my story, you're probably wondering if I am a full-fledged sex addict in dire need of more therapy or even sex-addiction counseling. Well, I want to assure you, without hesitation or equivocation, that the answer is no. No, no, no. When you get to be as powerful and important as I am in our nation's capital, multiple sexual conquests are part of the game, as natural as breathing the thick Washington air. In fact, it's common knowledge that the number of conquests is indicative of one's power, arguably the most universally recognized trading currency around town.

Hell, for a man in my position – especially at my age – thinking about sex and trying to have sex as often as possible is perfectly commonplace. It's part and parcel of the capital culture, The way I look at it, every day you don't have sex with someone is one less day in your life you will have sex with someone before you die. My career wasn't always this full of infidelity. But in recent years, due to circumstances beyond my control, I had been womanizing more than usual.

Back to the narrative. As I brain-scanned my options, I realized I didn't have many, especially at this late hour, unless I drove all the way back down to the Hill and stopped at one of those meat markets like Proposition, where I could conceivably capitalize on my fame and score quickly – probably within an hour, max – depending on how desperate I was feeling and how many potential power-crazed female predators were lurking about at the bar, holding court in their skimpy, revealing attire and waiting to meet a man with my stature and gravitas. While that was fine in theory, I wasn't feeling that desperate.

Truth is, I was trying not to stray with total strangers as often as I used to. I knew this level of cheating was becoming unfair to Juanita. Even though we had our marital problems, and frequent interpersonal dysfunction, I was still doing my best, day in and day out, to make our relationship survive in some way, shape or form. And I knew in my heart that she was, too. I also understood deep down inside that hooking up with random strangers for one one-night stand after another carried significant risks besides various sexually-transmitted diseases and disconcerting morning-after regrets. Especially in Washington, where you could end up running scared all over town, hiding from a wacky lobbyist, staffer, politician or intern who'd always fantasized about converting a one-night fling with *moi* into a serious relationship, a stalker situation, an evil blackmail scenario, etc. Worse yet, I could make the mistake of ending up in bed with a high-profile name-dropper hell-bent on including me as a footnote in a tell-all article, screenplay or thinly disguised novel they were writing about the perversion of power and morals and ethics on the banks of the Potomac. For the sake of my career as well as my wiener, these scenarios had a lot of risk and little reward.

Which meant I had only one practical option tonight. Candy. Oh, Candy, here I come.

I raced uptown in hot pursuit and shot over to Tenleytown, pulling into the parking lot behind Thongs R Us, a local strip bar on a downscale stretch of upper Wisconsin Avenue across the street from the National Cathedral, which made it easy for Thongs R Us patrons to pray for their sins right after committing them.

Thongs R Us had always been – and remains to this day – the most upscale national chain of classic gentlemen's clubs for men like me, who have no interest in being gentlemen. It featured young, minimally clad, amazingly flexible, highly paid strippers who entertained the wealthy, power-hungry, sex-starved clientele before leaving the profession after a couple of years, presumably to become highly paid lobbyists or senior Congressional aides.

"Is Candy working tonight?" I asked Frank, the greasy-haired, greasy-faced, turd-shaped maître d', as I walked through the velvet-roped entrance, barely escaping the rain that had started to cascade down from the sticky summertime sky.

"Sorry, Mr. King. Candy's not here tonight," he answered. "She's working a private party at the State Department. But Tina is here."

"That stinks," I said. "But I suppose Tina is better than nothing," I added, with zero excitement.

"Most customers think Tina is plenty fine," said Frank.

"To each his own," I said. Candy was my favorite. Tina was not. Candy was hot and bubbly and fun and easy to talk to. Tina was not. Not even in the ballpark.

As Frank sat me down at my usual table, in front and just to the left of the stage, Tina, speak of the devil, walked out and started strutting her stuff. Despite the nice stuff, and it was unquestionably nice, her onstage presence didn't inspire me in the slightest. And why was that? Because, to be perfectly frank, she had a bad attitude, most likely stemming from her strong opinion that somehow she was God's gift to the strip-club profession: an Australian bombshell who pole-danced at night while purportedly making the Dean's List at Georgetown Law School during the day.

When I first saw Tina strip at Thongs R Us, probably about a year ago, I approached her after the show and offered to get her an internship working for Attorney General Casey in the Justice Department, which she coldly rejected by remarking, "He's a fascist."

When I asked if she wanted an internship in *my* office, as a research assistant, she recoiled: "Venereal disease sounds more appealing." Ouch.

When I ran into her once at some reception she was performing at on Capitol Hill and tried to exchange some innocuous pleasantries, all she could say in response was: "You're a lousy tipper."

Tonight, as Tina unwrapped herself from a pole and slid off the stage, I hailed a waitress and ordered a Scotch. But before I could savor my first sip, I felt an unwelcome tap on my shoulder. Kramer, the bottom-of-the-barrel political consultant from hell, plopped down right beside me without even asking if I felt like some company. Outside of the Grim Reaper, there was no one I wanted to see less at this second of my life than the loathsome loser Kramer and his royal fetidness.

"Hello there, Burtie Boy," he said joyously. "What brings you to Thongs R Us on this rainy night? Shouldn't you be at the White House with the rest of the rich and famous?"

"Hello, Harold," I sputtered, my eyes scanning the room for another empty table or the nearest "Exit" sign. Shit, Kramer had me trapped. Unless, of course, I knocked him unconscious. Which I could have justified in court as an act of legitimate self-defense, given how assaultive his personality could be.

Plan B. I forced myself to expel a series of fake dry coughs and snot-filled sneezes, a trick I had learned shortly after arriving in town. Nothing worked to extricate oneself from a jam in a jiffy better than acting like a highly contagious germ-machine. The scientific research was incontrovertible: the bigger the windbag, the bigger the germaphobe.

"Are you okay, Burt?" asked Kramer, who seemed genuinely concerned, having been sufficiently convinced by my less-than-convincing acting. "You sound terrible. I was there at your ASSPAC speech the other day. You were terrific, despite the riot. Were you sick then, too?"

"I've been feeling terrible all week," I lied. "I've been battling a real bad bug, and I can't seem to kick it."

"Have you gotten tested for bovine flu? Or early signs of Exploding Head Syndrome? Aren't you on your cellphone all the time?"

"I wish it were only the bovine flu or EHS. My doctor thinks I may have a contagious form of Functionitis or perhaps Iglometosis – the real bad kind."

Kramer leaned back, visibly alarmed as he double-checked my facial expression to see if I was messing with him. Even though I was, he had no idea. Few people can keep a straight face under extreme duress like I can.

I snorted in and out through my nostrils, winced in pain and hacked again.

"I don't think you should get too close to me," I moaned. "I'd hate to get you sick. This bug is a real bitch."

"Hey, before I leave," Kramer said, shifting uncomfortably in his seat, "can I ask you something?"

"Sure," I sighed, hiding my euphoria.

"Why do you hate me so much?"

"What sort of question is that?"

"A real good one," he replied. "Look, Burt. We've known each other forever. We've both been in this business a long time. It's a small world we run in. And you've never ever helped me out. You never return my calls. You never throw me any referrals. You never toss me your scraps. I want to know why you despise me."

Needing a break from this unwelcome confrontation, I took my eyes off Kramer and glanced at the dressing-room door, where Vanna the Vampire, dressed in her warmup robe, was stretching out her body in preparation of taking over the stage from Tina and delivering her rather unimaginative necrophilia routine that I had witnessed countless times before. I squinted at Kramer with 50 percent indignation and 50 percent exhaustion.

"I don't hate *you* specifically, Harold," I said, in between another series of phony coughs. "To be perfectly honest, I basically hate everyone in general, including myself. Ask my wife. I'm an equal-opportunity hater. It's how I manage to survive."

"For real?" he wondered stupidly.

"For real," I confirmed with sufficient surety in my voice. "Now get the fuck out of here and leave me alone. I came to see strippers, not self-pitying shitheads like you."

I congratulated myself as Kramer bounded up from his chair and bolted away. Free at last. Free at last. Thank God almighty, I was free at last.

For the next hour or two, or possibly three, I sat and drank my Scotch straight-up, blissfully alone, thinking deep thoughts about nothing in particular. Until I had an epiphany. I had never before scored with a stripper at Thongs R Us – or a stripper anywhere, for that matter – but that did not mean it could not be done. I had never faced a challenge I could not meet.

With plenty of Scotch in my system, I had no reason tonight not to go for it. Sure, I might have had a better shot scoring with Candy because we kind of knew each other, but since she was off tonight, I had to focus on the feasibility of the obvious No. 2 option, which was Tina – and which was going to be a serious long shot. More like a Hail Mary pass with no time left on the clock.

Given Tina's supersized ego and previously displayed distaste for my existence, I needed to come up with a brilliant, foolproof, exceptionally persuasive and irresistible approach. I rubbed my temples, engaging in extensive protracted analysis, barely enjoying the barely enjoyable stage show unfolding in front of me, until finally, I had a strategy and was ready to execute.

After last call at 1 a.m., Tina and two of her colleagues completed their last three-way dance and walked off the stage to a smattering of applause in the nearly empty club, where I was waiting with a handwritten note inside a rolled-up hundred-dollar bill. "We need to talk," it said. "Official government business."

"Whatever," she blurted over her shoulder, sauntering past me to her dressing room. "I'll be back in 10 minutes. I need to change."

When Tina reemerged in jeans and a T-shirt, I was the only patron still left in the club – if you didn't count two shit-faced foreigners in suits passed out at their bottle-strewn tables.

"What do you want?" she asked in a not-so-friendly voice.

"You," I said. "I want us to be friends."

"Are you drunk or just stupid?" she said, heading toward the "Exit" sign.

"Probably a bit of both right now." I laughed.

"I am done for the night. And so are you."

"Can't we just go somewhere and talk?" I tried.

"The answer is no," she said defiantly. "As in, no way. I have too much pride and self-respect to even talk to you, King." She spit out my name with a snide staccato.

"How's law school going?" I inquired, trying to change the subject.

"Fine. Now leave me alone. I gotta go home and study." She started walking faster to the door.

"Can I buy you a drink?" I offered.

"I don't drink," she snorted. "And all the bars are closed. Including this one."

"Can I at least give you a ride home?" I begged.

"Nice try, King. My car is parked outside."

"Are you sure you don't want to go somewhere and hang out? You know, we could talk about politics, world affairs, race relations, the lack of justice and equality in our highly flawed society – whatever you prefer."

"Not with you. Didn't you hear me?"

"Would you like a sneak peek at the President's big speech tomorrow?"

"I'd rather watch TV alone. Or clean my bathroom, for that matter."

I checked my watch. The window of opportunity was quickly closing. Time for a last-ditch effort.

"Can I pay to play?"

"Huh?"

"You know, make it worth your while. Help you pay your rent, help pay your tuition."

"What do you mean, make it worth my while?" she gasped. "Are you kidding? What sort of person do you think I am, King? Do you think I'm a hooker?" To underscore her fury, she kicked me on the shins.

"Of course I don't," I said, blocking her foot from hitting me again. "I think you're ambitious, hard-working, principled yet prudent, idealistic yet pragmatic, success-oriented yet possibly debt-ridden due to excessively onerous student loans."

"Don't be a dick," she muttered, trying to regain her composure.

"But that's who I am," I reminded her.

"Suppose I could use a little extra cash?" she said after reflecting for a moment.

"How about I pay you $1,000 for hanging out at your place? And maybe a back rub."

"How dare you insult me like that!"

"$5,000. Toss in a front rub."

"Goodnight, King," she snickered as she stomped away.

"Okay. Ten grand. No rubs. Just good, poignant conversation."

She turned on her heels and looked at me. "Ten grand and a paid internship this summer at the Supreme Court."

"Shit," I sighed. "You sure know how to drive a tough bargain."

"And White House VIP Tour passes for my entire family when they visit me later this year."

"C'mon, Tina. Is that it?"

"Premium seats to a Redskins game, preferably against the Cowboys, 50-yard line, waiter service, all-you-can-eat and drink coupons."

"Anything else?"

"Nothing I can think of right now."

"Fine," I said, as I offered my hand to seal the deal. She chose not to shake but pushed me gently toward the door.

"You can follow me back to my place," she said.

"What an honor!" I said as we headed out.

"I wish I could say the same," she sighed.

I escorted Tina around the corner to a dimly lit parking lot where she climbed into her car. Then I walked back out to the street and got into mine. Or that was the plan, at least, until some evil bastard jumped out from behind my car, egged me in my face and then had the audacity to shoot me in the ass, which caused me to scream in excruciating pain, which apparently caused my assailant to gas me, which apparently caused me to black out.

When I finally emerged from my unconscious state, I faced multiple surprises. I was in a hospital room, not at home; Juanita was at my side whispering to a doctor; and my head and my back and my ass were throbbing so bad they felt as if they were each, individually, about to burst.

I attempted to ask what was going on, but not a single word emerged from my mouth. My head was groggy, my throat was dry and, for the first time in my life, I could not summon the strength to speak.

"How do you feel?" the doctor asked as Juanita gave me a half-hearted kiss on the cheek, which was unexpected and comforting, especially considering the undeniable naughtiness of what I had been doing at Thongs 'R' Us after bolting from the White House.

"What happened to me?" I managed to get out in a hoarse whisper. "Why am I here?"

"You got shot, honey," cried Juanita. "Someone shot you."

"I got shot? Huh?"

"You got shot in your tush with a BB gun. Right in the middle of Tenleytown."

"Why would anyone hurt me?"

"Criminals are crazy these days," Juanita said. "They want to take more than your money. They want your life."

"Ughhh," I groaned, as my mind clouded up and I started to fall back sleep, too tired to absorb the magnitude of what was happening, thanks to what I learned later was plenty of Percoset.

A little while later, I was shaken awake by Juanita.

"What are you doing?" I said, dazed and confused. "Can't you see I'm sleeping?"

"Someone is here to see you," she answered.

I tried valiantly to sit up but failed, due to severe ass pain. So I rolled over on my side and waited for my brain to focus. Unfortunately, it did, on a large, lumpy, unshaven guy who approached me with trepidation, flashing an official-looking ID and badge that my still-blurry eyes could not handle reading.

"Hello, Mr. King. I'm Detective Ganges, D.C. Police. Second District."

"Ganges...Ganges...Hmmm." I knew I knew that name from somewhere. Oh no, I wondered. Could it be a relative?

"You may know my older brother, Rocco Ganges. He's the national political reporter for *The Washington Scandal*."

And one of the biggest sleazebags in the history of modern journalism, I thought but had enough self-control, for once in my life, not to say.

"Why are you here, Detective?"

"It's about the note."

"What note?"

"The note your assailant left on your body."

"There was a note on me?"

"Sure was. Stapled right on your butt. Right above where you got shot."

"No wonder my ass hurts so bad."

"I bet it does," Ganges said, "between the BBs and the staples."

"What did this note say?"

Ganges cleared his throat. "Okay, the note said, and I quote: 'Look, America! A hole in the ass of one of America's biggest assholes.'"

"What?" said Juanita.

"Are you kidding?" I asked, hoping he was.

"I wish I were," Ganges said. "But I'm not. Do you want to see it?"

Before I had time to answer, the detective pulled out a plastic evidence bag. It was sealed up, but the hand-scrawled letters were still plainly visible. As was what looked to be a distinct splatter of my own blood. It was upsetting enough to make me pass out – or maybe just collapse back into a deep sleep for a few hours, until Juanita woke me once again.

"C'mon, Burt," she said, rubbing my head. "Wake up. It's 6 a.m. and time for us to go home."

"I can't. I need to sleep."

"The nurse said the hospital needs this room for some guy with a real bullet wound."

"Tell them to go fuck themselves," I bawled, with all the indignation I could summon. "*My* bullet wound is real, too."

"Whatever you say, Burt," Juanita said, trying unsuccessfully to calm me down. "Whatever you say."

And that's the last thing I remember hearing before I faded back into peaceful obliviousness on the night I got shot, a traumatic event that will forever haunt me – along with everything else that happened next.

Thursday

I woke up in my mile-a-millisecond hyper-panic mode, not sure where I was. As my eyes darted around the vaguely familiar room, and my brutally sore sphincter expelled some early morning gas, I considered for an instant the possibility that last night's insanity was only a dream – until the raging pain in my limbs reconfirmed that it was not. My head was pounding, and my ass ached all over.

I tried shouting for Juanita but couldn't raise my voice enough for her to hear me, wherever she was. My mind drifted in and out until I finally broke out of my fog and figured out my location: I was covered in blankets and lying on my side in our living room, not on our trusty, luxuriously comfortable couch but on some odd, uncomfortable contraption, a hard-as-nails hospital bed that Juanita must have felt compelled to rent for my convalescence. Fortunately, she had correctly positioned it right in front of our 144-inch plasma TV, one of my favorite material acquisitions of the current calendar year. It featured 12-foot 4-D images that blew away even the most realistic forms of reality. But I still felt like shit. Given the depth of my current state of agony, I would have been much happier on my couch, which, unlike this ridiculous hospital bed, would have lessened rather than exacerbated the extreme discomfort I was experiencing.

Now, I liked my wife. I liked our condo. I loved my killer TV. But perhaps my greatest love at this time in my life, especially when I was tired or depressed or both, was my super-premium overstuffed leather couch. Deep, sensuous Italian cow skin, stitched tight from the corpses of eleven cows but with sufficient give to be either supportive or womblike, depending on my needs. So, so cuddly, it was the perfect place to veg out, watch the boob tube and drift away to sleep. If only I could someday find an equally perfect soul mate to love as much as I loved my couch.

"Roll over, Mr. King, so I can change your bandage," said a monstrous, mustachioed 300-pound-plus female nurse who propelled herself toward me like a shark. "Gotta keep your butt wound clean so it don't get infected."

Before I had a chance to fight back or shield myself from her onslaught, she grabbed my shoulders, flipped me on my belly and ripped open my robe, exposing my wounded ass in its full glory. Without offering a single word of warning or even a token bit of comfort, she tore off my bandage with zero concern for my well-being, visibly enjoying the chance to abuse me.

"Damn, that's the oddest ass wound I've ever seen," she proclaimed. "I've seen more than my fair share of gunshot wounds, but you look like you got shot with nails."

"He got shot with BBs," said Juanita, who arrived on the scene with Populace in tow. "Good morning, Burt. How are you feeling today?"

"Terrible," I said in search of pity. "I haven't been in this much pain since that time my mother hit me in the face with a tire iron after I got a C in sixth-grade math."

After the nurse dressed my wound and slapped a new book-size bandage on my butt, I tried to sit up. No way. The pain was unbearable. I gingerly lowered myself back onto the bed. I knew would be spending the day imprisoned in this room, lying on my side, stewing, and depositing as many painkillers and assorted numbing agents into my bloodstream as possible.

"How long am I gonna be laid up like this?" I asked Juanita. "For a month?"

"I doubt that long," she answered. "Dr. Cutter will be by later to check on you."

"Since when does that bastard make house calls?"

"Since I offered his family and a few close friends of his choice a private VIP tour of the White House, with you as their personal guide."

"Won't that be a joy," I said, dreading the thought. "I can hardly wait for his eminence to arrive."

Despite the clear sarcasm in my voice, Populace had heard what he considered to be a lie and, as a result, reflexively peed all over our insanely expensive living-room antique rug, hand-stitched by the artisans at Oregon State Penitentiary over a decade earlier.

THURSDAY

"Anyway," Juanita continued after commanding Matilda, our newest and possibly most incompetent housekeeper of all-time, to attempt to remove the urine puddle from the premises, "if Dr. Cutter gives you the green light, you could be back at work tomorrow. Aren't you supposed to be flying off to California?"

"Yes. I gotta get out of here. I mean, I gotta get out there. Big meetings with important clients. An awful lot is hanging in the balance."

"I bet," Juanita said, slyly mocking my self-congratulatory importance.

"When do you expect Dr. Cutter to bless us with his presence?" I asked. "Soon, I hope."

"His secretary called to say he'll stop by sometime between this morning and 8 p.m., whenever he has time. Apparently, he's overbooked and in great demand."

"Wonderful," I snapped. "I'll just wait for him to descend from the heavens on the wings of an angel to save the day."

"Lighten up, Burt," said Juanita. "He'll get here when he gets here."

"This is more ridiculous than waiting for the cable guy. Waste a whole day of my life sitting around on my ass because my quack doctor is such a busy guy. I bet he feels extra special making one of his most important patients, if not his most important, wait forever."

"What's the big deal?" said my increasingly exasperated wife. "You're gonna be stuck at home taking it easy all day today. So do the world a favor and calm yourself down. Don't forget, you're really fortunate. You could have been killed last night."

"If I had been killed, would that have upset you?" I asked Juanita twice as obnoxiously as I should have. "Would you be missing me right now?"

"I don't know, maybe for a minute or two," she said as she walked out. "But I'm sure, sooner or later, I would have found someone better to love."

Juanita was still pretty sexy when she was pissed at me.

Moments later, my lovely wife returned with the videophone. She said it was Big Al.

"Take me off video," I instructed her. "I can't let anyone see me in this condition."

"Christ almighty! What happened to you, Burt?" said my rightfully panicked limited partner. "Are you alright?"

"I'm fine," I assured him. "If you didn't know, Burt King is bulletproof."

"That's what I hear," said a relieved Big Al. "Because if you were ever killed, Slice & Dice would be doomed."

"How right you are," I confirmed.

"Can I assume you're not coming in today for the PDC meeting?"

Damn. I didn't want to miss that one. PDC was a particularly prickly client. But, given the way I was feeling, I knew I was not getting out of bed in the foreseeable future.

"Sorry, I can make it in."

"Should we reschedule?" he asked. "I'm sure they'd understand."

"Hell, no," I said, rejecting his notion. "You can handle it. Just stick to your guns on the script and don't let anyone push you around."

"No problem," said Big Al, pleased with the trust I had in his abilities to stage-manage one of our biggest corporate clients, the Prepaid Death Consortium, a nationwide chain of for-profit hospitals offering quick, easy assisted-suicides for seriously ill Americans who couldn't afford to see a doctor. These guys had been making obscene profits for the longest time, ever since health insurance became virtually unaffordable for 99 percent of the people. Hey, it's survival of the fittest, right?

"Okay, Big Al, I have to go recuperate. Good luck with the meeting, and let me know how it goes."

"Are you going to postpone your California trip tomorrow?"

"I think I'll have to, but I'm not sure yet. I'm waiting for my stupid doctor to pay me a visit. All I know is that I'm a mess."

And so began one of the most inhumanely boring days of my life. Worse than the most boring day of high school, when I sat in detention for seven hours after telling my history teacher, Mr. Fanuck, that he was an embarrassment to the teaching profession, after he sent me to the principal's office after I told him to go fuck himself after he slapped me after I gave him the finger after he flunked me on a term paper in which I argued that history class was completely worthless, because anything that was in the past was irrelevant and inconsequential to the present or future. Whoever said that those who are ignorant of the past are doomed to repeat it, or something along those lines, totally missed the point: Why would anyone give two shits – or even notice – that they were repeating something from the past if they never knew about it in the first place? Even to this day, I subscribe to this Theory of Irrelevantivity, in direct opposition to my nocturnal nemesis Einstein. And I will defend my views to my dying day.

As I recuperated in bed for what felt like a millennium, I logged more hours of TV than I ever had in my life. And it was insipid. Actually, it was torturously insipid, which was the worst kind of insipid – exceptionally more taxing than most of the other things in life I usually found to be insipid.

First I watched two reruns of *Death Row Executions*, a reality show on the Death Network. In both episodes, the criminals, one male, the other female, met their makers via lethal injection, which was dull as hell to sit through. All these felons did was slump in their chair before they went into cardiac arrest and died. Not suspenseful in any way, shape or form. I much preferred when *DRE* televised a live decapitation or firing-squad execution from some foreign country, but there was nothing of that kind to enjoy.

Next I watched *America's Most Dysfunctional Marriages*, one show I could count on to make me feel better – albeit temporarily – about my own marital travails. The episode I saw on this day was a testament to how horrific marriage could be even when I wasn't personally involved. The case centered on a wife who came home early from work and caught her husband in a four-way with her sister and her mother and her brother. When she was asked by the on-air reporter why she'd decided to put up with this indignity and stay in her troubled marriage, she said, with supreme confidence: "I'm gonna stand by my man and work through this, because he makes good money. Sure, he made a mistake, but I appreciate the fact that he kept it all in the family."

Then I watched *Maximum Security Iron Chefs* on the Food Network, the most popular prison cooking show on TV, featuring gourmet cooks who happened to be incarcerated felons with a penchant for brawling with fellow contestants in the caged-in kitchen. I was a fan because each battle was as bloody and entertaining as Ultimate Fighting – but even more dangerous, thanks to the use of kitchen knives and other assorted utensils. Sadly, this episode lacked any meaningful drama aside from two ugly incidents, one in which the challenger was eliminated for burning a judge with an illegal propane torch he claimed was for Bananas Foster, and a second in which two sous chefs badly scalded each other's respective faces with huge pots of boiling water.

After that, I flipped over to my myriad porn channels but came up empty-handed. I watched the latest installment of *HookerSnooker*, a new game show from England in which high-class, high-priced hookers played Snooker, which is kind of like billiards, except the players were buck naked. Honestly, this sounds better in theory than it is in reality.

Just after 4 p.m., halfway through a segment on *Badass Grandma's of Detroit* – about a rough-and-tumble cocaine ring run by senior citizens on the mean streets of the Motor City – lo and behold, by the grace of God, my personal physician, Horatio Cutter, M.D., came waltzing in, live and in person, to examine me.

"It's about time!" I groaned.

"Nice to see you too, Burt," Cutter replied before flashing his trademark and completely insincere smile.

""Where the fuck have you been?" I was not amused.

"Doing the Lord's work," he said, clearly reveling in his own bullshit. "Helping heal all the sick and insured rich patients who can afford my aggressively priced, largely unreimbursable premium fees."

"I can't imagine many people besides me can pay what you charge."

"Well, then, that's their loss, right? By the way, Burt, my VIP house calls have to be paid in cash. Up front. As I tell all my patients, if you don't have the dough, then I gotta go."

I yelled for Juanita, who came running in. "Your friend, Dr. Cutter here, is trying to rob us blind."

Juanita didn't seem to mind. "Whatever it takes to get you better, honey," was her inappropriate response. "How much do we owe you?" she asked, surrendering to Cutter's appalling display of *rapacity*. (Note: I love the sound of that word – it's much fancier than saying "greed" all the time.)

"Let's say one grand for the exam," said Cutter, "another grand for the house-call service charge, and I'll pay for the valet parking in your garage out of my own pocket. Deal?"

Two thousand dollars and 10 minutes later, after glancing ever so briefly at my raw, gaping butt wound, Cutter was out the door, leaving me with a prescription for some extra-strength painkillers and a pronouncement, to my surprise and delight, that I was officially fit for work and travel.

"Just one thing, Burt," he said before departing. "Try to take it easy, and, please, no crazy sex for a day or two."

"Don't worry, Dr. Cutter," said Juanita. "That won't be a problem."

Easy for her to say.

Despite Cutter giving me a clean bill of health, I was still feeling crappy and intensely stir crazy. After exhausting my television remote and all other available options, I decided to do something new and different, something I had never ever tried before: I, Burt King, was going to write some impassioned poetry, inspired by my encounter the night before at the White House with the singularly eminent poet John Paul Pippin, who was probably lying drunk in some jail cell somewhere.

It took me almost a half hour, but my first effort yielded this opus:

Me and You

I am me

And you are you,

Which means we have zero in common.

THURSDAY

Except maybe the air we breathe.
Too bad.
Your loss.
But don't go feeling all sad and sorry for yourself.,
Admit the truth.
Accept the truth.
Embrace the truth.
The truth that confirms,
Without a doubt,
That I am better
Than you will ever be.
Such is life.

The next several poems I wrote that afternoon took me even longer, nearly an hour in total, which was fine by me, because killing time was my highest priority.

<u>Satisfaction</u>
I can't get no satisfaction
I can't get no satisfaction
And when I try
To be sly
And I lie
And I cry
I still can't get no
Stupid satisfaction.

<u>The Fire Within</u>
Harboring hateful feelings
Toward heinous individuals
As Rage rushes through my body,
I am a warrior,
Forever fighting,
Hellbent on obliterating
Every enemy who dares to stand in my way.

<u>Mother Dear</u>
Why did you?
Why didn't you?

I AM BURT KING

How could you?
How dare you?
Why did you make me suffer so?

<u>*Falling Leaves*</u>
From graceful trees,
Autumn leaves,
Sparkling with color,
Fall quietly to the ground,
Floating at their own peaceful pace,
As the soft healing wind blows,
Ever so gently.
Creating momentary beauty,
Until they shrivel up and die,
Like Ed Ravitch in Rhode Island,
After my negative ads destroyed that prick's campaign,
And his marriage.

<u>*As Time Flies By*</u>
As time flies by,
Marriage becomes harder,
As time flies by,
The tensions mount,
As time flies by,
The pressures build,
As time flies by,
The urges are aroused,
As time flies by,
Even the ugly women look hotter,
As time flies by,
I can't resist,
As time flies by,
My fly opens,
In a rush of animalistic passion,
I am powerless to stop
All the sex that unfolds.

THURSDAY

As I reread my masterpieces, my pride surged with well-deserved self-approbation – until the phone rang and Juanita came rumbling in, interrupting my creative process and rushing me back to reality.

"It's for you," she said. "He says he's Todd McNamara, CIA deputy director of operations."

I knew his boss, but I didn't know anyone at the agency with the name McNamara. "Why would he be calling me?"

"What's up, McNamara?" I asked. "Are you spooks investigating the assassination attempt against me? Was it an international conspiracy? Am I a marked man?"

"I'm sorry about what happened to you," the caller said with a heavy lisp. "But to tell you the truth, Mr. King, I am not with that CIA. I'm calling from the Continental Insurance Agency, the other CIA, with an unbelievably special offer for you on new-term life insurance, to protect you and your loved ones if one day you actually do get killed or suddenly keel over and croak."

"I'm hanging up now, you jerk!" I screamed, as loud as possible for a yeller to yell. "Do you fucking know who you're fucking telemarketing? Do you know how powerful I am and what I could do to you if I wanted to? If you ever in a million years call here again trying to sell me anything, even a bar of soap, I will have you crushed like a bug."

I hung up and tried to calm down by closing my eyes, breathing deeply and envisioning one final ode I could compose on this trying day. I wanted something memorable, with an off-the-charts profundity that would invoke the best verse humans had ever heard, as good as anything John Paul Pippin was capable of creating, even better than when he performed "Defecate" at the White House. And just like that, out it came from my brain, radiating pure, blissful brilliance.

<u>The Roll</u>
It spins and spins,
Sometimes once, twice or three or more times a day,
Depending on how much greasy food I've eaten.
Soothing, cleansing, soft yet firm.
Without it I would be trapped.
I sit alone on my seat of power,
Grasping its grace,
Sitting, Waiting,
Pushing, Wiping,

> *Flushing, Swirling,*
> *Rising, Washing*
> *Thanks to premium soft-tissue toilet paper,*
> *I can do my business,*
> *Rise with impunity,*
> *And walk away,*
> *Free at last,*
> *Relieved,*
> *Free for now.*
> *Until nature calls me back again.*

I knew I couldn't top that, so I quit my artistry and resumed my unproductive channel surfing, looking for something, anything, to watch. I must have fallen back to sleep due to all the painkillers and tedium, because the next thing I knew, I was rudely awakened by the sound of the living-room doors flying open. In marched two Secret Service men accompanying the First Lady, Zoey Strump. Surprise, surprise!

I shot up in bed and covered my scantily robed body with blankets to camouflage as much flabbiness as possible.

"Hi, Burt. How are you feeling?"

"To what do I owe the honor of your visit, Zoey?"

"The President and I heard about what happened to you last night, and we were worried. Very worried. I was in the area, so I came by to find out first of all how you're doing, and second of all. why on earth you were at a strip bar named Thongs R Us last night instead of at our White House dinner."

"Thanks for your concern," I sputtered. "I'm terribly sorry I had to leave the White House early, but I had to check on an undercover surveillance operation we were conducting on some douchebag running against one my most vulnerable clients, Senator Fischer from South Dakota. Hell, we have to keep our Senate majority intact, right?"

"Whatever you say, Burt," Zoey snickered.

To her credit, Juanita intervened to ease the tension. "Can I bring you some tea, Zoey?"

"Thank you, that would be lovely," she said. I, for one, acutely appreciated Juanita's hospitality at this moment – further proof that my wife had no apparent knowledge of her husband's unrequited love for the First Lady of the United States.

"So you claim you were working at Thongs R Us?" Zoey asked with sufficient sarcasm once Juanita had left to make tea.

"What do you mean, 'I claim'? Of course I was."

"So you deny what Povich wrote on his blog this morning?" said my inquisitor.

"Please spare me what he said. He's a pathological liar. And a stalker to boot."

"He says he has confirmation from a well-known political consultant that you were carrying on at Thongs R Us last night, enjoying yourself among the nakedness, and then, after it closed, you were seen across the street, soliciting sex from child prostitutes in the parking lot of the public library."

"That's insane," I argued. "A ridiculous lie."

"Are you sure?" Zoey asked with a cruel smirk.

"All I know," I said, switching gears, "is that I am lucky to still be alive."

Zoey stared into my eyes, trying to measure the veracity of my statements. "Did your assailant really shoot you in the butt with a BB gun?"

One of her Secret Service agents muffled a chuckle from the back of the room.

"What's so goddamned funny about me getting shot?" I asked with annoyance.

"Nothing, sir," he replied, clearly embarrassed.

"No, c'mon," I countered. "What's so hilarious about getting shot? Do you think this is some kind of joke? I could have been killed."

"Chill out, Burt," said Zoey. "It could have been worse."

"I doubt it. This was pretty bad."

Zoey laughed. "To tell you the truth, I find the whole thing rather comical."

"And why do you find my near-death experience so funny?"

"Think about it, Burt. You are such a drama queen – I mean, drama *king*. You are beyond self-absorbed, and you act as if everything you do automatically qualifies you to be the center of attention, the most important life force in the universe."

"What are you suggesting, Zoey? That I put myself at death's doorstep on purpose?"

"Feel free to form your own conclusions. All I know is that if you had done the right thing and stayed at the White House and not left early to amuse yourself at a scummy strip bar, none of this would have happened."

"You're saying I'm to blame?"

"Aren't you?" Zoey gave me one of her self-righteous sighs, reminding me once again that she regarded the halo over her life as far superior to mine.

Happily, Juanita walked back in with the tea, officially ending this painstaking, needlessly argumentative conversation and reducing the level of discourse to amiable banter, basically a low-energy tea party. After 15 minutes of this inanity, Zoey jumped up, wished me a speedy recovery and fled through the door with her armed entourage, leaving Juanita and me to fend for ourselves with a lot of nothing as the rest of my rehab day slid slowly by.

I finally heard back from Big Al right before dinner. The PDC clients loved the script of our new spot, which featured my inspired new message for the masses: "Are you sick and tired? Have you lost all hope? No worries! Before you suffer any longer, please call us, your friends at PDC, for a free consultation. We can help you and your loved ones make your death much easier than your life."

Chalk up another home run, another shot way out of the park, for yours truly!

By the time I took my nighttime dose of valium, packed my carry-on suitcase, ditched the crappy hospital cot and slid into my own bed, I was almost halfway back to form. I was feeling a lot better and regaining my swagger, grateful to still be alive and grateful to still be Burt King, the best bad-ass political brain in all of humanity, for now and most likely forever.

My greatly improved mood was punctured by a late-night call, which experience had taught me was rarely, if ever, good news. It was Simmons, the deputy political editor of *The Washington Whisperer* which was always bad news.

"Sorry to call you so late, Burt, especially after you got shot, but I need to ask you a question."

"It's after 11 p.m. Have you no decency?"

"Something's up, we're on deadline and I need your comment."

"Hit me with it," I said resignedly.

"In your spare time, when you are not at work, are you a pimp for a transvestite prostitute?"

"What?"

"One of our interns Googled your name to fact-check a piece on the Canfield campaign, and there is a Burt King from Washington, D.C., listed as the proprietor for Bipartisan Transvestite Escort Services, which advertises itself as featuring 'Bipartisan Big Shots Who Will Blow You All Around the Beltway.' Ranks first on Google's search results, so it must be true, right?"

"Go blow yourself," I said. "And that's on the record."

"C'mon, Burt," Simmons pleaded. "Tell me what's going on here."

"I'd be happy to," I lied. "When I'm not talking to you and your journalist jihadist friends, or advising the most important people in Washington, yes, I am running a transvestite escort service. Do you like that catchy slogan about how my escorts are bipartisan? Well, I can assure you that we are the only bipartisan professionals in town. In fact, right now, by calling me at home this late at night, you are eligible for a free trial offer with any one of our transvestites. Can I send someone over to your home right away?"

"So are you denying it's you, Burt?"

"Yes, I am denying it's me, Simmons. Don't you putzes at *The Whisperer* have anything better to do with your time than Googling transvestite hookers?"

"I guess not," he said before hanging up.

I've spent a good chunk of my professional life defending my character, but I had to see this one for myself. I clicked on Google and searched my name, and sure enough, there he, or she, or it was for the entire world to see:

Bipartisan Transvestite Escort Service

Ranked #1 among members of Congress and high-ranking White House officials, BTES offers the largest selection of high-powered, bipartisan transvestites, including she-males you've never seen, all hand-picked by the owner/operator, the incomparable Burt King, political consultant extraordinaire. For the discerning client who wants to explore the inner workings of power behind closed doors.

My enemies knew no bounds. You had to love this town.

Despite all the drugs, and despite my overall state of exhaustion, it took forever for me to wind down for the night. Especially with Juanita talking in her sleep again. First came her relentless moaning, as if she were in pain or having sex with an elephant. Then came the groaning, as if she had been injured. Then came the shrieks, which were unsettling, to say the least.

"I'm gonna kill you, Burt!

"I have a knife, you son of a bitch! Can you see it?

"Go ahead, Burt, you ass," she chortled. "Make your move and I'll make mine. I'll slice you into a thousand pieces.

"I am leaving you, Burt. I want a divorce!"

I tried nudging her gently to interrupt her disturbing train of thought. Her dreaming about killing me was not exactly relaxing. I was getting exceptionally tense just listening to her violent rage.

I lay there, listening to her go on and on, desperately willing my unwilling self to fall asleep and end this miserable fucking day. However, I was woefully unable to calm my angst, lower my blood pressure and relax enough to have my eyes and brain shut down and take the rest of the night off.

This was a job for Max Morrison. I grabbed my radio and tuned in to my favorite maestro of miasma.

"We need to put every single immigrant in jail," said Morrison's gravelly, self-assured voice. "Starting with the Arabs and Chinese. Then the Canadians. Lock them up and throw away the key."

"I hear ya, brother," said one enthusiastic caller. "Screw those termites. We need to just exterminate them as soon as possible, before everything good gets infested."

"Why not?" said the all-too-happy-to-oblige host. "We have to take America back. This is our land, not their land."

"Hell, you should run for President, Max," said the caller. "Only you can protect us from them."

"Thank you, sir. That's very nice of you to say, and I appreciate – and never ever take for granted – all the support I get from listeners like you. To tell you the truth, running for President is something I have thought about from time to time. I know I could be an outstanding Commander-in-Chief. I know I could lead our nation and destroy our enemies at home – and around the world. But, to be impeccably honest, I can't afford to take such a massive pay cut at this time in my life. Not now. Maybe in a few years."

Even though Morrison made those caustic comments the other night about the President, perhaps he wasn't such a bad guy. I rolled over in bed and wrote myself a note to call him in the morning and offer a free, no-obligation consulting session to discuss his Presidential ambitions. I had met him once, in passing, several years ago at some forgettable reception at George Washington University, and despite his distaste for the President, I unequivocally believed he had all the right raw stuff to be a formidable political presence – with my masterful guidance, of course. Such an exciting prospect even aroused a little tingle down below.

"Go ahead, next caller."

"Good evening, Max. What should we do about the Jews?"

I waited with bated breath to see how Morrison would respond, but he never did. Instead, I heard shouts, a struggle, two bangs and a shriek from what was obviously something bad that had broken out in his studio. After a few more seconds of on-air commotion, there was silence. No sounds from Morrison or anyone else.

I sat up in bed, completely baffled. A minute later, a strange voice spoke into the microphone:

THURSDAY

"We, the people, are pleased to announce the capture of Max Morrison. Consider this a public service. Stay tuned to this station for further developments."

I freaked out so bad, I nearly fell out of bed. First Chief Justice Adams had been kidnapped, and now this? What the hell was going on around here?

Friday

The previous 24 hours of mayhem had made me restless and way too fidgety to sit around. It was time to leave behind all the craziness and bullshit and kidnappings in D.C. It was time to hit the road. As bad as my butt still hurt, I was beyond stir-crazy. I needed to get back out there in America and do my thing.

Before my fiasco at Thongs R Us, I had been genuinely looking forward to my one-day West Coast swing to San Francisco and Los Angeles. Sure, for most mere mortals, it was an excessive amount of flying in less than 24 hours, but not for *moi*. These were two good cities for high-profile, lucrative clients in a state whose electoral wackiness and volatility I'd always understood. I'm proud to say that in all my years of consulting in California, none of my candidates had ever lost an election, a distinction that none of my consulting competitors could claim.

I especially liked Los Angeles, where I felt at home and knew my star power was appreciated by the politically active, ostentatiously obsequious studio execs, actors, producers, agents and showbiz hangers-on who understood that Washington and what remained of Hollywood were two very similar planets, both consumed by an eternal quest for power, influence, status and sex with young things half one's age. In the spirit of full disclosure, I should also mention that I pictured my life story as prime material for a movie, which is why I sucked it up and curried favor with all those film-industry clowns whenever I met them. I knew they would someday be slobbering all over me to help them put my inspiring life story on the big screen in 4-D. In fact, by the time you read these words, I will hopefully have signed a deal to make my life into the blockbuster movie, TV show and video game it rightfully deserves to be.

San Francisco, where I was flying first, was fine, too, except that it was a little too rough around the edges for my taste. A nice place to visit, whether you were gay or weird or not, but I would never have wanted to live there, especially since two-thirds of the city's residents were homeless and begging for a living. Kind of a downer. But certainly not my concern. I also missed the days when the Golden Gate Bridge was actually a bridge, before it was purchased by Target and turned into a giant supercenter store.

I took the 6 a.m. flight out to San Francisco, arriving at SFO a little after 9 a.m., just in time for my limousine to miss the worst part of rush hour. By the time I got in the stretch and flipped on the TV, speculation on the Morrison and Adams kidnappings dominated the news. A ransom note had been emailed to D.C. Police, demanding $1 million and a truckload of tofu for the prisoners' release – but it had turned out to be a hoax perpetrated by two stupid teenagers from Catholic University who'd been arrested and were on their way to jail for the rest of their youth. Thanks to the recently enacted "Crackdown on Crime Bill," impersonating a kidnapper was a serious felony in all 50 states and the District of Columbia.

"We are investigating all possible leads," I watched District Police Chief Qadaffi say unconvincingly. When asked if the Morrison kidnapping was definitively linked to the kidnapping of Justice Adams, Qadaffi replied: "Beats me. If I knew what was going on, I would tell you what was going on." A response that gave every wealthy Washingtonian an excuse to call their security consultants, buy more guns and upgrade their surveillance systems.

My first stop in SF was the Mandarin Omnipotent Oriental, where I would have coffee with California Governor Dora Waltz, after which I was scheduled to accompany her to City Hall for the inauguration of the city's spanking new mayor, and one of my up-and-coming clients, the honorable Clem "the Cowboy" Hoskins. Or, as Hoskins liked to say, (thanks to my wit, which never ceases to amaze me) "There's a new sheriff in town!" or "If you want law and order, I'm your man!" or, in homage to his Bay Area progenitor, Clint Eastwood's Dirty Harry, "Go ahead, punk! Make my day." I'll never forget how the audience went wild when my boy Clem whipped a pistol out during that first debate with his poor sap of a sissified opponent. The damn election was over before it had even begun.

Hoskins was Silicon Valley rich, telegenic and enjoyed playing hardball, which meant he had a good future on the American political scene.

"You know, Burt, I'm convinced I can be President," he told me the first time we ever met.

"Why don't you try being mayor for a few weeks and then we can talk?" I suggested. I admit, I like my prospective clients to be self-confident, aggressive and rich enough to afford me, but they also need to be a little realistic. Rome wasn't built in a day, and I'm not exactly a miracle worker – although I repeatedly come close. However, Hoskins had everything he needed to go far in politics, and if he did a halfway-decent job as mayor of this unruly city, his electoral possibilities were endless.

On the other hand, Waltz, my first-term Governor of the Golden State, was a disaster, having needlessly squandered the high approval ratings I bestowed upon her after her resounding election win. Her short time in office had been an unending series of moronic policy decisions, bad hires and stunningly wrong-headed political miscalculations. As we sat down to have coffee in an opulent, sprawling suite with a panoramic view of the San Francisco slums, I figured I had, at most, an hour to stop her from self-immolation. To add gas to the fire, there were multiple stories online this morning quoting former confidantes, ex-aides and recently fired household servants, that Waltz was disillusioned with the state of politics in California and was on the verge of resigning.

"What the hell is going on with you?" I said after we sat down.

"I don't know, Burt," she said, as if she really had no clue. "Did you see all the negative press I'm getting?"

"I did," I fibbed, "and you probably deserve it." I actually hadn't bothered to read the stupid stories, but I didn't question their veracity. Waltz's eyes said it all. "You look like shit. The bags under your eyes are so big, they look like they're gonna burst."

"Thanks for the diagnosis. Is this what I pay you for?"

"Among other things. Go ahead, tell me what's wrong."

"Basically everything," she said softly. "The voters hate me. My husband hates me. My kids hate me. Even my biggest supporters hate me. I can't sleep at night. I'm depressed. I've managed to ruin my entire life."

"But other than that," I said, trying to inject a little humor into a tense situation, "is everything else okay?"

"Yeah, right, Burt," she said, sufficiently annoyed. "Everything is just dandy."
"Well, do you want my high-priced advice?"
"Of course I do. Why else would I even meet with you?"
"Because you enjoy my company?"
"Hardly."

I paused to amp up the dramatic effect. Staring deep into her eyes, as if I were intensely examining her predicament, I took a deep breath and unleashed the following barrage, expressly designed to get her attention.

"With all due respect, Madame Governor, you are a fucking mess."
"That's all you have to say?"
"That's all there is to say."
"Then why don't we end this highly unproductive conversation, Burt? We have nothing further to discuss. I have plenty of problems without you being such a jerk."

"Stop feeling so pathetically sorry for yourself, Waltz," I said. "All this self-pity is killing you. For heaven's sake, you are still the Governor of the great state of California, you are still rich, and you still haven't lost your attractive looks and magnetic charm, despite being a rather advanced-middle-aged mom on the downside of 50. If you ask me, you've still got a great future if you want one. But stop being, you know, such a pussy. No offense."

She didn't respond at first. I could see I was pushing her buttons. But she kept silent for a long time, as if she were truly absorbing the magnitude of my unusually salient advice. Finally, she cleared her throat and spoke softly:

"I really, truly hate this job. I honestly do. You know I wanted to be Governor forever, and now that I've finally reached the pinnacle of achievement and won the damn election and reached my goal, fulfilling and even exceeding my wildest dreams, I discover that this whole thing sucks terribly."

"What whole thing?" I asked, discreetly checking my watch. We had to be in our seats at City Hall for Hoskins's inauguration in 40 minutes. This salvage job was gonna be one helluva rush.

"Being Governor of this state is the pits. Beyond hideous. All I do is go to interminably boring meetings, slash budgets that have already been cut to the bone, chase donations 24/7 from a bunch of leech-like lobbyists and sycophants, and then, to top it all off, I have to spend every single day misleading the people, telling them with a big smile that I can help solve their problems, when I know deep in my heart that I can't do one goddamn thing to make their wretched lives any better."

"That's not your fault," I said, "which means it shouldn't be your concern."

"It's not about assigning blame. It doesn't matter whose fault it is. I am hopelessly stuck in a depressing, dead-end job."

"That you wanted badly and spent nearly $100 million of your family's fortune to win."

"Fine. Can I get a refund? Can I turn in my keys and get my money back?"

In the course of my career, I'd seen some extreme cases of candidate burnout before. And I recognized all the common symptoms – glassy eyes, disheveled look, crying, excessive angst, binge drinking, abnormally high levels of indiscreet philandering. But this one was a doozy. If I were going to fix Waltz, I needed to shake off the jet lag, get my brain firing on all cylinders and give it all I had.

"Please consider for a second the platform you've got," I argued. "You are the Governor of a gigantic state of 35 million Americans, not even including all those illegal immigrants we're rounding up and deporting at this very moment. Think about your power! Think about your influence! Think about your image. Think about what you stand for. You're a political goddess to the people, especially the vocal minority who support you."

"But the reality is," she countered, "I stand for nothing. I have accomplished nothing. And worst of all, I feel nothing. I am numb to the job. And to my life."

This was beyond baffling. Off-the-charts levels of despair, combined with a profound sense of nothingness. I racked my brain for an answer. "If you don't mind me asking, Madame Governor, are we talking menopause here?" I asked.

"What did you say?" she retorted, becoming agitated.

"You heard me, Governor. Have you really become this existential, or are we talking about female problems that may be clouding your thinking and your ability to rise to the occasion and do the job the voters elected you to do? Are you experiencing wild mood swings, hot flashes, whatever?"

In retrospect, maybe – just maybe – I pushed a little too hard.

"Fuck you, Burt! Fuck you!" she hollered. "You're out of line. You're offensive. You're fired."

"What did you say?" I asked, becoming agitated myself.

"You heard me. You're fired. I am sick and tired of you and every ridiculous thing you say and do."

And just like that, Governor Waltz stormed out, leaving me sitting there like a fool. But instead of chasing after her and apologizing, I finished my coffee and did some quick math in my head, analyzing the opportunity cost of keeping this babbling psycho-woman as a candidate when she was most likely a one-termer

– at best – and paying me the lowest retainer of any of my gubernatorial clients, a paltry $496,000 a month.

"Screw this," I said to myself. "One door closes, and a dozen other higher-paying ones invariably open."

I shook off the unpleasant interlude, went downstairs and grabbed a cab over to the Hoskins inauguration, which went off without a hitch, except for Waltz shooting me a couple of dirty, dagger-like looks – and one audible snicker – from six seats away, until I finally stopped looking over in her direction. I knew she would miss me more than I would miss her. Her loss would be my gain.

Although I had reviewed an early draft of Hoskins's inaugural speech, I contributed very little verbiage, save for one key closing passage that I gave him as a gift and was pleased to see he kept in, presumably as a tribute to me and our burgeoning relationship:

"Ladies and gentlemen, as many of you know, I have a gift. I can see very clearly into the future. Make no mistake about it. Our enemies are evil. They are the scum of the earth. They will try as hard as they inhumanly can to defeat us. And I swear on my life, with all my heart and all my might, that I will hunt them down, one by one, by any means unnecessary, and capture them or kill them whenever possible until they are all gone, and all the good people in San Francisco who have a place to live can sleep at night, safe and sound. That is my irrevocable commitment to you."

When Hoskins mouthed my words, the aroused crowd, more than five thousand strong, jumped to their feet and roared their approval, as I knew they would.

After listening to Hoskins's slick, thick oratorical brilliance, I spent the rest of the inauguration ceremony tuning out all the banal pomp and circumstance, which included way too many other dignitaries droning on from the stage about this or that. I don't mind writing this crap for my clients -- or listening to them deliver it -- but I'm too busy to waste my time sitting through shit I didn't write emanating from the lips of politicians who aren't clients. Whatever they say or do is just white noise to me. So I passed the time sitting in my uncomfortable folding chair, as my still fresh ass wound throbbed with frequently piercing pain, alternating between random daydreaming and answering the cascade of emails piling up on my BrainBerry, giving me an excruciating headache.

The second the unmercifully long proceedings finally ended, I shot up from my seat and got ready to race to the airport. The good news was that Senator Frances "Skip" Frump, California's senior Senator and a longtime Slice & Dice client, pulled me aside and asked if I needed a ride. The better news was that he, too, was flying to Los Angeles for a fund-raiser. The best news was that he was flying private aboard an Orefice Pharmaceutical plane, which had an extra seat for me, with all the food and drink I could consume. The bad news was that, unbeknownst to me until after I accepted his offer, the Senator desperately needed my help to solve a problem. A big problem.

Well before being elected to the Senate 28 years ago, Frump was thrust onto the national stage as a highly decorated military hero, a made-for-me prime-time television legend who earned a Bronze Medal for his heroic bravery after saving 25 of his fellow soldiers during a particularly bloody battle outside Oslo in the war against Norway, a brief but intense conflict over underwater oil reserves that America needed and captured after a week of warfare, effectively reducing the price of gas consumers paid at the pump by as much as 25 cents a gallon for an entire year, according to the H&R Block Congressional Budget Office. This was a huge sacrifice of human life but it laid the groundwork for Frump's political career.

Riding a tidal wave of pro-America, pro-military, pro–fast food, anti-immigrant vitriol among California voters, Frump became a popular, impossible-to-beat Senator who skillfully combined his cool, intensely focused demeanor and larger-than-life stature with a tough law-and-order message, which, as you've learned by now, was a cornerstone of all the successful candidates I'd built over the years. The bottom line is that no candidate of mine ever lost a race for any office, including town dog catcher, because they were perceived as being too tough when it came to punishing evil criminals for their heinous misdeeds. Or too patriotic when it came to waving the American flag while threatening to flog the heathens. Or too supportive of fast-food restaurants in their fight against zoning restrictions or their unrestricted use of saturated fats. Or too extreme, especially in the border states, about sending hapless immigrants packing, regardless of their age or excuse.

Years ago, I had given Frump the nickname of "Friendly Bastard," which he always said he liked. But today, as we were chauffeured in his police-escorted extra-stretch limousine to the airport, California's most popular pol was clearly not his normal self.

"I have a big confession to make, Burt," was his opening salvo, delivered in hushed tones so the driver couldn't hear us.

"Are you leaving Polly and announcing you're gay?" I guessed, based on a feeling I'd had about him for some time. "That's certainly not a negative. It actually might improve your already-high poll numbers, particularly in this state, if we spin it correctly."

"No, everything thing is fine on the home front."

"Did you commit a crime, Skip? You know, bribe a law-enforcement officer or rob a 7-Eleven or something like that?"

"No. Not even close."

"Then what, if you don't mind telling me so I can stop guessing, do you have to confess?"

"Let me put it to you directly, Burt."

"I'm waiting."

"I've been the victim of a blackmail attempt."

"Are you joking?"

"No."

"What are you being blackmailed about?"

"My military record."

"It's beyond impeccable," I reminded him. "Off the charts. Your last poll showed that 86 percent of all registered voters in California vote for you because they admire your heroic military record."

"I wish it were that simple."

And then Frump dropped the bomb. The shit bomb of all shit bombs.

"You know that Bronze Star I earned in Norway?"

"Of course. Doesn't everyone?"

"Do you want to know the truth?"

"Better late than never," I assured him.

"I didn't deserve my medal. The whole thing's a fake. Complete fiction. My father, may he rest in peace, gave my commanding officer $1.5 million to buy me the medal. It was a flat-out bribe. My dad and I knew that if I came home as a war hero, it would jump-start my political career and open all sorts of doors. And the sad thing was, he was right. Now, nearly 30 years later, someone who knows the truth is threatening to blow the whistle and bring me down – unless I pay him $5 million."

Fuck me, I thought. "Hold on here! You're telling me now, after everything we've been through, that you aren't a war hero?" I gasped. "You're saying you didn't risk your life to rescue your comrades in that infamous firefight outside Oslo?"

"It's pure fiction."

"Were you even in Norway?"

"Chill-lax, Burt, I was there for the worst days of Oslo. My life was on the line like everyone else's in that brutal battle. We got ambushed. Norwegian drones blasting us to bits. Bullets flying everywhere. A tragic number of dead and wounded. By far, the worst experience of my life. But contrary to popular belief, I was not technically on the front lines, leading the charge, in harm's way, saving lives, being heroic under fire."

"Then what were you doing?"

"Cooking a big beef-stew dinner back at base camp, about five miles away."

"You were the cook?"

"And I swear, a damn good one at that. No one made a meaner chili, beef stew, Bolognese sauce or carrot cake. My grandma taught me well."

Usually, I can anticipate sudden crises. But this one sucker-punched me. I felt like retching.

"You've got to be kidding."

"I wish I were, Burt. I wish I were."

"And is the commanding officer the one blackmailing you?"

"No. He's been dead forever. It's his loser son, some parasitic professor at Stanford, whom he must have told before he died. He's the perpetrator."

"Along with you."

"What are you implying, Burt? I am not the bad guy here. I've been an outstanding Senator from the great state of California. I've served the people exceptionally well. I am not a villain. Hell, I'm the victim. I didn't ask for this to happen. I'm the one being attacked. I'm the one whose professional career and livelihood are being threatened. Some deranged lunatic out there is doing something bad to *me*."

My stomach started churning in overdrive, making its final preparations for blast off.

"You wanna know what I think, Skip?"

"Of course I do."

"I'd say you're toast."

"Toast?"

"Yeah, toast. Burnt toast. Your political career is history. When this gets out, you will have no choice but to fall on your sword and resign. And spend the rest of your life living in shame."

"That's it? That's my only choice?"

"You have no fucking choice. You've dug your own grave here. Now hop in and make yourself comfortable."

"C'mon, Burt. What about coming clean and saying I'm sorry for mischaracterizing my wartime experience? I could cry at a nationally televised press conference, check myself into rehab for some unspecified addiction and somehow try to ride this whole thing out."

"Sorry, Skip. Even if you apologize personally to every man, woman and child in California, write a best-selling confessional and become a devoted born-again follower of every single religion ever created, you will not erase this stain on your character. It's time to resign and start a new chapter in your life. There's no other way to say it."

"But what will I do? All I know is how to be a Senator."

"Maybe you could make beef stew for a living. Or try your hand as a lobbyist – that is, if any of your soon-to-be former Senate colleagues will even speak to you."

Senator Frump burst into tears and started dry-heaving as we arrived at the private air terminal at SFO and pulled up to the sleek private plane, glistening in all its splendor on the tarmac.

"You have to stop crying," I said, patting him on the shoulder. "You can't open this car door and be seen in public with tears streaming down your cheeks. I'll admit you're in big trouble, but that doesn't give you the right to cry like a baby."

"You have to help me, Burt," he sobbed. "You have to help me figure something out."

Such a pathetic sight. Even though he refused to accept it, he had no one to blame for his downfall but himself. Having said all that, he had been an excellent client and a good Senator. Out of loyalty, I plumbed the depth of my overtaxed brain for some sort of answer. I could only think of one potential against-all-odds solution.

"Okay, Skip, stop being a baby and calm down."

"Why should I calm down? You just said I'm completely fucked."

"Listen up. Let's say, for the sake of argument, that I arranged, hypothetically, to have a former CIA operative – whom I may or may not know from a consulting gig I once did in Dubai – track this fellow down at Stanford and possibly terminate him."

"Terminate him?" Frump seemed shocked.

"Yes. Just a routine termination. It wouldn't be the first time that some college professor in this country was gunned down for having controversial views."

"And then what?"

"Nothing. Case closed. I realize this scheme seems complicated and will cost you a considerable sum, but it just might do the trick."

FRIDAY

Frump stopped crying. His red eyes stopped tearing, and his breathing returned to normal. He cracked a small smile. And then he reached over in the backseat and began hugging me too tightly, a human sign of affection that I had always abhorred, probably because, as every shrink I had ever seen had instantaneously deduced, I was never hugged as a child. Hit, yes. Verbally abused, without a doubt. Ignored, certainly. But hugged by a parent? Never, ever.

After extricating myself from his unwanted embrace, I made a fast judgment call. As much as I wanted to fly private to L.A., spending the next hour with a broken-up, needy and uncomfortably clingy Frump was no longer a viable option. I would rather have gotten poison ivy on my pecker. Had dinner with Juanita's parents. Or, for that matter, visited my mother.

"Driver," I commanded, "after we let the Senator out, please drop me off at the main terminal. I need to catch the next shuttle to Los Angeles." Which I did, leaving the discombobulated Senator on the curb and saving me a lot of aggravation, if not time.

It worked out well, because Boris Pavlov sent me an urgent text to call him, which I did. He bragged to me that his operatives had already signed up 11 Senators and 25 members of Congress to buy into our newly hatched "Let's-Set-Up-a-Dummy-Foundation-in-Order-to-Buy-Control-of-Congress" plan.

"Not bad for a week's work," I said.

"The Pavlovs are Kings of the World," he bellowed in his typical understated manner.

"Congratulations, from one King to another," I remarked before boarding the plane and hanging up.

On my mercifully brief flight, which was so overcrowded that even the standing-room-only seats were SRO, I couldn't help thinking about how long I had gone without sex: a whopping two and a half days and counting. Lest you consider me some deviant sex addict, let me point out that, as the history books show, most of our nation's most famous political figures had a healthy libido and were well-known, unapologetic philanderers: Washington, Jefferson, Clinton, Clooney, Eminem, etc. Maybe a highly active sex life was a sign of above-average greatness, a measure of distinction, a characteristic that was part and parcel of a true visionary, a leader of a nation that wanted badly to be led. Or maybe not. Maybe, as my ex-attorney told me after we'd walked out of divorce court together for the last time, "Your big problem, Burt, is that you think with your dick."

Which isn't the worst thing in the world. Because if that's the case, it means that I have been blessed with two brains – one in my head and the other in my crotch, which gives me, technically speaking, 100 percent more mental firepower than your average Joe.

I touched down at LAX and headed to baggage claim, where I found my over-excited greeter, who proudly displayed my name on a sign he waved at every passenger exiting the concourse, even though I knew he knew damn well what I looked like. How could anyone not?

"Hello, Mr. King," the college-age kid gushed when he saw me. "My name is Ramon Smith, and it's my great honor to meet you."

"Yeah, whatever," I said, without a whiff of kindness. "Where's my damn car?"

"The driver is meeting us out front," he said. As Ramon unnecessarily reminded me when we climbed into the backseat of the limousine, we were heading over to Westwood to the main campus of UCLA, which used to stand for the University of California at Los Angeles – until last year, when it was purchased at a foreclosure auction by the Chinese government and rechristened the University of China at Los Angeles. This afternoon, I was to give the 11th annual "McDonalds Fast, Fried & Fresh Lecture" on "The Responsibility of Power" at the prestigious Scope Mouthwash Graduate School of Political Science.

I reached for my BrainBerry, basically to avoid having to talk to my fawning escort.

"All the tickets are gone for your appearance, Mr. King. It's a complete sellout."

"What did you expect?"

"If you don't mind me asking, sir, what are you going to lecture us about?"

"Nothing personal, but I *do* mind you asking. I'm getting paid to deliver my lecture to a large, adoring audience at 4 p.m., and you're not getting a free preview now, no matter what you do."

"What if I pay you?" he said, taking out his wallet.

"No way."

"How about if we have sex?"

"What?" I said, not completely convinced I had just heard what I thought I'd heard.

Ramon snuggled up next to me in the backseat and started rubbing my leg.

"What the fucking hell are you doing?" I yelled, jerking his hand away and elbowing the perverted punk in the gut.

"I'm terribly sorry, Mr. King," he said, writhing in pain and surprised by my rebuff. "I didn't mean to upset you. I was just trying to do the right thing."

"The right thing?" I asked incredulously. "Coming on to me, Burt King, is the right thing?"

"I thought so," he stammered, highly embarrassed. "My friends and I read on the Povich blog last night that you are secretly gay and prefer to make passionate love with young Republicans like me."

Great, here we go again, I thought to myself. Another round of insidious disinformation from Povich and his evil co-conspirators. "Do you believe every goddamn thing you see on a blog?"

"Usually."

"Then I don't care how smart you are or where you go to college or who you're willing to blow to get ahead – you're an imbecile."

"But Povich swore on his blog post that he had irrefutable video evidence that deep down inside, you are secretly gay. Just like me. And secretly Socialist. Just like me. So why don't you like me if, according to Povich, you're just like me?"

"Hey, I'm telling you that I'm neither gay nor Socialist. I'm just being slimed by some full-of-shit blogger. And even if I were gay, it wouldn't be any of your goddamn business. Now get out of this fucking car. Right now. You're giving me a horrible headache."

"Mr. King, we're driving on the highway," he pointed out.

"The 405, right?"

"Exactly," he said.

"Which means you shouldn't have too bad of a walk back to campus. Now get the fuck out of the car." I reached over and yanked open his door. The limo driver shot me a look in the rearview mirror, but I gave him one right back. In the interest of his own job security, he kept right on driving, which was the prudent thing to do when I was highly pissed.

"Go ahead, Ramon. Jump!" I said, as I shoved his body toward the now more-than-half-open door. "Time's up. Get out of here!"

"But I could seriously hurt myself."

"Not my problem," I said, shrugging.

"Please have mercy on me, Mr. King. I bet we're going 60 miles per hour."

"That's nice to know," I said, thoroughly disinterested. "The traffic here usually sucks."

"But I'll rip my new suit," he whined.

"Also not my problem," I pointed out. "I bet your parents will send you money for a new one."

"What if I break my arm? Or my leg?"

"Use your other one," I said. "Now, I will count to three and you will jump out of this car, or I will personally see to it that the Chinese powers-that-be expel your sorry ass from UCLA, and that nothing good will ever happen to you – professionally and personally – for the rest of your miserable life."

"I beg you, Mr. King, don't do this to me." His eyes were welling up with tears.

"One..."

"I implore you," he cried.

"Two..."

In retrospect, I felt a little bad when the poor kid jumped out right before "Three." As best I could tell looking over my shoulder, he landed fine, rolled over once, slid into the grassy berm and appeared unhurt – although he was right about ripping his suit. At least another car didn't run him over when he ricocheted off the pavement. He was pretty lucky. This episode would teach him an excellent life lesson: Never assume something about someone just because you read some horseshit on a stupid blog.

Me being gay. How insulting! How humiliating. Yes, I have plenty of gay friends and gay clients, but they definitely know *I'm* not gay – not that there's anything wrong with it. I'm proud to be a hetero, and a damn active one at that – a strong supporter of macho penile power to be shared on an exclusive basis with members of the opposite sex. Burt King, gay? No way. No how.

I had already been in a hideous mood before this provocation; now I was fighting mad. I had to defend myself. I had to fight back and put an end to this specious speculation. I had no choice but to unequivocally reconfirm my heterosexuality, my masculinity, my virility, my inner Elvis and to discredit my doubters and slanderers and gay-baiters. And I had to do it in a hurry.

I had a little under three hours until I was officially due to speak at UCLA. I figured I could skip the pre-event reception I had been invited to attend with the faculty and high-roller donors. After considering my options, I made an executive decision and ordered the driver to run me by the Beverly Hills Three Seasons hotel (which used to be called the Four Seasons, until global warming pretty much wiped out winter throughout the U.S., except in Alaska and when the occasional snowstorm hit Hawaii).

It took forever to slog through the typically horrid Los Angeles traffic. It took more than forever to get through the security checkpoint at the entrance to the green zone encircling the Three Seasons. A first-rate hotel, but a pain in the ass to get in and out of ever since the tragic Beverly Hills Uprising two years ago, in which the high-end luxury stores on Rodeo Drive were burned to the ground by a mob of super-rich Japanese shoppers who were angry about having to pay new tourist taxes on their purchases. As I waited in line around the block to gain entrance to the hotel, I felt nostalgic for the Beverly Hills of yesteryear, a gigantic playground for the American rich and their credit-card-crazed shopping orgies. What a shame that Beverly Hills had become an armed fortress, full of metal detectors, barbed-wire fences and private security patrols to keep its streets safe from criminals and unwanted minorities of one kind or another. Still, when a man of my stature came to Los Angeles, the Three Seasons was well worth $2,500 a night, especially with the beautiful, tastefully decorated rooms, perfectly fluffed pillows, sensuous sheets, impeccable service and one-of-a-kind sauna, which featured the best mud baths I'd ever had.

But this was going to be an emergency stopover, not an overnight stay. I would be spending the night flying home on the red-eye, as I had the usual slew of important meetings, conference calls and assignments in desperate need of my attention back in Washington.

I ran inside and saw, much to my delight, the famed, indispensable concierge, Serge, who knew me well from all my previous stays. After exchanging handshakes and a modicum of pleasantries, I told him about the unfortunate incident that had just transpired.

Serge shook his head sympathetically. "Astonishing," he muttered. "That kid must have the world's worst satellite gaydar."

"Satellite gaydar?" I wondered.

"C'mon, Mr. King, you don't know what satellite gaydar is? It's like GPS – you know, Gay Person Satellite. Advanced gaydar."

"Oh," I said, without a clue.

"The reality is that gay people, like me," explained Serge, "can tell without a doubt when someone within 100 feet is also gay. And I have no doubt whatsoever that you are not."

"Are you positive?" I asked.

"You are as straight and narrow as they come, Mr. King. Not that there is anything wrong with being straight and narrow. Not everyone is fortunate enough to be gay."

"Thanks, Serge," I said, somewhat relieved. "Is there any chance at all my body could accidentally give off a little bit of gay essence that might set off someone's gaydar?"

"I swear to you, Mr. King – and you have to trust me on this – that no gay person in their right mind would ever think for an instant that you were gay."

"Guaranteed?" I asked.

"100 percent guaranteed," said Serge, taking my hand, which I yanked away, uncharacteristically nagged by self-doubt.

"I'm still not feeling good about this," I said. "Something is not right inside my head. I feel like I have to prove to the world – and to myself – that I'm not gay."

"Fine. Whatever you say, Mr. King. Why don't you just tell me what you need?"

I paused and thought about both the simplicity and complexity of this profound question.

"I think I need to do it, and I need to do it in a hurry."

"Do what, specifically?" asked Serge, trying his professional best not to smirk. I knew he knew damn well what I was thinking.

"Do it!" I said, pointing to my groin. "I need a woman and I need one now."

"Oh," he sighed as if surprised, which he wasn't. "I must inform you that it's the policy of the Three Seasons hotel not to make recommendations of this nature."

"But for VIP guests like me, you will, right?" I said, handing him $100.

Serge surveyed the rotating security cameras in the lobby to ensure he was not being watched. Convinced the coast was clear, he pocketed the bill. As if I really cared right now about his discretion. "Okay," he whispered. "Go check in, head up to your room and freshen up, and I will make a few inquiries to see who might be available. As you know, Mr. King, she won't be cheap, but she will be worth it."

"What are prices like these days?" I wondered, doubting he would actually answer.

"Three grand for a basic tune-up. But remember, you get what you pay for."

"Do I get a discount with my American Express Triple X Platinum Card??"

"Sorry, no discounts on these special orders," Serge said apologetically. "Would you like to go ahead with your purchase?"

"Sounds like a plan." I shook Serge's hand, slipped him another $100 and hustled across the lobby to the elevators.

After a half hour of fretting, there was a knock on my door. I opened it and found myself staring right into the eyes of a past-her-prime but suitably-beautiful-for-my-needs blonde dressed for work in a perfectly uninspired blue corporate business suit.

"Hello," she said, rather officiously. "My name is Norita. Or Tiger. Or Mommy. Or whatever you care to call me. Can I come in? My clock is ticking."

"So is mine," was my lame response. "I don't have all day."

"You couldn't afford me all day," she teased.

As my rent-a-date strolled in and sat on the bed, I asked why she was wearing such conservative attire. As opposed to a more traditional hooker outfit.

"This is the Three Seasons in Beverly Hills," she explained. "Hotel security requires that we obey their dress code. Their rules apply to all of us in, shall I say, in the personal-services business. When you get right down to it, we have no choice. If we want to work the bar or lobby areas or have access to the elevators, we have to go with the high-class corporate look."

"Makes sense," I said, losing interest in the topic. "No tramps here, right?"

"As far as I know...." She paused. "How can I help you today, Mr. King?"

"Did Serge tell you my name?" I said with aggravation, realizing that any anonymity in this delicate situation had become an impossibility. Didn't anyone around here give a damn that I had a reputation to protect?

"Don't get mad at Serge. He told me your name was John Doe."

"Then how do you know who I am?"

"How could I not know who you are?"

"You lost me." I was getting annoyed. We were supposed to be screwing, not talking.

"Look, you and I share an awful lot in common, Mr. King."

"Like what?"

"We have powerful clients, outstanding professional skills and extensive contacts."

"Yeah..." I said, trying to comprehend.

"And," she continued, "we both charge exorbitant rates and, just to confirm, neither of us accepts credit cards, right?"

"Okay..." I added rather meekly.

"And we'd rather be called 'consultants' or 'experts' instead of 'prostitutes.'"

"Ouch," I sighed, absorbing the impact of what she'd just said. "I guess so."

"Out of curiosity, how much do you charge an hour?" she asked.

"I don't charge by the hour. I usually charge by the day."

"And how much is that?" I could tell she was dying to know.

"As much as $50,000 dollars a day for consulting work. Three or four times that amount if I give a speech and subject myself to questions from the audience."

"Wow. That's insane. I'm significantly less expensive. But definitely a lot more fun."

"Glad to hear," I responded, as I sat down next to her on the bed.

"Okay, Mr. King, time to get busy, since we're both busy people," she said. "I know you have to be at UCLA soon."

"How did you know that?"

"Trust me – I have my sources."

"I bet you do. Now tell me, Norita or Tiger or Mom – actually, I prefer Tiger – what are you offering today? Any specials on the menu?"

"Whatever you're willing to pay for. I am an equal-opportunity indulger, as long as it's legal in the state of California and conforms to generally-accepted P.I.M.P. principles, which, in case you're wondering, stands for Prostitutes International Morals and Practices."

"And if it isn't legal or in compliance?"

"Then you pay twice the prevailing rate of the closest legal approximation, provided, of course, you use protection, don't hurt me or yourself and finish in time for me to be downtown in 90 minutes for my next appointment. As you know, the traffic in L.A. stinks."

"Deal," I said, no longer in the mood for any further dialogue.

It probably won't surprise you, dear reader, to learn that although my wounded ass was still bandaged and a little sore, I had standard, not kinky or categorically outrageous sexual relations with that hooker. I really had no choice. I had to clear my head and confirm my non-gayness, and a half hour later, I had completed the task, paid Tiger for our romp, sent her on her way and was joyously scrubbing myself extra clean in the shower.

I didn't realize it at the time but there was one aspect of our encounter, which was, in retrospect, unusual compared to my prior dalliances with hookers: About halfway through our sexcapade, I could have sworn I heard someone from the room next door yell: "Zoom in Camera #5," which was odd but not as odd as when I heard the same voice yell" Cut! That's a wrap!" the moment we were finished.

"What the hell was that?" I asked Tiger.

"Nothing, honey," she said.

Despite that one hiccup, when all was said and done, I did what had to be done. After an emotionally taxing day, I, Burt King, was ready to rock the house at UCLA.

A short while later, my limo sailed down Wilshire, arrived in Westwood and parked next to the Nigerian National Petroleum Corporation Institute of Ethics Lecture Hall at UCLA, smack dab on the main quad. Before entering the pompously distinguished, ivy-covered edifice, which reeked of aged knowledge and youthfully exuberant innocence, I paused on the stairs to suck up some smoggy Southern California oxygen. As I was prone to do after committing a marital sin,

I pulled out my phone and called Juanita, ostensibly to check in, but in reality to purge myself of any lingering guilt for my latest lapse of marital fidelity.

"Hello, Burt," she said, sounding not particularly pleased to be hearing from me. "What's up?"

"Nothing, really," I said. "The usual craziness. Do you miss me?"

"Not particularly."

"What do you mean, 'not particularly'?"

"Lots going on here."

"Like what?" I wondered.

"Personal stuff."

Uh-oh. Something was not right. I braced myself. "Can you be more specific, Juanita?"

"I spent the day thinking about things and talking to my parents and Dr. Rabinowitz."

"Who's Dr. Rabinowitz?" I interrupted.

"Our marriage counselor. You know, the one we see every week."

"Sorry. I forgot."

"I'm used to that, Burt. Which is why I've made a decision."

"About what?" I murmured, before being distracted by a tap on my shoulder and an eerily familiar voice cooing softly from behind, stopping me in my tracks and inducing me to unintentionally hang up on my wife.

"It's so great to see you again, Burt."

Even before I wheeled around, my silent stalker alarm went off. Fuck. It was Huffington.

"Hello, Muffy," I said with profound regret. "What an unpleasant surprise!"

"I'm so excited to see you," she said, giving me a sexually charged hug, too tight and too long for comfort, which I found way more unnerving than inviting.

"Are you following me?" I asked. "You're supposed to be on your way to your new life in Sacramento, not Los Angeles."

"Relax, Burt. I am not following you. I was meeting with my agents at ICM and heard you were in town for your big lecture, so I thought I'd stop by, hear you speak and reconnect."

"You have an agent?" I said, as my stomach started to churn.

"Two actually. One for my pending book deal. Another for my pending movie deal. And both men are terrific. They loved my ideas. And I think they love me."

"I bet they do," I whined, looking at my watch so as not to look at her face. "Excuse me, but I need to get inside."

"Knock 'em dead, Burt," she purred. "I'll see you in there. I look forward to hearing what you have to say to the youth of America, our next generation of leaders. I know they'll learn a lot from you. Like I did."

"Thanks for your kind words," I said, starting to pull away, not caring at this second if she was being sincere or slyly bullshitting me.

"Keep in mind," she teased, "if you want to hook up later, you can call me on my cell. I'll be staying at the Three Seasons, a hotel I know you're intimately familiar with."

"How do you know?"

"Just a lucky guess."

"Sorry, but I'm flying back to Washington tonight on the red-eye."

"Your loss," she pointed out. "But if your plans change, maybe we could meet for a quick drink. I could introduce you to my sister. I'm meeting her at the hotel before we go out."

"You never know." But I did know one thing for sure. This babe was bad news.

I raced inside, leaving Huffington behind. Hopefully forever. As beautiful as she was, and as shallow I could be in these self-serving situations, I could smell trouble a mile away, and this one was starting to stink. I could only imagine the role my likeness would play in her books and movies and late-night talk-show appearances. No, thanks.

Inside the lobby, I received a VIP greeting from Duck Kim Fong, the former Chinese Ambassador and current Dean of Political Science at UCLA.

It was good to see Fong again, and his respectful bow temporarily took my mind off the trouble I had left on the steps outside. I had known the Ambassador forever and had done millions of dollars in lobbying work for the Chinese government when he was running the show for them in Washington.

"The King is in the house," he laughed. "And not a moment too soon. It's show time."

"Let's get going," I said. "Time to mold some young minds."

"Or warp them," he replied. "Wait till you hear my sterling introduction."

"I can't wait."

There were, by my estimation, more than 1,500 devotees packed inside the auditorium. I was given a standing ovation when I walked inside – not the loudest one I've ever received, especially when compared with ASSPAC, but a B+ one nonetheless. By the time I ascended to the podium, after the Ambassador had introduced me as "the single most influential force in all of Washington, an adviser to the biggest stars in government and one of the most connected, consequential men in modern American history," I was pumped.

With my ego mightily stroked, I spoke without notes, neatly adapting my standard "I am the legend of Burt King" stump speech to incorporate these spontaneous nuggets of brilliance:

"As great as I am – and I don't take that lightly – and as powerful as I am – and I don't take that for granted – and as wealthy as I am – and, trust me, I am wealthy beyond belief – when I was your age, I was a confused, miserable, pimply-faced, plump fuck-up. I basically despised every aspect of my life. . As a result of this childhood trauma, I had zero confidence in my intelligence or abilities or sexual magnetism. So don't despair. No matter how miserable some of you might be at this moment in time, there is hope. If you are relentless in pursuit of your goals and passionate about doing everything possible to eradicate anyone and anything that stands in your way, you can be successful beyond your wildest expectations. That's the beauty of the American dream. If I can turn out as amazingly well as I have, there sure as shit has to be hope for you, too."

I basked in the glory of the standing ovation a little more than usual. This had been a tough week, and I appreciated the chance to indulge in some extra gratitude. I suppose I may have detected a handful of boos amongst all the rousing cheers, but I sloughed them off. That was the price I paid for being Burt King.

As is customary when my honorarium was well above average and I was strutting my stuff at a not-for-profit or educational institution, I agreed to take 10 minutes of questions from my acolytes.

Which, in retrospect, was 10 minutes too many.

The young punks in the audience waiting in line at the microphone to ask me questions were nothing more than heinous bastards, setting me up, trying to humiliate me. They definitely ambushed me, hitting me hard and way below the belt, assaulting me with their ridiculously obnoxious, offensive, so-called "questions" before being cuffed one at a time and carted away by the uniformed security personnel.

"Mr. King, did you really piss in your pants at your Bar Mitzvah?"

"Mr. King, did your wife really find a roll of unused condoms in one of your suits earlier this week?"

"Mr. King, are you helping the Speaker of the House hush up another sex scandal, this time involving an intern?"

I heard someone gasp somewhere in the back. It was probably Huffington, but I couldn't pick out her face in the crowd.

"Hey, Burt!" cackled another one of the protesters. "Are you and your wife making any progress in your marital therapy?"

"Is it true you offered to pay a stripper for sex right before you got shot?"

"When was the last time this week you cheated on your wife?"

"Did you assault an innocent blogger in the lobby of Slice and Dice?"

"Have you ever engaged in inappropriate racist behavior with a parking-lot attendant in your building?"

"Are you plotting with your Russian mega-clients, the Pavlovs, to buy the Senate?"

"Does your mother still hate you?"

"How can you work for the President when you lust after the First Lady?"

"How can you live with yourself?"

For one of the few times in my life, I didn't know what to do. I froze in shock at the podium, feeling naked, betrayed, and violated and trying my best to maintain my dignity and composure. Which was easier said than done, especially when the shaving-cream pie hit me right in the face, signaling an abrupt end to my lecture. These spoiled little shits were infuriating. Was this what America was coming to? Were these acne-faced asswipes the future leaders of our great nation? If so, I'd be glad to be dead when their day arrived.

And who fed them such detailed information about the inner-most secrets of my life? Was it those CIA pricks, still bitter about a few classified secrets I inadvertently passed on to some North Korean clients two years ago? Was it some media twit who was after my ass because he or she resented my stature and success? Was it the work of KGB double-agents hired by the Pavlovs or perhaps one of their enemies in an attempt to keep my ego in check by torching me in public? I had no fucking idea.

All I know is that after wiping my eyes and face, I stomped off the stage to a chorus of jeers and boos, which I assumed were directed at the miscreants by my supporters.

"I'm so sorry, Burt," said Ambassador Fong, who was burning with rage. "I assure you that every single one of these infidels – and their accomplices – will be hunted down and prosecuted to the fullest extent of the law. At the very least, they will be expelled from UCLA."

"I would assume nothing less, Ambassador," I said as I toweled off. Luckily, my face had taken the brunt of the flying pie, and my top-of-the-line suit and shoes had been largely spared. As bad as this day had been, it could have been worse, since I had no extra clothes to replace the ones I was wearing. Trying to console myself with this singular bit of good fortune, I said a hurried goodbye to Fong and headed outside to the safety of my limo, eager to get to my last appointment before heading back to LAX to catch the red-eye home.

Next stop: the Harlots hotel lobby bar in Santa Monica, where I arrived early for a belated reunion with Karen Schumacher, a former political phenom and ex-client from Nevada who had flown in to pick my brain about a theoretical comeback run for Congress. Even though Schumacher was rich beyond belief – in a league miles ahead of even me, thanks to the gazillions of dollars her grandfather and father had made opening casinos in high schools across America, a last-ditch effort to keep bankrupt school districts from shutting down – I was only meeting her as a courtesy. What she wanted to do, I was about to tell her, was a pathetic pipe dream.

Thankfully, I had a few minutes free to myself before I'd have to be a truth-teller, so I ordered a glass of wine at the bar and rested my weary brain by watching the cacophony of cable news on the TV overhead.

Still nothing new or substantive to report on the kidnappings of Max Morrison and Justice Adams. Lots of idiotic theories, no clues and scant evidence of anything even remotely meaningful.

"This country is going to hell," said Schumacher, approaching me from behind. "And not even Burt King can save us from ourselves."

"Hello, Karen," I said. She actually looked a lot better than I thought she would, especially given everything that she had gone through.

"Hello, Burt. Long time, no see." She leaned over to give me a peck on the cheek, which I managed to rebuff by faking a sneeze.

"Why the resistance to a simple sign of affection?" she snarled. "You're gonna give me a complex."

"What are you talking about?" I said too defensively to appear innocent.

"You know damn well what I'm talking about. Cut the shit."

"Nothing personal. Nice to see you again. Now how about we dispense with the pleasantries and get down to business?"

"So, how do I look, Burt?" she asked. "Even though you're not my type, I'm curious. Do you find me sexy?"

"Unbelievably so," I lied. "If I weren't married, I'd be trying every trick in my book to seduce you."

"I bet that's the book of all books."

"It is," I replied, "but it hasn't been written yet. It's all in my head."

"I'm sure it is," she snickered.

"So, if you think I'm sexy," she continued, "why am I having such a hard time finding a real man to mount me?"

I was tempted to say something along the lines of, "The way you look, not even a horny dog would mount you," but again showing uncharacteristic restraint, I bit my tongue and remained silent, as tough as that was for me to do.

If you hadn't noticed, Karen Schumacher and I had a weird vibe between us. Always did. Always will. The problem is that whenever I see her or hear about her, all I can think of is the unassailable truth that Karen Schumacher used to be Keith Schumacher, before he retired from Congress and transgendered himself into political oblivion after announcing, over my strenuous objections, along with his despairing wife's, that he was a woman hopelessly trapped inside a man's body.

As I stared at her overtly manly facial features, I thought back to when Keith Schumacher was initially elected to Congress, in a stunning upset of a 10-term incumbent in a race I never thought he could win, even with my help. If he – she – hadn't quit politics so abruptly to switch genders, Schumacher would have been by this time, at the very least, Governor of Indiana or Senator from Indiana, on his way to becoming a Presidential contender or, at a minimum, a top Vice Presidential prospect on every Presidential aspirant's short list. He had political stardust sparkling all over him.

"What are you thinking about, Burt?" Karen said, interrupting my daydream. "Me or some other politician you're lusting after?"

"I'm thinking, Karen, that you are beyond crazy to even be contemplating a comeback. As good as you look – and I can assure you that you are still good-looking – this ain't gonna work. America just isn't ready for this. No way, no votes."

"C'mon Burt, you gotta help me. You gotta do this race for me. I want to get back in the game. I feel better and freer than ever before. I have what it takes to win. I want to be a Congressman again. Then a Senator. I know I can be the comeback kid."

"Or comeback queer," I suggested, failing to bring any levity to the situation. She slapped me hard across the face once and then again for good measure, bringing shocked silence and stares from everyone nearby who had previously been minding their own business.

"Fuck your attitude and all your self-righteous bullshit, "she howled. "You're dead wrong. My time has come. I can get elected again. Just look at my tits."

And with that, the once-honorable Congressman Keith Schumacher of Indiana rose to her feet, stood straight up on her chair, tore off her shirt, unbuckled her bra and scared the bejeezus out of me and everyone else in the hotel lobby.

"Why don't you believe in me anymore, Burt?" she cried, her meltdown degenerating further. "Don't you remember? We were unbeatable together."

"That was then, and this is now," I pleaded. "Things have changed. Please sit down and put your clothes back on before you humiliate yourself anymore."

"So what do you think of my ta-tas?" Schumacher asked, cupping her breasts, seeking my approval.

"Very, very nicely done," I lied, worried about what she might do next. "After what I've seen today, I can say with confidence that you have a much better chance of becoming a swimsuit model than you do of winning a comeback race for Congress."

Schumacher sat down and slowly dressed herself. Then she put her head down and started rubbing her temples, as if the magnitude of my message was starting to sink in. "Okay, Burt," she said finally, looking up at me all dewy-eyed. "If you do my race, I'll pay you triple what you usually get. Along with a $5 million signing bonus."

Fuck me. She knew my weakness. "Okay, you got a deal," I said, knowing when to surrender, go for the close and get it done. Hell, if it turned out to be the abysmal failure I knew it would be, I could always quit the campaign a month before Election Day, discredit the candidate's ethics and disavow any role or association with the forthcoming Election Day debacle. Been there. Done that.

We shook hands. Exactly what happened in the next couple of seconds still remains a mystery. But I knew this immediately: I was hit in the head by a flying shoe, followed by a hunk of cheese that had the smell and texture of a cheap French Brie.

"What the hell!" I yelled, rising from my seat and turning around just in time to see a well-dressed man lunging at me with what appeared to be a cheese knife.

"Die, you motherfucker!" he screamed, as he tried to slash me.

My mother, in one of her few benevolent acts, had taught me a couple of basic karate moves before I entered the 9th grade, so I could defend myself, albeit temporarily, against the everyday onslaught of assorted punks and predators who roamed the halls of our high school. Faced with this cheese-knife-wielding madman, my killer instinct kicked into gear, and I grabbed my assailant by the hair, slapped his knife away and karate-chopped him to the ground, where he smacked his head against the leg of a conveniently placed couch. As he lay there, stunned, gasping for breath and trying feebly to stem the trickle of blood coming out of his nose, I placed my shoe on the back of his neck – primarily for dramatic effect and to impress the crowd of gawkers, who were now staring at me in shock, waiting to see if I was actually going to kill him.

I chose not to. Despite the heat of the moment, I recognized, out of the goodness of my heart, that I was way too busy – and way too rich and famous – to subject myself to a protracted manslaughter trial, even if all of my actions were completely justified on grounds of self-defense.

"You suck, King, you pig," said the man, trying unsuccessfully to shove my shoe off his neck.

"Who are you, and why did you attack me?" I demanded to know, as hotel security guards came running out of nowhere, presumably to rescue me from this highly unfortunate and unexpected altercation.

"You deserve to die!" he said.

"Well, you're gonna die if I decide to stomp you to death with my beautiful shoes."

"You don't remember me, do you, King?" he sputtered, as a security guard gently pulled my foot off him.

"Can't say that I do," I responded without equivocation.

"South Dakota Senate race, 18 years ago. You ran my opponent's campaign. Ran ads saying my wife was a slut."

"Was she?" I asked, as the guards cuffed him.

"It doesn't matter," he whined. "That was our private business. What does matter, you Satan, is that she was so humiliated by what you did to her – and what you did to us – that after I lost the race, she killed herself."

"Hmmm…" I paused. "Still doesn't ring a bell. But from what you're telling me, it sounds like my guy won the race. And in the final analysis, that's all that counts. Have fun in jail, you low-life loser."

And with that, the fool was taken away – but not before he said he hoped I died a painful death. Thankfully, his harsh words did not hurt me at all. If that was his best shot, I was lucky. It could have been worse. He could have had a loaded gun.

"Are you okay, Burt?" asked Schumacher, putting her hand on my shoulder, which I brushed aside, not wanting to needlessly feminize an incredibly macho encounter.

"Are you okay, Burt?" asked Muffy Huffington, who approached me from behind with a video camera, proving beyond a reasonable doubt that she was stalking me all over the greater Los Angeles area.

This may have been surprising on one level, but not as surprising as what happened next.

"What are you doing here?" I demanded to know.

"Filming a pilot for my reality show, *PolitiPorn*," she said with great pride.

"Wonderful," I scoffed.

"In fact," she continued, "I'd like to interview you and Ms. Schumacher about what just happened here."

"Even more wonderful," I added.

"But first I want you to introduce you to my sister, who's co-producing my TV show. Burt King, I'd like you to meet my sister, Penelope."

Sadly, the woman I turned to greet was no Penelope. I knew her as Tiger, the call girl I had sex with earlier this afternoon at the Three Seasons. Same woman. Different outfit.

I'm not sure what happened first – the blood draining out of my face or the sweat pouring from it – but it didn't matter. I had no choice but to flee this hideous scene as fast as I could.

"Goodbye, Karen," I told Schumacher. "I'll call you when I get back to D.C."

"Goodbye, Muffy," I told Huffington. "I'll have my lawyers call you when I get back to D.C."

"Goodbye, Tiger," I said stupidly, but by then my faux pas Freudian slip was inconsequential. The only thing that mattered to me at this second was getting to the airport, getting on an airplane, getting my ass out of this God-forsaken town and getting back to my domain, my hood, my one-and-only Washington, D.C., my home.

I collapsed the second I settled into my ultra-premium elite royalty-class seat on Qatar Air. Whenever I was in a jam and had no choice but to slum it and fly commercial with the common people, this was the way to go. All the gourmet food and wine I could drink. Attentive, personalized service served up by attractive stewardesses (nothing against the manly women and womanly men who too often fill those jobs). Plus, a fully reclining, halfway-decent bed that beat those cramped sardine-like contraptions on other airlines. On this red-eye, all I wanted to do was disconnect, decompress, sleep and recharge my weary soul.

I'd had plenty of long days before, but this had been one of the longest. Three flights totaling 7,000 or so miles, too many meetings in SF and then L.A., and one *Fuck Me* moment after another. They way I kept score, life was full of *Fuck Me* moments – where you got fucked over by one thing or another – and *Fuck You* moments – where you got to fuck over someone else, either for your own personal gain or to satisfy your hunger for revenge, or, on occasion, both. The *Fuck Me/Fuck You* dichotomy of life was far more believable than all the pretentious bullshit philosophy I had been forced to study in college. Plato and Homer and Springsteen – hell, even the latest and greatest President or Pope – had nothing on me when it came down to developing my own homemade, profound theories on why things were the way they were.

Since you're probably wondering, Burt King's overarching, umbrella theory of life, when it comes right down to it, is made up of three simple words: *I Am Me*. That's right, you heard me. *I Am Me*, which, for those of you who need help, translates into: *My brilliant essence is my being*. Or in plain English: *I am the straw that stirs the greatness of my drink*. Or in other words: *My superiority in life is a force of nature that will not stop unless I am stopped, which is impossible for anyone to do*. Unless, of course, someone kills me. Which would stop my monumental accomplishments dead in their tracks. Because I would be dead, not alive. Which means I could no longer lead or inspire or have sex, even though my posthumous legend would live on for eternity.

Although history will most likely acknowledge the incredibility of my genius forever, even after I am dead, the reality is that I cannot perpetuate my greatness on my own or control my destiny if I am not alive. Makes sense, eh?

Back to earth. I must have fallen asleep even before the plane took off, thanks to my already-fried brain overtaxing itself into exhaustion thinking deep philosophical thoughts. The next thing I remember is waking up in a hot sweat and shrieking: the hallmark sign that another Einstein nightmare had terrorized me in my sleep.

This one had been unusually horrific. I had gone to visit my mother in her nursing home. As I walked into her room, Einstein, who must have been hiding behind her door, clocked me over the head, knocking me unconscious. When I came to, I found myself tied up, splayed on a spit and being roasted over an open fire, as my mother and Einstein looked on with glee.

"Please don't kill me," I pleaded, twisting slowly in the fire, helpless to do anything as my body began to burn. "I'm too important to die."

"You've deserved this for a long time, son," said my mother, with the icy look of a serial killer and showing no remorse whatsoever for barbecuing her only child.

"You've been a terrible waste of a human life, Burt Stein," said Einstein. "So tonight we've decided to slow-cook you to death and then grind your fat-ass carcass into ground meat so we can make meat pies out of you and enjoy you for dinner, along with a fine Chianti."

"What's wrong, Mr. King?" asked the flight attendant, who must have heard my blood-curdling scream. "Are you okay?"

"I hope so," I whispered softly, trying to decipher the meaning of this latest assault on my psyche. Suffice to say, I was afraid to fall back to sleep for the remainder of the interminably long and lonely flight. If I didn't sleep, I didn't risk encountering Einstein, and as tired as I was, it was a decision worth making.

When we finally touched down at Washington's Abu Dhabi National Oil Company Airport, known ages ago as Dulles Airport, I was dog tired, on the verge of being comatose. I took a short nap in the limo on the ride home, where I would say hi to Juanita, chill out for awhile on the toilet, shave and shower, before heading right back to work. No matter the circumstances or obstacles that stood in my way, "Bill, baby, bill" had always been and would forever be my motto.

But despite my best hopes and intentions that the rest of my day would unfold as planned, of course it didn't. As some wise man once said, "The best-laid plans of mice and men always get fucked up, and then you get fucked over." Yes, more fuck me moments were right around the corner.

Saturday

When I walked off the elevator and into our condo at 7 a.m., Juanita was nowhere to be found, which was highly unusual, considering how late she liked to sleep.

Where could she be? I asked myself, as I double-checked every corner, closet and bathroom, which took some time, given our expansive floor plan. Our bed was unmade, which meant Juanita had most likely left in a hurry. Although she never really did much around the house – we, like most people in our class, had maids to pick up after us – Juanita, unlike any of my other wives, always made the bed. I never understood why but she did.

I walked back into the kitchen and saw a pile of unopened mail on the counter. My eyes focused on the letter on top. I could tell by the distinctive handwriting that it was from Howie Evans, my long-lost college roommate from freshman year at Bangalore U. Beyond brilliant in all things scientific, which, to this day, I proudly and defiantly know nothing about, Howie Evans was a genius, a madcap inventor, schemer and wackjob of monumental proportions, his only downside being the fact that he was despairingly shy. To the point of being the most socially awkward human being I had ever met in my life. To the point of being a complete loner, incapable of knowing how to make a friend or keep a friend or even how to strike up a conversation. So I made him my personal project – and my friend.

And as he reminded me repeatedly, I was literally his only friend in college, his only vehicle for social interaction for the entire four years.

That was way back when, before Evans went to grad school to study engineering at Stanford, got a job in Silicon Valley, bounced around for awhile and then had the good fortune to invent the most revolutionary technological device ever: the Libidometer®, a hand-held, high-tech modern marvel that measures libido levels of anyone or everyone around you.

If you're not lucky enough to own a Libidometer® or are ignorant about its very existence, you might be interested to know that it utilizes low-level electromagnetic frequencies to track human libido levels from up to 500 feet away. Like radar for romance. So whether you're in a bar, an airport, an elevator, an office, a church or jail, if you're single – or even if you're a married horndog – you can get a quick read of the potential sexual action around you. In my younger days, I used it extensively and was one satisfied customer. It didn't guarantee that you'd get laid, but it gave you everything you needed to ensure you were fishing in the right spot. I should point out that I had no need for such a thing once I'd made a name for myself. Women gravitated toward me naturally because of who I was.

Despite his resounding professional success, incredible wealth and lavish early-retirement lifestyle, Howie Evans not-so-surprisingly never made another friend in college or anytime after graduation. "Friendship is not my core competency," he once confided in me, pointing out that he remained completely incapable of having friendships, let alone simple conversations with the butlers, cooks, housekeepers and gardeners who worked for him at his giga-mansion in Puerto Vallarta, where the Pacific Ocean was his backyard. And since my anti-social freshman roommate was indebted to me for being his only friend, he insisted on sending me a thank-you check every year.

When the first check arrived years ago, I called Howie to thank him but said I couldn't accept it, which caused him to cry. Ultimately, I cashed it because I didn't want to hurt his feelings. Plus, I wasn't rich yet and needed whatever money I could get my hands on.

I tore open Howie's latest envelope, tossed aside the note, because I knew what it would say ("Hi Burt! Thanks for being there for me! Enjoy!"), and looked at the check amount: a flat $500K. Not bad at all, considering all I ever did for the guy was be his friend.

"God bless the Libidometer®," I reminded myself, as I thumbed through the rest of the mail.

Given that 99.9 percent of the mail we received was junk mail, I was surprised to see a second handwritten envelope addressed to me. It had no return address – and I soon discovered why.

Burt King –

You are hereby ordered to appear in court to face charges of crimes against humanity. Stay tuned for more details.

See you soon, jackass!

"Big whoop," I muttered, not sure what to make of this bizarre missive. "I suppose someone else is out to get me. Same old story."

I got up to make some coffee. Needed it bad. Had to stay awake. Had to get ready for work. And that's when I saw the note. The note of all notes. It was taped to the front of the refrigerator.

To my soon-to-be ex-husband –

In recent days, I have learned that my worst fears about you being a good-for-nothing, obnoxious, self-centered, sex-addicted jerk are true. Which means I am fed up and outta here. See you in court, you bastard.

P.S. Seven years of marriage was six and a half years too many. By the way, you suck in bed. Also, I took Populace with me. He never liked you. Neither did my parents.

I tried my best to breathe but couldn't. My knees buckled, but I steadied myself. What the fuck was Juanita doing? My heart began to palpitate. My penis recoiled at the suggestion that I sucked in bed, which I knew in my heart and in my loins was patently false. At that instant, I came to the realization that my latest marriage, my latest and best attempt to maintain some semblance of marital bliss, was officially over, disintegrating in the blink of an eye right before my very eyes, an obvious metaphorical double-dipping but one that is eminently justified to illustrate a supremely hurtful point in my life – or, if not in my life, at least in the recent history since my last marriage had collapsed.

Whenever I was under assault, and this jet-lagged morning was no exception, my killer instinct was to fight back – in this case, to respond vigorously to Juanita's attempt to undermine my confidence and impugn my unassailable character. Was I perfect? Hell, no. Did I occasionally cheat on her? Hell, yes. Sometimes once a year, sometimes once a month. Sometimes, during especially stressful moments of weakness, once a day. But if the history of our civilization was clear about anything, it was clear about this: A man's gotta do what a man's gotta do to stay virile and alive and sexually active. And that's all I was doing – being a man's man, the kind of guy whose penis principle was plain and simple: Use it or lose it.

I tried valiantly to regain my composure and imagine my life without Juanita. And after a few minutes of thinking through all the angles, fantasizing about the pure beauty of a single man's "do whatever I want to do whenever I want to do it" lifestyle – and thanking God repeatedly that I had gotten Juanita to sign an iron-clad prenup protecting my sacred assets – I concluded that everything, once this marital mess was cleaned up, was going to be alright. For me, getting divorced was never that stressful. Getting married again always was.

And fuck Populace. That needy, neurotic dog was a royal pain in the ass. And a chronic urinator to boot. Good riddance.

I summoned the strength to rise up again and resume my pursuit of maximum-caffeinated coffee. As I strolled by the kitchen island, I noticed a business card just sitting there on top of the counter. It was from Ganges, the D.C. detective and lead investigator on my butt-wound case.

Why was Ganges's card sitting there? Was it from the other day when he came by to see me? Or had he returned again yesterday to see Juanita when I was in California?

There was only one way to find out.

"Ganges," he grunted on the phone.

"King," I grunted back. "Burt King. Gunshot victim."

"I know who you are," he said without a trace of levity. "It wasn't technically a gunshot, you know. BB pellets are hardly bullets."

"BB guns can kill," I reminded him.

"So can a bee sting. It just depends."

"That's a technicality and beside the point. Look, Ganges, were you at my house yesterday?"

"Yes. As a matter of fact, I was."

"For what reason, may I ask?"

"I wanted to speak with your wife."

"Professionally or personally? Are you in love?"

"Are you joking, King?"

"Usually when I use that line, yes. Today, no."

"And why is that?" For the first time, Ganges seemed interested in our conversation.

"Sorry, none of your damn business."

"Then why are you calling?" Ganges said.

"Why were you with my wife?"

"I wanted to ask her some questions, as part of our ongoing investigation,"

"About what?"

"I wanted to get her perspective on who might have wanted to hurt you."

"You mean, who might have wanted to shoot me?"

"Sure. Do you have any enemies? You know, people who really don't like you."

"Wake up, dude," I said. "Half the free world fucking hates me. Three-fourths of the people in this town wish I were dead. But they're not the ones who pay my bills."

"That's essentially what your wife told me."

"Speaking of which, have you seen my wife?"

"Like I said, I saw her yesterday afternoon, around 4 p.m. I was with her for about 20 minutes."

"Did she tell you anything else of interest?"

"No. Not at all. However, she seemed to be in a shitty mood."

"She certainly can be moody."

"Anything else you want to know, King?"

"No, thanks, Detective. I'm all set."

I shat, showered and shaved, got dressed and headed out. Before departing, I looked blankly at Populace's empty cage, not for any nostalgic reason but to reconfirm that I no longer had to take care of either one of my needy bitches. As I drove toward the office, I tried to locate Juanita on my Hummer's custom GPS navigation system. Unbeknownst to her, I had had a GPS tracking device planted inside her newest diamond-encrusted BrainBerry before I gave it to her as a present, which allowed me to surreptitiously monitor her movements around town whenever necessary. I rarely used it, unless she was running late to meet me or I was worried she was spending too much time shopping at the mall or I thought she had the audacity to be screwing around behind my back.

Sure enough, Juanita's tracking signal came in loud and clear. Interestingly, the Google Satellite People Finder™ map showed she was on Pennsylvania Ave., one block from my office and heading due east, straight at Slice & Dice. She probably wanted to cause a scene at my office in front of my staff by balling me out or serving me with some bullshit papers alleging some bogus marital misconduct.

As I sped toward the office, I braced myself for a messy public confrontation – one I was sure I would win. Then my phone rang, temporarily distracting me from my prefight preparation.

"Is this Mr. Burt King?" asked the adolescent-sounding crackling voice on the other end.

"Maybe, maybe not," I replied coyly, not wanting to blow my cover by confirming or denying the allegation until I knew exactly who was calling.

"This is Francois Pelepoop, the assistant deputy undersecretary to the prime minister of Canada."

"Yeah, right. And I'm the King of England," I said, hanging up on the moronic, crank-calling, stupid-ass teenage prankster. My country was at war with Canada, I didn't have any Canadian clients, and even if I knew any high-ranking Canadian officials or liked any Canadian people, I never ever would have given them my cell number. I figured some punk was trying to punk me, and I would have nothing of it, especially with the way this shitty day was going.

My phone rang again. This time I checked the caller ID before answering and didn't recognize the number.

"Damn it, who is this?" I demanded to know.

"Mr. King, this really is Francois Pelepoop," the caller said in a marginally less juvenile, rather officious, genuine-sounding kind-of-Canadian-French accent. "Can you speak to the Prime Minister?"

"The Prime Minister of what?" I said, still not entirely sure what was going on.

"The Prime Minister of Canada."

How very strange. How utterly unlikely. "Tell me his name, Mr. Poopoloop, or whatever you said your name was, so I actually believe you are who you say you are and not someone trying to entrap me for one of those ridiculous reality TV shows."

"The Prime Minister of Canada is George Christian LaPierre. He met you eight years ago when he sat at a State Dinner at the White House, five years before the war began between our countries and four years before he was elected Prime Minister. His wife's first name is Francine. She said you hit on her."

I remembered this White House dinner, one of a thousand I had been to. Less so LaPierre, who was unremarkable and eminently forgettable for a head of state. But Francine, his hot, highly flirtatious wife? Yes, I remembered her.

"Good-looking redhead, right?" I said. "A real ball of fire."

"That's right, sir," said the caller. "I'm handing the phone over right now to her husband, Prime Minister LaPierre."

I pulled the Hummer over to the side of the road, idling in front of a fire hydrant. I needed to concentrate with everything swirling around my head.

"Bonjour, Mr. King," said the Prime Minister's voice, a voice I immediately recognized from all of his wartime propagandistic utterances broadcast on American TV. "How are you?"

"Fine, Mr. Prime Minister," I snapped. "Is it cold in Canada today?"

"It is, Mr. King," he said, not appreciating the tease. "As you know, thanks to your American sunshield, every day is cold in Canada. Plenty dark, too."

"As *you* know, Mr. Prime Minister, we love our military might here in the U.S. Our sunshield technology is a huge competitive advantage."

"I can see that it is," he said.

"Are you enjoying our little war, sir?"

"Not at all, Mr. King. First, it's not a little war. Thousands of Canadian and American young men and women have died. Second, it's costing both of our countries trillions of dollars at a time when neither of us can afford it. Third, and perhaps most importantly, our two nations should be friends, not enemies. The way things used to be."

"Then give us your damn oil," I said as patriotically as possible.

"Then give us back our sun."

"Then respect our superiority."

"Then respect our sovereignty." He was being such a baby.

"With all due respect, Mr. Prime Minister, why would we ever agree to such an outlandish request?"

"Enough is enough," he stammered. Let's make peace, not war."

"Is that why you're calling me?"

"Yes, Mr. King. The Canadian government, under my direction, would like to hire you on a confidential basis to help us negotiate a behind-the-scenes peaceful resolution to this terrible conflict."

"Wait a second. Let me make sure I understand. You, the Canadians, want to hire me to represent your national interests and broker a truce with my most important client, the be all of my end all, the President of the United States?"

"Precisely."

"In other words, you want me to represent your evil and inferior empire in negotiations with my humble and proud nation, in a time of war, a time of great danger to our national security and standing in the World Power Ranking."

"Yes. That is my intent."

"Which really means that you want me to ignore the best interests of my own country and my own business and use my unparalleled high-level influence to help Canada save itself from eventual annihilation at the hands of our troops?"

"Whatever you say, Mr. King. We would very much like your assistance."

This was a no-brainer.

"No can do," I said with proud defiance. "For one thing, I will not in good conscience work for an enemy state. And I cannot ethically, emotionally or financially leverage my relationships with the White House, Pentagon and State Department to help finish a conflict that is arguably in America's best interests to continue until the bitter end."

"But what if it never ends, Mr. King?" said the Prime Minister, who I could tell was getting peeved. "What if this war goes on forever? What if our children – and their children – never see the sun again?"

"While that may be sad on one level, it's not the worst thing in the world for my country and my clients to have a war that never ends. You know as well as I do, Mr. Prime Minister, that a good war can bring a nation together and keep people focused on an evil adversary."

"Okay, Mr. King," he said. "Just to be perfectly clear: You are saying unequivocally that you will not represent Canada at all in this urgent matter."

"Yes. That is correct."

"Even for a $2 million-a-month retainer and a $25 million bonus if a peace treaty is signed within 90 days?"

Ouch. He'd hit me where it hurt. A slap shot to my private parts, exposed without a cup. A veritable dagger to my heart. "That's some proposal!" I remarked after doing the math. "Maybe I can reconsider. Give me a few days to think about it." Note: I am such a bad ass negotiator I could burst with pride.

My call-waiting clicked. I checked the number to see if it was Juanita, but it flashed "Hernandez" and a Miami area code, which intrigued me enough to thank the Prime Minister for his call and promise him a response by the end of the week. Playing hard to get always paid off.

"Who's this?" I asked, picking up the other line.

"Burt," said a tearful voice. "I am beyond fucked."

I was not used to hearing Anthony Hernandez, the new elected wunderkind Governor of Florida, use profanity or lose his cool. And right now, he was doing both.

Hernandez was the quintessential rags-to-riches poster child, one of my favorites. His middle name was even Horatio. Born dirt poor in Cuba, raised in abject poverty in the slums of Miami, orphaned at 12 when both of his parents went to jail for trying to murder each other, grew up in a foster home, flipped burgers at BahrainBurger after school, taught himself about business by reading books when he wasn't working, got a full scholarship to Harvard, returned home to Miami, bought a floundering shoe store and parlayed it into the Southeast's largest discount shoe chain, which he ended up selling to some Chinese company for $100 million. A veritable hero in the Hispanic community, a rising national star and, soon, I predict, the Presidential front-runner for the Republican party and ultimately the first Hispanic President of the United States.

In his election-night victory speech last year, which I flew out to witness since I had seriously wordsmithed it, he was beyond marvelous: "And I thank my fellow Floridians for this unbelievable opportunity to serve you, to be your humble representative as Governor of the great state of Florida. I thank you from the bottom of my heart for giving me the chance to live the American dream, the dream that every immigrant tries to achieve from the second they set foot into this remarkable country." Best of all, he gave the entire speech in Spanish, much to the delight of more than 100,000 Spanish-speaking supporters who roared their approval that one of their own had made it so far. We knew his English-speaking constituents would be offended by his all-Spanish speech, but fuck them, because they voted for his opponents, who lost by 11 percentage points.

But now, something was rotten in the state of Florida.

"What's wrong, Governor?"

"It's over!" he cried.

"What are you talking about, Tony?" I asked, completely confused by the sheer panic in his voice.

"*30 Minutes* is after me. They're gonna nail me on Sunday night's show. I'm dead meat."

"Slow down and tell me what's going on."

"I can't right now. I have to go. I have to do what I have to do."

And with that, the Governor abruptly hung up, leaving me, his closest confidante, more than a little confused.

I speed-dialed Donaldson, his press secretary.

"So you heard, Burt. We're dead."

"Heard what?"

"He got busted."

"The Governor got busted?" I asked incredulously. "For what? DUI? Drugs?"

"Much worse."

"What could be worse?" I wondered. "Did he rob a bank or murder someone?"

"He's not Hispanic," Donaldson said matter-of-factly.

I held the phone away from my head and stared at it, speechless as the magnitude of this earthquake began to register.

"Excuse me?"

"You heard me, Burt," he shrieked in pain. "Anthony Hernandez, the Governor of Florida, the man I've dedicated my life to...turns out, he's not Hispanic. The psychopath has been lying about his heritage. Big time. And 30 Minutes has all the documents they need to destroy us. We are D.O.A."

"Shit! Shit! Shit!" I said, considering both the dire consequences for my client, who was officially dead meat, and the financial consequences for me. Not that Hernandez had been particularly lucrative thus far in the relative infancy of his career. But according to the media pundits and mega campaign donors, who ate up his heartwarming narrative, he was going to be unstoppable on his rocket shot to the top.

My head began to throb uncontrollably. I rubbed my aching temples but to no avail. "So, if Hernandez is not Hispanic –" I paused, still not believing it, "– what the fuck is he?"

"Can you handle the truth?" asked Donaldson.

"That's what I get paid to do," I reminded the jerk.

"Okay, Burt. Anthony Hernandez is as WASPy as they come, right off the damn Mayflower. He was born in Greenwich, Connecticut, as William Edward Howell III, if you can believe it. And the icing on the cake is that not only was he not Hispanic, but he was never an orphan, either. Or poor. Made the whole thing up. Even had his name legally changed to Hernandez for the sole purpose of helping him get into Harvard as an affirmative-action, full-scholarship-worthy hardship case. Worst part is, his parents were in on the whole thing, just to help him get ahead. Those sick schmucks are still living in Greenwich."

"You're telling me Hernandez fabricated his ethnicity and his entire life story, just to get into Harvard?"

"Gets even better."

"How could it?"

"Believe it or not, he has a juvenile criminal record. He never worked at McDonalds in high school. But he sure robbed a few. Until he was caught and did a year at a juvenile detention center in Hartford. Until his dad's friend, Connecticut Governor Adams, had him sprung and his record expunged, all in exchange for approximately $5 million in campaign contributions over two years."

"The media is going to fry him."

"It's over, Burt. Thanks for the memories."

"And his supporters are going to hang him."

"Unless he kills himself first."

Minutes later, as I finally pulled into my office driveway, I heard on the radio that Hernandez had done just that, apparently right after he hung up on me. According to Big Al, who was smoking while pacing nervously outside our building, presumably waiting for me, CNN even had footage of the dude jumping right off of his 42nd-floor balcony. Splattered all over Brickell Avenue. What a tragedy. What a shame. What a horrible waste of talent. Worst of all, his campaign still owed me nearly $250K from a recent polling and branding project, which would now be next to impossible to collect.

I didn't know whether to ask Big Al about Hernandez committing suicide or Juanita's whereabouts. But first things first.

"Have you seen my wife?"

"Oh, yeah," Big Al said gravely. "Juanita took a baseball bat to your office, told us all you gave her multiple STDs and said we're insane to be working for such an evil human being."

"Is she still upstairs?"

"No. She finished what she came here to do in less than five minutes, said goodbye and stormed out."

"Did she say where she was going?"

"No, and we were afraid to ask. She was furious. Are you having marital problems?"

"Seems so," I said, a little offended by the personal nature of the question.

"Can I park your car, sir?" interrupted a new, young, clean-shaven valet I had never seen before, who looked too young and too educated to be parking cars.

"Where is Jones?" I demanded to know.

"He's gone, sir," said the valet. "Quit last night. Called the manager and said he'd met the love of his life online and was too busy having sex to come to work."

"I'll miss that guy," I remarked to Big Al. "I liked his moxie."

"Excuse me," said the valet. "Jones left a message for you, too."

"Really?"

"He said: 'Tell Burt King I said thanks for everything.'"

"What in the world is that supposed to mean?" I asked.

"Could it have something to do with this?" the valet said, handing me a printed out profile page from some online dating site, which I stared at, grasping to decipher its significance. It featured a photo of Jones and Juanita, buck-naked, locked in a passionate embrace.

This was a shocking blow, to say the least. It instantaneously sucked all the air out of my body. I fell to the pavement.

"Are you okay, Burt?" asked Big Al, as he put his arms under my pits, lifting me off the ground.

"I'm certainly not okay," I admitted. "Would you be okay if you just saw what I saw?"

"Probably not," said Big Al.

"Fuck me," I muttered. "Fuck this. Fuck them. Fuck me." Look at that! One of my best poems ever, an kind of, sort of haiku, smack dab in the middle of a crisis. Who would have thought? My poet friend Pippin would have been impressed.

"I will kill them both with my bare hands," I announced.

"Just be careful," cautioned Big Al.

I stumbled back into the Hummer, fired up my dashboard monitoring devices and tried to zone in on Juanita's tracking signal. I located her right away, heading north on Rock Creek Parkway, presumably heading back to our condo, which she wrongly assumed would end up as her condo. I knew for sure it would be mine, no matter how many judges my lawyers had to bribe.

I tried to maintain some semblance of composure as I tracked my prey, but that proved to be impossible. I was enraged. After all I had done for this woman – after all I had done to give her access to my world – this unspeakable betrayal, this unconscionable assault on my stature and pride was how she said thanks? By running off with my parking attendant? Fine. There would be hell to pay for both of them. No one, in a million years, ever got away with crossing Burt King like this.

Within a microsecond, I was in hot pursuit, barreling down the Rock Creek Parkway at maybe 70 miles an hour, snaking around the Kennedy Center tent city for the homeless, dodging a few middle-class stragglers who had staggered across the road at the risk of becoming road kill, and ignoring those pathetic, politically correct protesters waving placards supporting moronic, sissified notions such as "Food For All" or "Health Care For All" or "Peace Now" or, my personal favorite, "Yale Divinity School Grad Will Work For Food." I had no pity for these fools. Only for myself.

I was zooming past the Virginia Avenue exit, getting angrier and angrier, when out of nowhere, some crazy old lady in a big beat-up Buick blew by me in the left lane, barreled into me, tore off my passenger-side mirror and then swerved over to the right, cutting right in front of me. I slammed on the brakes as hard as I could, but it was too late; I smacked the bitch's fender. Unfuckingbelievable. I pounded my fist on the horn to send a long, heartfelt "fuck you" message, but the oblivious offender kept right on going as if nothing had even happened. Hit and run, 101. Another infuriating example of the decline and fall of our civilization.

"Take a deep breath," I told myself. "Calm down. Don't blast your blood pressure. It's just a mirror on your Hummer, probably less than four grand to fix." But it was humanly impossible for me to suck this one up. Screw that! This was no time for calm. It was time for decisive action. It was time to fight back. As my elderly aggressor would soon discover, I could play that way, too. Bring it on! It was time for her to experience road rage, Burt King-style.

I hit the gas and caught up to the Buick, which was now in the right lane as we passed the Georgetown ramp toward the Pennsylvania Avenue exit. I pulled up alongside her in the left lane, rolled down my window and thrust my third finger at her, letting loose with a firestorm of expletives, despite my realization that the target of my venom appeared to be pushing 80 years old and bore an uncanny resemblance to my great Grandma Eleanor, whom my mother would unmercifully drag me to visit in the nursing home when I was a child.

"You must hide, Albert," Grandma Eleanor would say, jabbing me in the chest with her finger. "The CIA will kill us if they find us. They're evil. So is your mother, my only daughter, who had great potential, until she married the terrible loser who happens to be your father. By the way, did you steal my sour cream?" It was my first encounter with dementia, which, in retrospect, proved to be perfect basic training for advising politicians who flitted from reality to fantasy and then back again by the minute.

As I flipped off the elderly woman in the Buick, she had the audacity to give me the finger back – and then, without warning, she stepped on her accelerator, intentionally ramming my Hummer on the side and snapping my body back with a bang. I struggled to keep control of my vehicle but it spun around, slid off the road and came to a stop on the grassy berm by the edge of Rock Creek Park.

I sat there in my battered and bruised Hummer, dazed and confused, rubbing my aching neck and trying to assess this increasingly violent confrontation. In my rearview mirror, I could see the Buick pulling up just behind me in the grass, with its emergency brake lights flashing. Cars on the parkway whizzed by. I wondered what was coming next. This road-rage experience was, by far, more intense than all of my other road-rage experiences combined. I quickly calculated that the key thing here was to defuse the situation: apologize quickly for my outburst, jointly inspect our respective vehicles for damage, exchange insurance information and then get the hell out of there and keep anything uglier from transpiring – especially anything that could end up online, getting unwanted publicity and giving my enemies even more ammunition for their relentless, malevolent attacks on my character.

I looked in my rearview mirror and saw granny step slowly out of her car. As she approached the Hummer, I tried to anticipate her next move. I was ready for anything.

Except for the handgun she shoved in my face.

"Who the fuck do you think you are?" she yelled. "How dare you curse me like that! Such profanity! I should call the cops on you."

"Why did you cut me off like that?" I said, as kindly as I could, being mindful of who had a gun and who did not.

"I didn't cut you off, you prick."

"You're the one who's wrong," I responded emphatically. "Now please put your gun away, and let's have a rational conversation about all this."

"I'd rather kill you right here, right now!" she said, with sufficient bravado to start me sweating.

I pictured my face plastered on the home page of every media outlet in America, alongside a story detailing how an 80-year-old lady had gunned me down in what she termed "a legitimate act of self-defense." This was not exactly how I visualized my last day of life on earth. So unfair to me and my legacy. So unfair to Juanita and her credit-card bills.

Not wanting to provoke my assailant any further, I shut my mouth and let her assert her authority. Which she did – by sliding her gun barrel back and forth across my forehead.

"I should do the world a favor and kill you," she said.

"Sorry ma'am," I said meekly. "I apologize if I offended you. But let's try to be honest with each other. History will show you did, in fact, cut right in front of me on the Parkway and side-swipe my ultra-luxury vehicle, causing an accident that easily could have killed me."

"That would have made me a true American hero," she said aloud for her own amusement.

"How dare you impugn my character!" I said, probably a little too aggressively.

"If I let you live, you better stop your bullshit!" she said. She was twirling her gun around on her finger, demonstrating surprisingly dexterous firearm-handling skills for a senior citizen.

"Okay, okay, I'll stop," I said, shifting into a charm offensive.

"Yeah, punk. I bet you will."

"No, really, I will," I begged. "I apologize sincerely for saying or doing anything that has unintentionally annoyed you."

"Are you making fun of me, Sonny?" she asked in a creaky, grandmotherly voice, mocking me big-time. "Do you think I'm joking around here? Do you think I'm playing a game? Would you like me to go ahead and blow your brains out just to prove a point?"

"Please stop threatening me," I answered. She pointed her gun right at my groin, which I found even more unnerving than when she had pointed it at my head. "Look, lady, I'm sorry for giving you the finger. And I hope you're sorry for cutting me off back there. Why don't we simply apologize to each other, shake hands and get on with our respective lives?"

"You wish, Sonny," she huffed. "I know who you are, you sleaze bag. The more I think about it, the more I think I should kill you now, put us out of your misery and teach you one final lesson before you burn in hell."

"C'mon, lady! Be reasonable," I begged. "Why can't you accept my apology, so we can resolve this dispute and call it a day?"

"Easier said than done," she said. "My problem with you is not going to end just because you want it to end."

"What?" I asked, with a rising sense of disbelief. "Then how does it end?"

"Give me your wallet and your watch, and then maybe I tell you how it ends."

"Huh?" I mumbled, trying to get my bearings. "Are you robbing me?"

"I sure am. You don't think I can get by on Social Security alone, do you? Fifty bucks a month couldn't feed a dog, let alone a person. You guys killed Medicare to pay for your stupid wars, so now we have no health care, and I have to mug idiots like you and turn tricks as a hooker to buy food and pay for my husband's prescriptions. Now give me your goddamn wallet and watch before I blow your fucking brains out."

Uh-oh. Time to shut up and do as the angry geezer said.

"Fine. Here's my wallet," I said, handing it over. "And here's my watch, which, as you may have noticed, isn't any ordinary watch. It's a Rolex."

"Big whoop," she said unenthusiastically. "I'll get a grand at most for it."

"That's crazy. I paid 95 grand for it."

"These things are a dime a dozen at area pawn shops. I'm not the only one in town who's busy robbing rich people."

"Whatever," I sighed. "Now, if you don't mind, how about we wrap things up, end this highly unpleasant mugging and go our separate ways?"

"I do mind. In fact, now that you mention it, this mugging isn't over. It's just beginning."

"Say what?"

"C'mon, Burt, time for us to get going," she said, pointing her gun once again at my nose.

"How do you know my name?"

"Who doesn't in this stinkin' town?"

"That's true," I said with well-deserved pride.

"Okay, cut the small talk. I need you to step slowly out of your gas-guzzling, environment-killing, obnoxious monstrosity of a car and follow me. Then no one gets hurt."

"Excuse me?" I said.

"You heard me. Get the fuck out of the Hummer. Time's a-wasting."

The cars racing by on Rock Creek Parkway had no idea what was unfolding on the side of the road. Neither did I.

The elderly goon pulled her gun away from my face, put it in the pocket of her long coat and motioned at me with her index finger, as if I were a dog being summoned by its owner to follow.

I stepped down from the Hummer stepped gingerly around to the rear of her car. She followed one step behind, her gun shoved in my back.

"Get in," she ordered, as she hit her car-key remote and the Buick's trunk opened wide. "Hurry up."

"Your trunk? You want me in your trunk?"

"Glad you understand English, King."

I looked forlornly at the steady traffic passing us by, but no one slowed down to see what was going on. Congress was in session, which meant all the drivers were either yapping on the phone, picking their noses, daydreaming about writing memos, shopping online or more likely, gambling online. I realized I shouldn't expect a single person to be kind enough or curious enough to pull off the road to offer me any assistance in my time of need.

"But I don't want to get in your trunk," I whined. "Not only will I suffocate in there, but I'll wreck my back, as well as my clothes. Do you realize this is a custom-made Italian suit I'm wearing?"

SATURDAY

"Last chance, King," she growled. "If you'd like to stay alive, do as I say. Otherwise, I'll shoot you and toss your corpse into the trunk. Either way, you're getting in."

"Okay, I get it," I said, as I put my feet on the Buick's rear bumper and climbed tentatively into the trunk. She slammed the door closed on top of me, leaving me curled up in the fetal position, trapped in a sea of darkness with barely any oxygen for breathing.

As my captor started her car and pulled away, I wondered how long it would take for the police to notice my abandoned Hummer. Or for car thieves to find it, steal it and strip it clean. I tried to keep what was left of my composure. The future of the Hummer was the least of my problems.

The Buick drove and drove for what seemed like hours. I had no sense of where we were going. I could tell we were on highways for the most part, stopping at toll booths or whatever from time to time, as the car slowed down and stopped before accelerating, and at some point, I was pretty sure we were on a major highway, most likely Interstate 95. I was clueless, however, about whether we were heading north, toward Baltimore, or south, toward Richmond. I was in sheer agony. This was a million times worse than a long dinner with an insufferably boring client. My claustrophobia was overwhelming. And thanks to all the bodily abuse, my beleaguered back felt like it was broken in as many as five places. I tried shielding my head and my ass with my arms to keep them from smashing open like a rotten pumpkins.

To keep from going insane, I tried to relax by composing another poem. This wasn't one of my best, but given the dire circumstances, I was pleasantly surprised it wasn't one of my worst:

<u>Me B Fucked</u>
In a whole lot of trouble
If I die here right now
Will anyone really truly give a shit?
Why me be fucked?
Why couldn't it be someone else
Less important to our society
Less critical to our country's future
Like you?

Several hours or eons later (although my Rolex glowed in the dark, I no longer had it), the car pulled into what felt like a long, bumpy, gravel driveway. As we slowed to a stop, I heard a man's muffled voice ask: "Everything go as planned?"

"Perfectly," said my geriatric friend. "He's such an angry bastard, he fell right into it."

Into what? I wondered briefly, before I recognized that this nefarious old bag had induced me to commit road rage with her asinine driving on Rock Creek Parkway as part of some premeditated master plan.

The trunk door popped open, and an excessively bright flashlight shined in my face. I could see some guy in a ski mask, carrying a machine gun. He greeted me with this convivial salutation, "Get your ass out of the car and lie face-down on the ground, hands behind your back."

As I stumbled out of the trunk, wobbly from being cooped up for so long in such a cramped space, I tried to quickly look around but could see nothing except the dark contours of what appeared to be a run-down industrial building next to us.

"Get down on the ground, now!" said the man, as he blindfolded me.

"May I ask one question?" I said rather nicely, falling gently to the ground face-down while the masked man not-so-nicely kicked my hands behind my head.

"What?" he replied, clearly agitated by my audacity to ask anything.

"Where am I?"

"None of your goddamn business," he said.

"Would you be favorably inclined to tell me why I'm here?"

"None of your goddamn business," he repeated for my benefit.

"I beg to differ," I responded. "It is my goddamn business, because I'm the one here who has been kidnapped by some psychos for no apparent reason."

"How do you know there's no apparent reason?"

"Are you saying there is?"

"None of your goddamned business."

"Then I can unequivocally confirm that I am unable to comprehend what's going on here."

"Too bad," he remarked, in a tone that was progressively more menacing. "Now lie still while I tie you up, and keep your fucking mouth shut if you have any interest in staying alive."

The hag howled. "Look at this miserable shit. Maybe we should go ahead and kill him just to do the world a favor. A pro bono act for all humanity."

"Not yet," said ski-mask man, giving me even more pause. "Killing him is not in the cards. He's more valuable to us alive than dead."

"Are you sure?" she countered. "Didn't we vote that King deserved to die?"

"It was a poll, not a binding vote," he said. "Plus, things have changed."

"In what way?" she asked, confusing me even more.

"End of discussion," he said in his bossy best. "Until I say otherwise."

I found that mildly reassuring, given what had transpired thus far.

What happened next was cruel. The two of them dragged me inside the building and down a flight of stairs, laughing all the way, at my expense. I speculated on how long it would take anyone to notice if I was never seen again. A day? A week? A month? Never? The possibilities were endlessly humiliating. Maybe Juanita would go so far as to look the other way, deciding not to report my disappearance to the authorities because she was suddenly free to live a wonderful life totally unencumbered by my presence. Maybe Big Al would exploit my disappearance to take over Slice & Dice.

"When will the Commander be joining us?" the lady asked, as another door creaked open and I was shoved into what felt like a damp cellar with a hideously cold floor.

"Any minute," the man answered. "He's down the hall welcoming our other guests."

I wondered what that was about as he chained my left ankle to what must have been another chain attached the wall. Before long, my butt was stiff, my back was aching and I got pissed off and started farting. My stomach felt like it had consumed a super-size chicken-and-bean burrito. A stress-induced grease-bomb waiting to explode.

"Stop it, King," said the man. "You're stinking up the joint."

I started to lose it. "Ask me if I care, douchebag."

"What did you just say?" said the lady, clearly irked.

"You heard me, you dicks. Now let me out of here so I can get back to where I was and what I was doing before you had the balls to abduct me for no apparent reason. You are messing with the wrong person."

And that's the last thing I remember saying before one of them decided to whack me in the back of the head and knock me unconscious.

I woke up with a splitting headache, still blindfolded, my hands and legs still immobile, still in the same dark, damp room, which sure smelled like a mildew-filled basement. My back was off-the-charts killing me as well, throbbing as if my tormented spine were on the verge of tearing away from the rest of my body.

"Are you the one and only Burt King?" asked a new voice, a deep, phlegm-filled one that spewed cigarette smoke as it spoke, no more than two feet from my face.

"Before I answer your moronic question, do you mind putting out your cigarette?" I asked without really asking. "I'd prefer not to inhale your secondhand smoke and put my own health at risk."

"I hate to break it to you, King, but your own health is already at risk, by virtue of us kidnapping you. In the grand scheme of things, whether or not I smoke right now is immaterial to your health."

"It's disgusting."

"You're disgusting."

I chose to remain silent, which was agonizing in its own right.

"Time to get started," said my inquisitor. "Smile, you're on camera."

"You're videotaping this?"

"Yes, we are. For posterity."

"If that's the case, can I take a second to comb my hair? I can't see a thing, but I'm sure I look disheveled. Any chance you have a stylist around to help with makeup?"

The room filled with laughter. Not mine.

"First question," he said. "Are you willing to admit that you are the one and only Burt King, the Prince of Darkness of American Politics?"

Was that supposed to be an insult? Or a compliment? The more I thought about it, the more I liked that "Prince of Darkness" label. No one had ever called me that before – at least as far as I knew. It sounded rather important, impressive, foreboding. Plenty of gravitas and not a small amount of sex appeal. Absolutely worth trademarking if I ever escaped.

"Okay, yes," I answered slowly. "Yes, I am Burt King. I am the Prince of Darkness."

"Do you admit you are the bastard who sells power and influence to the highest bidder? The most corrupt man in Washington."

As infuriating as this jerk was, I found his overt hostility to be perversely humorous in such an exasperating moment.

"Are you implying I'm a bad person?"

"Aren't you?"

"Maybe yes. Maybe no. Depends on which answer gets me out of here fastest."

"It's not a question of which answer gets you out of here the fastest," said the voice, taking umbrage while reminding me who was in control. "It's a question of which answer gets you out of here alive."

"Okay. Cut the crap. Stop your threats. I'm getting sick and tired of this utter nonsense."

"We are, too," said the voice. "And so are the American people."

"Meaning what?"

"Spare us the bullshit, King. We both know who you really are, what you represent and why you're here."

"Not quite," I countered. "I know who I am, but why the fuck am I here?" What is this? Some sick joke gone haywire? A case of mistaken identity? What are you hoping to accomplish by kidnapping me? When I get rescued by the police or FBI or Army, you're all gonna end up dead or in jail – or in jail and then dead, when I call in some favors."

"Hold on a second, King." The voice was irritated. "I strongly disagree with your description of the situation. You have not been kidnapped. That implies we are holding you for ransom, which is not the case, because according to our exhaustive research and analysis, no one in your life cares enough about you to pay a kidnapper a penny in ransom. Therefore, you have not, in a traditional sense, been kidnapped. No, you have been arrested. For crimes against humanity, including but not limited to the perversion of democracy in America."

"You totally lost me," I said. "What are you implying?"

"Exactly what I said," said the voice. "Our country would be a much better place with you off the streets. You're a dangerous criminal, a master manipulator of the masses."

"Say what?" I grumbled, trying to absorb the absurdity of the situation, which was increasing exponentially.

"C'mon, King, come clean here," the voice said in a most patronizing way. "Be real. Just admit the truth."

"What truth?" I asked.

"You know."

"Know what?"

"You're a menace to society, a profoundly repugnant deviant who has perverted our democracy to benefit your tyrants while making millions for yourself. You cater to the ruling class and help them exploit their chokehold on power to hijack our government. You distort our elections so the rich can buy victory after victory while depriving honest, hard-working Americans of the opportunity to have any meaningful representation in their government."

"Is that all you got on me?" I asked with a yawn. "If I plead guilty in your kangaroo court, can I leave?"

"Not so fast, King," the voice rattled on. "Above all, you are an incorrigible criminal who pollutes our nation on every level. And these are only a few reasons why we decided to apprehend you. When future historians look back on your actions and assess the damage you've done to our society, they will agree we had no other choice."

"Are you done yet? Your rant is boring me."

"You're clueless, aren't you?"

"I guess so, if it makes you feel better."

"Don't play stupid. You know damn well all the reprehensible things you've done."

"Can you be more specific?"

"Okay," said the voice. "Do you want to play that game? Terrific, we'll play it."

"What game?"

"True or false, King: You have cheated multiple times on your five different wives, most recently Juanita."

My bravado deserted me, leaving me speechless as my mind raced with disconcerting possibilities. How did these clowns know about my marital conflicts? Sure, D.C. is the gossipiest town in the universe, but marital strife is as commonplace as infidelity or corruption. Hardly the stuff of headlines.

"It is conceivable that I've had my share of marital issues," I said defiantly. "Not that my personal life is any of your fucking business. But my current wife and I are doing fine, thank you." Yes, that was a lie, but when your life or your reputation or lucrative clients are in danger, it's permissible to lie.

"That's not what Juanita is telling her parents and friends," the voice said with joy.

Initially, I figured this guy was bluffing. Unless Juanita really was telling people about our problems. Conspiratorial theories flashed through my mind. Were my kidnappers spying on us, or was Juanita, my sweet, estranged Juanita, somehow, someway connected to this terribly hostile act of aggression against me? I found it hard to believe, but I had to ask.

"Out of curiosity," I said ever so calmly, trying to catch my interrogator off guard, "is my wife involved in this kidnapping? Is she behind this atrocity?"

"Who knows?"

"Is Juanita involved? Did she hire you to knock me off?"

"That's not how the game is played. I ask the questions and you have to answer them."

"Or what?"

"Or I'll shoot you. Or maybe just cut off one of your pinkies for the first infraction."

"You're bluffing," I snarled, testing his mettle once again.

"Wanna bet?" cackled the voice.

"Sure. I'll bet you $10,000 that your threats are meaningless and you're nothing but a two-bit coward."

Too bad I calculated wrong, grossly overplaying my hand. A bullet whizzed by my head, and I screamed in fear, pissing in my pants and conjuring up traumatic memories of my ill-fated Bar Mitzvah. Thankfully, my mother had no idea I was still capable of wetting myself at my advanced age.

"You win," I sighed, biting my tongue after making such an agonizing admission.

"Yes, I won," he laughed. "My, oh my, that's a nasty wet spot you got there."

"You shot at me."

"Yes, I did. Now, I've only got a couple more questions, and then we're done."

"And then what?"

"Depends on how you behave."

"I'll behave."

"Good. So tell me, what gives you the right to be such an asshole?"

I tried to rock back in my chair. The rope tightened even more against my limbs.

"I don't know." I shrugged. "I just am. Maybe I was born that way."

"So you realize you're an asshole?" the voice said with mild approbation. "Sometimes we get criminals down here who don't even recognize how hideous they are."

"Wait, I never said I was hideous. Or a criminal."

"But you are," said the voice. "Even your mom agrees."

"Leave my mother out of this," I demanded.

"By the way, what did you think of her interview today on the American Association of Retired and Poor website?"

"Why would she give an interview to AARP?"

"To rip you a new one."

"You're kidding, right?"

"Here's what she had to say," explained the voice with glee. "I want to express my deepest regrets to the American people for giving birth to my son, Burt. If I had known then what I know now – if I had known then how Burt was going to turn out – I never ever would have had sex with my husband, may he rest in peace, that lucky bastard. I can't rest in peace until I die or my son does first.'"

"That's my mother for you," I admitted.

"She sure tells it like it is," said the voice.

"Tell me about it," I said.

"Unlike you, she seems honest."

"No comment," was my appropriate response.

"Okay," he continued, "time for our next question. True or false: When you die, you deserve to go straight to hell instead of heaven."

I took a deep breath, trying to retain any composure I had left. "What is this idiotic game? Some stupid TV quiz show?"

"Not exactly. Think of this as your trial. Actually, it's more like a tribunal – you know, like a military court. A speedy rush to judgment. More efficient, less time-consuming."

"Oh, I get it," I said. "Juanita's father is behind this. He sent you to protect his little baby girl from her big bad husband, right? Makes perfect sense. My bitter, ex-general father-in-law hired some of his old Banana Republic hatchet men to rough me up."

"I'm not at liberty to answer any more of your questions," said the voice. "But I can assure you that if you don't answer this question with either 'true' or 'false,' it will be the last question you're ever asked. So let me restate the obvious: You are going to hell. True or false?"

"I don't know and I don't care. I don't give two shits about heaven or hell. Or the past or the future. Only the present, the here and now."

"Wrong answer, King. Guess again or I will have to extinguish my cigarette in your nose. And that won't feel good, I swear."

"What the fuck? Okay, true."

"What's true?"

"If you want me to say it, I'll say it: I'm going to burn in hell."

"How right you are."

"How wet I am."

"Are you sorry for all your sins?"

"Whatever."

"Still the wrong answer, King," he said. I could hear him rising from his chair. "This is going to hurt you a lot more than it will hurt me."

The jackass grabbed me from behind, yanked me over to a sink of running water and shoved my head into the ice-cold liquid. As I screamed, my mouth and nose filled up with water and I started gagging. Real bad. Yes, I was being waterboarded in a dank, rank sink, an abominable form of torture that completely crushed what little was left of my dignity and resolve.

"Are you a bad man?" my inquisitor asked, as his goons dunked my head and bent my neck to the point where I thought it might snap and cause me instant death, which, at this juncture, did not feel like such a bad outcome.

"Yes, yes, I am," I hyperventilated, realizing that they weren't expecting me to argue with their condemnation of my being. "Burt King is a bad man."

"Do you pervert the political will of the people?"

"I suppose I do," I moaned.

"True or false? You are a heinous human being."

"For sure," I relented, in a necessary act of self-preservation.

"Good to hear you finally speak the truth, Albert Einstein Stein."

"That's not my name," I cried in between dunks. "I had it legally changed."

"Who are you kidding?" he responded.

I coughed up more water. "Go ahead. Call me whatever you want."

"Ready for the next question?"

"Do I have a choice?"

"Not in the least."

"Ain't that the truth."

"Okay, true or false: You are full of shit."

"False," I sputtered.

"True," I relented, less than a minute after being waterboarded once again. As far as effective forms of torture went, this particular method lived up to its well-deserved reputation.

"Just to confirm," said my grand inquisitor, "you, Albert Einstein Stein, do solemnly swear that you are full of shit."

"Yes, I do," I fibbed, bracing for whatever might unfold next.

"Good night, Mr. King," he said. I felt a syringe prick my shoulder. As I became groggy, I noted the irony of being pricked by a prick.

When I came to, I was still blindfolded and immobilized, but this time by a chain instead of a rope. Despite being unable to see squat, I could tell I had been transported to a different room while unconscious. Wherever I was stunk like mildew even more than the last place. I could hear a dripping pipe nearby, and my trusty nose detected the faint smell of a recent fart from someone other than me wafting through the decidedly sour air. I had company.

"Who farted?" I asked no one in particular.

"Not me," said an oddly familiar voice.

"Stop lying to me," I demanded.

"How dare you accuse me of farting?" said the voice. "Where I come from, whoever smelt it dealt it."

"Who are you?" I asked.

"That depends. Who are you?"

"I am Burt King. I'm sure you've heard of me."

"Are you *the* Burt King?"

"Live and in person. For the time being."

"Nice to meet you. I'm Max Morrison. A big fan."

Who would have thunk it? I had been kidnapped by the same people who kidnapped Max Morrison. These were some high-powered kidnappers. Impressive.

"Nice to meet you, too, Max," I cooed. "It's an honor."

"An honor?" he said as if surprised by my obsequiousness.

"I gotta tell you, I love your show."

"Really?" he said with surprise. "All that smack I say about the President and his administration doesn't offend you?"

"No, I find it entertaining. And I respect how well you connect with your angry callers. Your rage is authentic. It's contagious. It's combustible. Frankly, it's arousing."

"Why, thanks, Burt. If I weren't tied up, I would reach over and shake your hand. If you were a babe, I would kiss you."

"The feeling is mutual."

"You know, King," he continued, "I've followed your career closely. I've tried to model my manipulative skills after yours. I may not agree with anything you do, but I sure admire the way you do it."

"I swear, Max, you were on my list of people to call this week. I wanted to discuss your future."

"My future? What about my future?"

"If you ever get serious about getting into politics, I hope you'll come talk to me. We could go a long way together. I have no doubt I could take you all the way to the top."

"Shut the fuck up," said a new voice, highly peeved. "We're in some goddamn prison, not at the Palm having a business dinner."

"Who the hell are you?" I asked.

"Watch your language and show some respect. You're talking to the honorable Keanu Adams, Chief Justice of the United States Supreme Court, which even you should know is the highest power in the land."

"Says who?" I challenged the arrogant ass.

"Says me."

"Excuse me, your honor – and I use that term loosely – but the last time I checked, I was exponentially more powerful than you."

"Don't make me laugh, King," he laughed. "I could have you put away in a second."

"I could have you impeached in a second."

"Supreme Court Justices don't get impeached, you idiot."

"There's a first time for everything. Don't put it past me, you fool."

"You're reprehensible, you putrid political hack."

"You're awfully judgmental for a judge," I countered. "By the way, what's your net worth?"

"Take this, bitch," said Adams.

What felt like a humongous wad of spit crash-landed on my forehead. I did my best to wipe it off before I spit back in the general direction of the Chief Justice. But my missile must have missed because it failed to elicit the desired reaction.

"Go fuck yourself, King." Adams was officially unhinged.

"After you, your honor."

"Break it up," said Morrison, who I'm sure was enjoying every minute of this mano-a-mano tussle. "If we make it out of here alive, I promise to invite both of you on my show to continue this fascinating debate."

"That's fair," I assented, not missing a beat. "So tell me, our robed warrior of justice, why are you in here with us?"

"I have no idea," he said. "You two, I can understand. But me? It makes no sense whatsoever."

"Have you been charged with anything?" I inquired.

"Not exactly. But it's evident these nuts are pissed about some of our recent decisions."

"Like what?" Morrison asked before I could.

"My assailants were not specific. However, while they were waterboarding me, they did make derisive comments about our ruling last week to uphold the limited use of waterboarding in the workforce and in the classroom, provided the defendant had been accused of felonious behavior and read his Miranda rights."

"What's wrong with that?" asked Morrison. "When someone knows for sure that someone did something wrong, trials are worthless – a colossal waste of time and taxpayer money."

"Amen," I added. "Sorry to hear you got waterboarded. If it makes you feel any better, I did, too."

"That makes three of us," sighed Morrison. "Those fuckers said they didn't like how racist I was on my show. When I kept invoking my First Amendment rights, they kept shoving me under the water until I pleaded guilty."

"For what?" asked Adams.

"Polluting the airwaves," said Morrison. "How outrageous is that?"

"Decidedly outrageous," opined Adams. "But it does demonstrate the value of waterboarding."

We were interrupted by the sound of a bell ringing. I could hear footsteps approaching. "C'mon, boys," said an obnoxiously bombastic voice as the door opened. "Time for breakfast."

At last, a positive development. I was as hungry as a horse, wiped out from my humiliating night of terror and torture.

A phalanx of guards led us, shackles and all, out of our current room, up a flight of stairs and down another long hallway to some place we had presumably never been before.

As we walked in silence, we could hear the creeping sound of classical music coming from somewhere around the corner.

"What's the music for?" I wondered aloud.

"Perhaps they want to fête us before they kill us," said Adams.

"I knew it! I knew it," said Morrison, worriedly confronting the specter of his imminent death. "I'm too rich to die."

Finally we arrived at wherever we were supposed to be going. We were ordered to sit down on what felt like large, wooden dining-room chairs, the kind you would expect to see in an antique store. The guards released us one by one from bondage, removing the handcuffs along with the assorted chains. We were instructed to keep our blindfolds on or we would be shot, but I could live with that. Even though I couldn't see, I could move. I was happy to see tiny trickles of light filtering through my blindfold, streaming in from a room that actually had some windows – as opposed to the windowless dungeon from where we had emerged.

A flurry of shuffling feet signaled that more people were filing into the room. Something was afoot, but I had no idea what.

A gavel banged.

"I call this session to order," said a new voice, even more officious than the others that preceded him. I imagined myself seated around a giant banquet table, beautifully set, in an exquisite, high-ceilinged dining room, beautifully decorated like it was fit for a King – no pun intended.

The new voice was coming from the head of the table, as if he were the Big Kahuna, the one in charge.

"Welcome, everyone. Welcome!" he said. "Welcome to 'The Last Breakfast.'"

"What do you mean by 'The Last Breakfast'?" Morrison asked.

The voice chuckled. "Can I assume you are all familiar with 'The Last Supper'?"

"Yes," we muttered in unison.

"Then I'd like to personally welcome you to Your Last Breakfast."

"Does this mean we're about to be crucified?" asked Adams.

"You never know," teased the voice.

"Do you find this violation of our rights, this mockery of justice humorous?" I interjected.

"On a certain level, yes," said the voice, relishing the fact that he was in charge and we were nothing more than his bitches.

As I write these words and recount what happened next, it takes every ounce of my strength and intestinal fortitude not to tear up. Such was the pain I was forced savagely to endure.

The stupid bell rang again. "Breakfast is served," said the voice.

More footsteps entered the room. I could hear the clang of plates and glasses being brought in and placed in front of us.

"I'm starving," I announced. "What's for breakfast?"

"Your favorite dish," said the voice.

"How do you know what we like for breakfast?" Morrison asked.

"Don't worry. We know."

"That sounds ominous," said Adams.

"Perhaps," said the voice before continuing. "Before your entrée is served this morning, "I'm pleased to present each of you with an 18-ounce box of pitted prunes that you can enjoy right away. Full of fiber and rich with potassium."

"I hate prunes," Morrison moaned. "They're revolting."

"Tough shit," said the voice. "Each of you has five minutes to eat every single prune in your box."

"How many prunes are in each box?" I asked.

"About 75, give or take a few," explained the voice. "Bon appétit."

"Screw you," said an exasperated Morrison. "You will die for this."

"If you don't eat your prunes," the voice said, "*you* will die for this."

"Bullshit," Morrison added for good measure.

"Either you do what we say or, by the power vested in us, we will sentence you to death by execution."

"And if we comply with your preposterous demand," said Adams, "then what?"

"Then," the voice said slowly, "you are one step closer to freedom."

"What do you mean?" I asked suspiciously.

"Exactly what I said," the voice answered. "If you eat your prunes, you will be well on your way to being free."

"What do you mean by 'well on our way'?" Morrison said. "What's the catch?"

"There's no catch."

"How can that be?" I said.

"You'll see," said the voice. "Now, eat your prunes. They're sitting there right in front of you."

"We'll get sick and crap all over the place," Morrison said.

"Correct," said the voice.

"Fuck this!" yelled Morrison. "I can't take this anymore. If you want me to eat prunes, you'll have to kill me first."

And just like that, they shot Max Morrison dead. Right then and there. For refusing to eat his prunes. What a hideous way to go. But at least I was alive.

Adams began sobbing uncontrollably. I tried to keep my cool, operating as best I could in overdrive survival mode.

As I heard them drag Morrison's corpse away, I began chowing down on my prunes, one by one, trying to savor every succulent morsel, since it was theoretically possible that this was indeed going to be the last meal I ever ate. I was trying to be brave, but seeing, or rather hearing a fellow prisoner get murdered did not exactly give me a surfeit of confidence that I would survive this ordeal. If these crazies were calling this sick scene "The Last Breakfast," I rightfully had to assume it was conceivable that was going to be the case.

I could hear Adams munching on his prunes, as well. What seemed like an eternity later, the voice commended us for our compliance.

"Well done, gentlemen," he said.

"Can we go now?" I asked, fully cognizant that being freed would never be that easy.

"Almost," said the voice. "Just a few more odds and ends."

"Like what?" said Adams.

"Like this," said the voice. And with that, a gong began banging.

"Please stand, Mr. King," commanded the voice. Which I did, rather nervously, I must admit, bracing for the voice's next utterance.

"Do you, Albert Einstein Stein, operating under the alias Burt Heinz King, plead guilty today in person – and live on our worldwide webcast – to 1,000 counts of Crimes Against Humanity as well as Willful Perversion of Democracy?"

"Sure," I said, wanting to avoid a repeat encounter with waterboarding. "Why not?"

"Do you give us permission to enter into the public record your videotaped confession from yesterday?"

"Knock yourself out," I said.

"And last but perhaps most of important of all, do you, Mr. King, swear to retire from politics immediately, thereby saving all the oppressed and disenfranchised people from the irreversible damage you have done to our society?"

"Fuck, no," I answered. "That's a deal-breaker. What would I do for a living?"

"That's your problem, not ours," said the voice.

"I couldn't live without politics. I would shrivel up, then die on the vine."

"Would you prefer to die right now?" asked the voice, not waiting for a response. "Fine. Ready...aim...and...."

"Okay!" I shrieked. "If I agree to this, too, can I go?"

"You can go," said the voice.

"Then, yes, I swear to retire from politics. Once and for all."

"So help you God?"

"So help me and God and the USA." I hoped no one could see I was crossing my fingers under the table.

"Okay, Mr. King, your confession is accepted by this court. All you need to do now is relax your bowels, take a dump and eat your own shit. Then you will be officially released."

"You want me to eat my own shit?" I stammered.

"Oh, yes!" howled the voice. "It's show time."

"Meaning what?"

"The American people are tired of eating your shit. Now it's time for you to eat yours."

"Are you serious?" I asked in horror. "That's preposterous, not to mention immoral, illegal and unsanitary. You realize I could die from that."

"You will die if you don't do this." The voice was losing his temper. I didn't want to test his mettle like Morrison did.

"Then you swear," I said disgustedly, "on your mother's life, that if I comply with your abhorrent request, I'm completely and irrevocably free to go. No ifs, ands or buts."

"No ifs, ands or buts," the voice responded. "Provided, of course, you sign an unconditional release before we let you go, indemnifying us against any criminal or civil claims you might have as a result of this temporary detainment. As soon as you fulfill your obligations and sign those documents, you'll be heading back to Washington."

"What about me?" whined Adams, as I assessed my options, which looked to be nonexistent.

"We'll be with you in a minute," said the voice. "Assuming you shut up first and let us finish with King."

I will neither confirm nor deny the details of what happened next. But I'm sure you or someone you know has seen the video, which will live in infamy forever and is one of the most highly watched Internet sensations of all time.

Let's just say it was the most degrading thing I ever had to do in my distinguished life. It made me feel awful and dizzy, and I started puking uncontrollably.

The last thing I remember before being drugged again and put out of my misery was hearing Adams plead innocent to something like "Crimes Against Justice." Whatever that was meant to signify. While I dutifully pled out and took my punishment like a man, Adams chose to act like a big pussy, crying to his captors that he wasn't guilty of any crimes or misconduct. Until they apparently started yanking off his fingernails with a pair of pliers, which immediately caused him to reconsider.

I wasn't there to witness it, but Adams later admitted that he too was forced to eat his own shit before he was released. I should point out that even to this day, the video of his vile feat is nowhere near as popular as mine.

Some unknown number of hours later, I was trapped in a nightmare – another Einstein affair. Frighteningly, I was laid out in a casket, and Albert himself was staring down at me with scorn, getting ready to slam the door shut.

SATURDAY

"Look who's dead now," he panted, like a rabid dog. "I told you, fool, that you were eventually gonna get what you deserved. I've waited a long time for this day. The end for you is finally here."

I was awakened abruptly by a trunk door opening. Two goons lifted my bruised and blindfolded body out of the trunk, depositing me on the sidewalk.

As they sped away, I ripped off the blindfold and tried to detect my whereabouts. That was the easy part.

Those fuckers had the audacity to dump me in Lafayette Park, right across the street from the White House. In the middle of the night. In an oversized garbage bag. By a bench. Surrounded by hundreds of homeless schmucks sleeping, drinking or milling about. How humiliating for a man of magnitude.

I untied myself and crawled out, groggy and sore. My clothes were putrid, but I was alive. I asked the homeless guy sleeping on the bench above me what time it was.

"Can't you see I'm homeless?" he yelled. "I can't afford a fucking watch."

A nicer breed of homeless humanity stumbled by and graciously told me it was 3 a.m.

"What day is it?" I asked.

"Saturday night," he said, before shaking his head at me. "Dude, I can't believe you ate your own shit. What did it taste like?"

"It tasted like shit," I muttered as I walked away.

Like everyone else in the park at that hour, I was exhausted and broke. I limped my bedraggled ass down Pennsylvania Avenue to Slice and Dice, prevailed upon building security to let me in to my office and crashed on the couch. I would call the police in the morning, when I had the energy to gain my bearings and answer their battery of questions about my harrowing kidnapping. Sunday was never a day of rest for Burt King. And this one in particular would be no exception.

Sunday

I was out like a light when my private line started ringing incessantly. Despite my best efforts to ignore the intrusion, I had no choice but to stumble over to my desk and answer the goddamn phone. As soon as I grunted hello, the caller hung up. A short while later, there was a loud knock – really more like a pounding – on the front door of our offices. I could hear it all the way down the hall. My desk clock said 4:30 a.m., which was not a good time on a Sunday morning to have an unexpected visitor.

"Who could that be?" I grumbled to no one in particular as I waddled down the hall and looked through the plate-glass door.

It was the Secret Service. Two agents: one short and chunky, one tall and rail thin.

"What's going on?" I asked as I let them inside.

"We didn't know where you were," the tall one said. "The webcast of your torture ended abruptly, so we assumed you had been executed."

"I nearly was."

"That would have been a shame," he replied with a detectable deficit of sincerity. "Now that we know you're alive, Mr. King, the President needs to see you right away."

"About what?" I asked, conveniently forgetting the pledge I had made to my abductors about quitting politics.

"We have no idea, but even if we did, we're not authorized to discuss the matter with anyone, even you."

The short, chunky one remained silent. He seemed to be listening intently to whatever was being discussed in his earphone.

"Is everything okay at the White House?" I asked.

"Let's get going, Mr. King."

"Give me 10 minutes."

"How about five?"

"Make it six."

"Okay, but hurry up. And don't forget to call the D.C. police later. They're looking for you, too."

I jumped in my handy office shower, which I used only to clean myself up after mid-day flings or for emergencies, which was the case here. I let the water cascade over my filthy body and tried, as fast as I could, to scrub clean the soiled essence that clung to my skin and festered in my bodily cavities. I threw on an extra pair of clean khakis and a dress shirt that I kept in my office closet and tried in vain to comb what remained of the hair on my head. Despite the rush, I was ready for action, looking as good as I was going to look, considering I never looked that good to begin with.

The two agents escorted me down the elevator, flanked me as we walked briskly through the deserted lobby of my building and held the door for me before I jumped into their super-sized SUV. I was getting the royal treatment, and I could feel my groove coming back to where it deserved to be.

When I waltzed into the West Wing, I was ushered into the Oval Office, where I found President Strump and the First Lady sitting on a couch. Even Angus Doltish was there, the empty-suit Vice President who had virtually gone into hiding the day after he and Strump were elected, because that's where I'd decided he belonged, given how gaffe-prone he invariably was. As we knew too well from prior experience, as soon as the Election Day polls were closed, Doltish became an accident waiting to happen every time he opened his mouth. To put it bluntly: Until the re-election campaign headed into its home stretch, we had little use for his good looks and sex appeal with Southern women between 35 and 64.

On this night, more than any other night, everyone seemed to be in a foul mood.

"We're glad you're okay, Burt," the President said before dismissing his aides, with the exception of Scudder, his trusty, tenacious, effete yet astoundingly ineffective chief of staff.

"Can I please go home and go back to sleep?" asked Doltish. "I'm tired."

"Be my guest, Angus," snickered the President, as he turned his back on the Vice President and headed toward me.

"You must feel like shit," he said, smiling as he shook my hand. "Get it?"

"Very not funny," I said. "Lucky for you, I wasn't killed."

"I thought you promised your captors you were done with politics forever."

"I would promise anyone anything if my life were on the line. You would too."

"Agreed. A promise is just a promise."

"Anyway, I'm happy to be here, Mr. President," I lied. "What's going on?"

"Have you seen CNN?" said the First Lady.

"No, I was sleeping. I only watch CNN when I'm awake."

"Okay, then," said the President. "Check this out."

He flipped on his humongous TV. CNN was broadcasting live from the back steps of the Capitol, where a massive crowd of people was marching down the Mall, holding candles and chanting, "Strump sucks," backed by a ragtag band of drummers banging away with impressive rhythmic precision.

"What all this about?" I asked. "Another anti-war rally by those psychotic Canuck sympathizers? Don't those crybabies ever stop whining? Don't they have lives? Why don't they do the world a favor and emigrate to Canada?"

"These are not Canadian sympathizers," said the President. "And this is not an anti-war rally."

"Is it the gun-crazies, the anti-gun crazies, the militant gays or the anti-gay militants, or some combination thereof?"

"No, Burt," said Zoey, as if I were stupid.

"Is it those anti-male pro-choice pro-lifers?"

"No, Burt," said the President. "It's POPP."

"For real?" I was sufficiently flummoxed. As recently as last month, the FBI had led to believe that POPP, short for the Pissed-Off People's Party, had gone into hiding after we had successfully sabotaged their fledgling attempts to organize themselves as a legitimate political party. "I thought we'd pushed them to the brink of extinction. I thought we had confirmation their leadership had been decapitated."

"Yep, that's what we all thought," said Scudder.

"Clearly, we were grossly misled by the Intelligence community," Strump said, "and now the enemy is heading right this way, five-hundred-thousand strong."

"Have they been rallying all night?"

"Since midnight," said Strump, as he paced around the room. "They're vowing to hold a hunger strike around the White House until I speak to them."

"Let 'em starve to death," I suggested. "Or, on second thought, just order the Secret Service to shoot them. Those despicable crackpots don't vote for us."

"Shut up, Burt," said the President. He was getting testy. "Protesters dying from hunger around the White House gates would look terrible. And killing them would be even worse. The carnage would make me look callous."

"On the contrary," I said, wagging a finger at the leader of the free world. "You would look strong. Presidential. Decisive. Totally in charge. Why reward these nuts by talking to them or even acknowledging their existence?"

"I don't think these people are nuts," said the First Lady. "But they are mad as hell."

"About what?" I asked.

"About pretty much everything," Strump said rather despondently. "Did you see our latest tracking numbers?" he added, handing me some new polling data that I had not seen yet, due to my temporary incarceration.

"What are these maladjusted pansies upset about?" I said. "The usual bullshit?"

"Among other things," Scudder whined.

"What else is there for them to be mad about?" I wondered.

"Apparently, any number of things," the President said in a somber, seemingly depressed voice. "The war, the bad economy, record-breaking unemployment, rising crime, the crappy state of our schools, the fact that people have no health insurance and no savings and no confidence that I even know how to brush my teeth and floss, let alone lead our country. Which isn't fair, damn it. It's not like I have any control over the situation. It's not like I have the power to fix this crap. It's not like it's my fault these losers have shitty lives. Jesus, they need to accept the way things are and get over it. They need to stop blaming me personally. They need to stop holding me accountable. I'm only the President. Not their Lord."

"Take it easy, Mr. President," I tried in my best peppy voice. "Don't be sad. Things aren't that bad. Your approval rating may be in the toilet, but it's still two years away from Election Day. With my brilliant guidance, you'll eventually turn your presidency around. The press will pump you up after tearing you down, and before long, you'll be heralded as the Comeback Kid and win your re-election in a romp."

"Is that before or after pigs will fly?" said the First Lady, turning her back on me and stomping out of the room with Scudder in tow, leaving the two most powerful men in America alone together.

SUNDAY

"Fine," I said, trying to defuse the tension. "How can I help? What do you want me to do?"

"I need you to stop fucking around," said the President, "and write me a short speech that I can deliver to these protesters when they make it over to the White House gates, which, according to the Secret Service, will be in approximately a half hour. I want to be nice and cheery and acknowledge their presence and explain to them that I feel their pain. I want them to know that I care that they care. I want to thank them for their passion. And their patriotism. I feel I owe them that."

"So what you're basically saying is that you want to lie to them?"

"Why do you always have to be cynical?" he asked, giving me his dirtiest look yet.

"I am who I am because I was who I was until I became who I became, which is exponentially better than who I used to be when I wasn't nearly the success I am today. Got it?"

"Not in the slightest," said the President. "But that's irrelevant. What is relevant is that I need you, my top adviser and crisis manager, to get to work immediately. Give me the words to convince these lost souls that I am with them, that I hear them, that I empathize with their concerns, whatever the hell their concerns may be."

"With all due respect, sir, your approach is dead wrong," I argued. "Do you really want to set a precedent that every time a throng of unruly protestors converges on the White House, the President will drop what he's doing, even in the middle of the night, and meet with them face-to-face in a desperate attempt to address their grievances? I can assure you that this is a ridiculous recipe for disaster."

"I'm done debating this. Let's do what we have to do and move on. Show them I'm a man of the people. Show them I'm sympathetic to those infinitely less wealthy and privileged than me and, for that matter, you. Don't you remember the 'Power to the People' slogan we successfully rode to victory?"

"I remember, Mr. President, but that was only a slogan. It was effective messaging, not an oath. It's not real."

"Why can't we make it real, even temporarily?" he asked, as Scudder re-entered.

"No one has principles these days," I opined. "But I assume that's irrelevant to this conversation."

"Give it a rest, Burt," said Scudder, asserting himself for once. "I like the President's idea."

"You didn't even hear his idea," I reminded him. "You stepped out."

"I heard everything," said Scudder. "Did you forget that we record everything that goes down in here?"

"Oh, yes," I remembered. "Nonetheless, whether you agree with the President or not, two wrongs do not make a right."

"In this situation they do," said Scudder. "Majority rules. You're out of luck. Or should I say, you're shit out of luck."

"Fuck you, Scudder. You're paid to like his ideas," I pointed out. "You're the consummate Yes Man, which is why the President picked you as his kiss-ass Chief of Staff."

"Eat me, Burt," he answered, as the President grimaced. "Speaking to the protesters tonight is a brilliant strategy. They don't expect it. In fact, it's the consummate contrarian approach. Exceptionally retro. Shows tremendous self-confidence. Real compassion. The dead Presidents used to do stuff like this all the time."

"Okay," the President said, giving me the evil eye. "We're done arguing. Go write me a speech that makes me look good. If we hit a home run, we can bask in the media's glory all day long."

"I'll set Burt up down the hall," Scudder said, motioning me toward the door. He escorted me out of the Oval Office and into the nearby Cabinet Room. A couple of young punks from the speechwriting staff were there, presumably to take dictation. Which was fine, because I was low on fuel and in no mood to type or scribble down what I wanted the President to say. I needed to conserve my energy for the critical task I faced: the creation of inspiring Presidential rhetoric to appease the angry masses.

A few minutes later, I had singlehandedly built a soaring cathedral of monumental oratory so exalted that the President would be able to convince anyone of anything at anytime.

I told the speechwriters to go forth and conquer, and they left the room, obviously in awe, to put my genius into typewritten words for the Presidential teleprompter.

As I sat alone, soaking in another self-congratulatory moment, Zoey came barging in with a not-so-nice look on her face.

"What a goddamn mess," she complained after shutting the door. "I never thought the people would take to the streets like this. Maybe in some Third World country, but not in the United States."

"Big deal," I said, sloughing it off. "A few thousand wackjobs. Welcome to my world."

"A few thousand?" she scoffed. "Make it a few hundred thousand."

"Relax, Zoey. I've got this baby under control," I said, sitting down in the chair next to hers. "When the President utters my artistry, this too shall pass."

"And what if it doesn't?" she asked.

"Then some new problem will come along and make you forget about this one. It never fails."

"You better be right, Burt."

"Don't worry, I always am."

Zoey grinned, easing the tension. "Your arrogance amazes me. Don't you ever get tired of always being the smartest person in the room? It must be incredibly difficult to be such a legend in your own mind."

"What do you expect from someone as perfect as *moi*? If you've got it, why not flaunt it?"

"I liked you more when you were a nerdy, neurotic college geek. What happened to that guy?"

"Excellent question. According to most, if not all of my psychotherapists, in my sophomore year of college, some girl broke my tender little heart, which, coming on the heels of my miserable childhood, forced me to develop a tough exterior as a protective veneer to mask my rampant insecurities and fragile sense of self-esteem. Or something along those lines. How's that for an explanation?"

"Sounds like you've spent a lot of money on therapists over the last three decades."

"Millions." Which may not have been much of an exaggeration.

"And I assume that in your personal, psychotherapeutical narrative, I continue to play the role of the cruel collegiate vixen who came along ages ago and hurt your feelings forever."

"Correct."

"But as we've discussed numerous times, Burt, that's ancient history. Back then, I was happy to be your friend. However, that was all I wanted us to be at the time. It's not like I strung you along and manipulated the situation for the sole purpose of crushing you like a bug."

"Yet that was the net effect."

"Of what?"

"Of rejecting my advances."

"When you tried to kiss me after buying me an ice-cream cone? You call that an advance?"

"Yes, in my playbook at that time, it was a well-calculated advance."

"Jesus Christ, Burt," she huffed. "You were so naïve back then. If you thought that was some slick move, you blew it. You can't take a girl out on a first date, buy her an ice cream cone and expect her to fall head over heels in love with you. Maybe in sappy movies you can, but certainly not in real life. I think it's time, after all these years, you let this bizarre fixation go. You're an old man. You've got to move on. I know I have."

I struggled to contain my emotions, which appeared to be more uncontrollable than usual.

"Can't you see, Zoey? I can't move on. Can't you see I still have feelings for you? Now that I've been shot, now that I've been held hostage, now that I've been under siege and under attack, I can see everything more clearly than ever before. I've always known what I want out of life. And I want more than anything for us, you and I, to be together. Forever. In love. In bed. For eternity. Or, if that's impractical, I'll settle for a one-night stand. You complete me."

"Dream on, Burt," she said dismissively. "I have no desire to be with you in any way, shape or form."

"Even for a quickie?" I pleaded. "To satisfy an urge I've had forever?"

"You're crazy," she said, in a most accusatory tone of voice. "What about Juanita?"

"We're through."

"What?"

"Juanita and I are done. Well done."

"But you were at the White House together this week, right before your fiasco at Thongs R Us."

"It's over, Zoey. Put another divorce in the books for me. Live, love, lose interest, lie and then move on."

"How many is that for you, Burt? Three divorces?"

"Four, as of today. If you count this next one, it'll be five."

"Congratulations," she said, as if I had the time or inclination to be the butt of her joke.

Maybe it was the fact that I was sleep-deprived, or maybe it was because I was suffering post-traumatic stress from the worst week of my life, or maybe I merely lost my mind for an instant because I was being rebuffed by the most powerful woman in the country – but whatever the reason, I, Burt King, began

SUNDAY

weeping. Tears that I never knew I could produce started, without my authorization or consent, streaming down my cheeks.

I buried my head on the conference table, sobbing shamelessly. I let it all hang out, wallowing in record-breaking levels of self-pity. This was a sorry state I was in, no less embarrassing than having to eat my own shit in a live webcast.

"You better get a hold of yourself, Burt," whispered Zoey, placing her hand on my hand as I wailed like a baby. "You don't want anyone, especially my husband, seeing you like this. He needs you at your best. Our nation needs you at your best."

I wished she hadn't said that. I wished she hadn't tried to comfort me. I wished she weren't even there in the same room with me. But fate had conspired against me. Fatally, it seemed.

To this day, I'm not sure what possessed me to wheel around and kiss Zoey Strump on the lips. But when she recoiled and shrieked, "What the fuck are you doing?" my instincts told me I had badly mishandled the situation.

Zoey ran out of the room, leaving me dazed and confused. Until the President ran in and punched me in the face. Hard. Maybe I could have blocked his fist or hit him before he hit me, but given the fact that several gun-toting Secret Service agents ran in right behind him, I decided it was best to do nothing to get in his way, essentially giving him a free shot. As I picked myself up off the floor, I figured I had probably deserved it.

In a blur of vitriol and commotion, I was removed from the West Wing, bloodied and bowed, in handcuffs, which fortunately were removed well before I was escorted across the White House lawn and led toward the guard station by the street. None of the agents or police said a single word to me on my way out. It was like I was a dead man walking. Like I had gone from superstar MVP to syphilitic in the space of a second. The good news was that the handcuffs were taken off before I was expelled from the White House grounds, which came as a relief, given the gravity of my ill-advised maneuver. I assumed from the President's point of view, the less said about this awkward incident, the better. For everyone involved.

As I wobbled down the sidewalk on the other side of the White House gates, I could hear the clamor of the approaching crowd marching up Pennsylvania Avenue, hooting and hollering and thumping away. Soon I could see an emerging glow from the flashlights, candles and torches they were carrying, which punctured the eerie darkness.

I fought my way through the converging masses and made my way around the back side of the White House grounds. I wanted desperately to watch Strump deliver my verbiage over the giant loudspeakers that work crews were hastily assembling and aiming toward the street. Barring something extraordinary, this was undoubtedly going to be my last Presidential address ever, and I wanted to witness it in person.

In a weird, unexpected way, what I saw next brightened my mood considerably. Acres and acres of rabble-rousing men, women and children, of all races, breeds, creeds and colors, stretching back as far as the eye could see, gradually encircled the White House, covering the Mall like a sea of rodents. The people escalated their rabid chant of "Strump sucks!" but their venom subsided when they heard the President's voice crackling over the sound system. I doubt many of them were close enough to actually see him wave from the second-floor balcony of his private residence, but they sure as hell could hear him. In a prudent act of self-preservation, I approached a nearby vendor and purchased a "Strump Sucks" baseball cap, which I pulled snuggly over my head. No good would come from me being recognized in the midst of this angry mob.

"Good evening, my fellow Americans," said Strump, nailing in perfect cadence the first line I had written. "Or should I say, good morning, people, because the sun is about to rise over Washington. Welcome to the White House. Normally, I would be asleep at this hour. But I don't mind the fact that you've kept me up all night. And I don't mind the fact that you seem to think I suck."

The crown cheered on cue. As always, I had their number.

"To tell you the truth," continued the President, "you're not the only ones who think I suck. My wife and kids do, too."

The crowd roared again. That self-deprecating bullshit always worked wonders.

"I am here, live and in person, speaking to you because I care about you. I care about your lives. I care about your anxieties. I care about your problems. I care about your frustrations with the way things are. I feel your pain wherever you feel pain. And tonight I pledge to you, my friends, from the bottom of my beating heart, that I will work with you, day and night, to change things for the better – to change all that is bad into good, all that is wrong into right, all that is sad into happiness. Because you, my people, deserve to be happy. You deserve the best. You know it. I know it. We all know it. And working together, arm in arm, we will build a future that is brighter than ever before."

Despite my brilliant wordsmithing, the masses did not show their love. On the contrary, and to my chagrin, they stayed unexpectedly quiet. Until a growing chorus of a new chant spread like wildfire.

At first, I thought the crowd was yelling, "Pull it! Pull it! Pull it!" – as if they were playing tug of war or some other odd game.

However, as the proletariats' voices grew louder, I realized they were chanting, "Bullshit! Bullshit! Bullshit!" while the President dutifully kept reading my words.

"As a new dawn arrives in our nation," he continued, seemingly oblivious to the mounting vitriol spewing toward him, "we can change everything we need to change before it is too late to change because change is no longer possible. If we stand united, together as one, indivisible, with liberty and justice for all those who deserve it, nothing is impossible except failure. And we will not fail. No way. No how. No can do. We are too good to fail. Too smart to fail. Too American to fail. Instead, we will walk together from this day forward and fight together to make all your dreams and all our dreams and all my dreams come true. As we forge ahead, we must stay strong, we must stay together in spirit and in purpose – and we must heed the words and wisdom of Abraham Lincoln, who told our forefathers in a nationally televised address the night before the start of the Civil War: 'C'mon, people. Why can't we all just get along?'"

By this time, the President's words were barely audible over the rising contempt of the crowd. The White House speakers were soon overmatched. From my perch, I could tell that Strump was now cognizant of the profane jeering. His dependable fake smile had turned into a full-blown grimace, a sure-fire sign of heartbreaking dejection. He paused and took stock of the mayhem. He looked nauseous. Seconds later, hundreds of airborne tomatoes and eggs and shoes started flying his way. As the Secret Service encircled him, the President waved meekly and limped back into the White House. A supremely dazzling speech, tragically interrupted.

For as long as I live, and I hope that's an awfully long time, I'll never forget the craziness that ensued next. With the President gone, I had no patience to hang out with the rowdy, not to mention smelly humanity surrounding me. It was time to go back to the office. I had work to do and a career to salvage, even if I was persona non grata at the White House.

The sun was barely starting to rise. I figured I would cut through the crowd and walk toward Constitution Avenue, hoping to find a cab on the overrun streets.

It took me forever, but I found a gypsy cab up near 17th Street and climbed wearily inside. The cab hadn't even gone a half a block when I heard the explosion, the mother of all explosions: a massive, bone-shaking, ear-piercing blast that blew out the back window of the cab. For a split second, everything in Washington came to a grinding halt. Cars slammed on the brakes. People froze in their tracks, too stunned to scream. I jumped out of the cab and wheeled around, just in time to see a firestorm erupting over the Mall, covering the Chevron National Oil Rig in a thick billowing blanket of black smoke.

"Holy shit!" I wailed in disbelief. "What's happening?"

"Holy Mohammed," shrieked my cabbie, as he bailed out of his cab. "I should have stayed in Pakistan where it was safe."

Without any regard for me or his vehicle, the jerk bolted down 17th Street, covering his ears with his hands as multiple sirens began to blare, followed by a wave of smaller but no less worrisome secondary explosions.

I stood there in shock, smack in the middle of the street, transfixed by the havoc and trying my best to ascertain if what I was seeing was really happening. Sky-high flames engulfed the Rig, which had been built on the former site of the Washington Monument (after it was sold to private Libyan collectors a decade ago and then transported to Tripoli). Now, the most revered tribute to the United States' historic commitment to oil drilling, anywhere, anytime, began swaying, in all its phallic glory, wobbling back and forth, until it keeled over and crumpled violently to the ground, setting off another seismic blast that rocked the earth.

I regained my senses as best I could and tried to outrun all the crap coming my way. But I didn't stand a chance. After a few yards of alternately sprinting, then walking fast and wheezing, I felt like a dirty glazed doughnut, covered from head to toe in a wet, disgusting mix of black and white debris combined with my own perspiration, which, as was usual in times of stress, was pouring out of me. Then came the coughing, which made it excruciating to breathe, let alone think.

The sirens grew louder. Two military jets thundered by, unusually low to the ground. The buzz of helicopters drew near. There was no ambiguity about this: Washington was under attack. As much as I wanted to believe the Canadians were responsible for this mayhem, I knew it wasn't them. This was not a foreign aggressor; it was those homegrown terrorists who made the Pissed Off People's Party such an insidious threat to the stability of the USA.

Amidst the chaos, those malevolent protesters were scattering, scrambling in every direction, trying to escape the wreckage and the police and the insanity of the moment. If I had had a gun, and if I had known how to use a gun, I would have started shooting every single one of them until I had no bullets left.

A ragged posse staggered toward me, looking both astonished by the magnitude of what they had done and proud of the havoc they had wreaked upon our nation.

"What did you savages do?" I yelled contemptuously.

One of the protesters, a not-very-young woman in blue jean shorts and a tie-dyed T-shirt that said "Power to the People," shot me a quizzical look.

"What do you mean, 'What did you savages do?' How dare you judge us?" She got up in my grill, gesturing incessantly before making the rest of her inane point:

"Look around you, King. You helped make this mess. This is your fault, not ours."

Even if my cover hadn't been blown, I couldn't stand there and take their abuse any longer. "You are malevolent morons," I said, using at least one word in the English language I knew they were too imbecilic to understand. "And thanks to this act of destruction, you are criminals, too. You deserve to die in jail."

"That's hilarious," said one of the greasy men accosting me. "You are the one who deserves to die in jail."

What a joke! "Why don't you do the world a favor and go fuck yourself?" I recommended. And with that bold utterance, I turned around and started walking away as fast as I could, which was not fast enough, because I had taken only a few steps when one of the protesters grabbed me from behind and held me long enough for several others to block my path.

"Where do you think you're going?" said a menacing, heavily-tattooed woman wearing a "Strump Sucks" tank top.

This was not good. These nuts were out of their minds, and now they had me surrounded.

"Let go of me immediately," I demanded.

"Not so fast, King," a different woman shot back.

"Help!" I screamed at the top of my lungs. "Police! Help me, please!"

In an ideal world, the police would have materialized immediately to save my ass. This was not meant to be.

"Hey, motherfucker," said a voice with a nastily familiar ring.

I turned just in time to see Jones running toward me, plastered in soot and holding hands with Juanita, who looked luminous albeit disheveled, like she was having the time of her life.

"Welcome to the revolution," said Jones. "Ain't payback a bitch?"

"What are you two doing together?" I asked, not wanting to know.

"Everything imaginable," giggled Juanita, as she flipped me the bird.

"This is quite the reunion," said another excited voice entering the fray.

It was Huffington, who kissed me on the lips as her camera crew filmed away.

"Have you been stalking me?" I asked, knowing the answer without even having to ask.

"That's absurd," she said, taking great offense. "I've been covering you, Burt, not stalking you. Thanks to my investigative reporting and the riveting interviews I've done with Juanita, Jones, numerous clients, lovers, government officials and enemies, plus videos of us having sex and you having sex with my sister, *PolitiPorn* is sure to be the #1 TV show in America. I'm going to be a big star."

I was totally fucked. Trapped in a lynch mob with Jones, Juanita and, maybe worst of all, Huffington, who was recording every second of my seemingly imminent death. Thank goodness for the canister of tear gas that landed with a thud at my feet and exploded.

It's painful for me to recount what went down next. With my eyes burning, I ran as fast as I could, which wasn't very fast but still allowed me to flee. By the time the smoke – or, in this case, the gas – cleared, I had broken free. I had shed that goon squad and was a mere two blocks away from the sanctuary of Slice & Dice. Gasping for air due to extreme physical and mental overexertion, I bent over, trying valiantly to catch my breath, when a cop car pulled over and two uniformed assholes got out and tackled me to the ground. Which hurt like a bitch!

"Burt King," one of the cops said as he cuffed me, "you're under arrest."

"U.S. terrorists just blew up the Chevron National Oil Rig and you're arresting *me*? For what?"

"You know what you did."

"I had nothing to do with the explosion."

"No one bombed the Rig," said the cop.

"Then why did it explode?" I cried.

As I writhed in agony, face-down on the ground, the cop explained that, according to preliminary reports, Chevron engineers had been working all night to repair an underground gas leak when one of them accidentally dropped a cigarette butt in the work area, which caused the massive explosion that spewed what turned out to be a billion barrels of crude oil all over the Mall, from the Capitol to the Lincoln Memorial to the White House.

"So why am I in trouble?" I asked in disbelief.

"Because you are," said the cop.

I lost it. "This is insane. In the last 24 hours, I've been wounded, kidnapped, tortured, waterboarded, debased, insulted, humiliated, chased, and cheated on – not to mention forced at gunpoint to eat my own shit before a worldwide audience. And instead of apprehending the villains who perpetrated these repugnant acts against me, you have the audacity to accuse me, one of the most powerful people ever to walk the streets of this town, of breaking the law? Is there no justice left in America?"

"You have the right to remain silent," said the cop. "Anything you say can and will be used against you whenever we want."

"You can't be serious!" I cried to the cops, as a crowd of guilty bystanders gathered and began hurling obscenities at me.

But they *were* serious. I, Burt King, was arrested that day and charged with six counts of Aggravated Boorish Behavior for inappropriate physical contact with the First Lady – a felony punishable by up to six years in prison, which I'm sad to report I received, after a much-too-brief hearing before a military tribunal, featuring egregiously one-sided, self-serving testimony from the First Lady, as well as from the President, neither of whom ever spoke to me again.

The End
(Not Really)

Whoever said you can't go home again is dead wrong. Hey, look at me. I made a triumphant return to where I was born, back where it all began, in New Rotica, N.Y. And now I'm living a life of relative luxury, relaxing, recharging, and resting up for my inevitable return to prime time.

I must say I will always be thankful that, despite the stunning ineptitude of my legal defense team, whose gross negligence and obscene incompetence resulted in my conviction, my overpriced legal nitwits were at least able to pull some last-minute strings and get me into the RitzJustice five-star federal penitentiary for white-collar criminals that I referenced earlier in this story's Introduction. And yes, if you want to know the truth, I enjoy the stress-free living, gourmet cuisine and social activities. For the first time in my life, I'm in great shape. I work out daily at the Canyon Ranch spa facility, which is a fabulous perk for those of us fortunate enough to be incarcerated here, less than a mile from where I had the misfortune of growing up.

But don't cry for me, America. I will be back. Sure enough and soon enough. Maybe even in two or three years if I get paroled early for good behavior. Back in business. Back in power. Back on top. Doing my thing. Doing mighty fine.

So this is everything that transpired during this dreadful week. I thought you should hear the detailed truth directly from me. Now, I fully expect that my critics, who are as numerous as they are nasty, will trash my story. I will be accused of presenting a biased, self-serving account of these calamitous events. My prose will be pilloried for being pompous and pedestrian. I will be impugned for being arrogant and insensitive. I will be excoriated for showing no character or class from the first page to the last. I will be attacked unmercifully for failing to learn my lessons or evolve as a human being.

Yet, before we part company, allow me the opportunity to respond with a preemptive strike to these baseless assertions: I basically don't give a shit. If an author is judged harshly by his critics, who are insidiously jealous of everything he has accomplished, then so be it. I did it my way and I have no regrets. That's the reality of the situation – the whole truth and nothing but the truth. I may be in jail instead of in my opulent penthouse, but I take well-deserved pride in being who I am, wherever I am.

It's important for you to understand that, in true martyr style, just like Martin Luther Luther, Martin Luther King, Larry King, Gandhi, Hillary Clinton, Taylor Swift and other noble, notable Americans whose heroic acceptance of their martyrdom predated mine – I'm completely at peace with the fact that I was jailed. No one can deny that in a historical context, I am in excellent company.

After everything I've been through, I'm really not bitter. Did I deserve to be locked up in here? Of course not. I was in the wrong place at the wrong time in history – a scapegoat for Strump, the media and the woefully ignorant American people, who threw me under the bus when they needed someone to blame for our nation's fucked-uppedness.

But no worries. I swear I don't take it personally. Because I did nothing wrong. I have no regrets and nothing to apologize for. If you can't live your life doing whatever you want with whomever you want, whenever you want to do it – acting upon your deepest impulses, urges and desires – what's the goddamn point of living?

As far as the First Lady goes, she clearly could have handled my imprudent kiss much better. She could have looked the other way or pretended it never happened. However, by hosing me the way she did, Zoey Strump ensured that my lifelong lust for her was extinguished once and for all, which has been liberating and downright cathartic.

Even my Einstein nightmares are few and far between. He hasn't terrorized my psyche for months, ever since I dreamed he was my date at Juanita's wedding to Jones, which did eventually happen in reality.

THE END (NOT REALLY)

Unfortunately, those two traitors waited to get married for nearly a year after my divorce from Juanita was finalized, which ended up costing me $15 million in alimony, legal fees and to settle her claims of excessive marital torture. As a highly unpopular felon, I knew no one had any sympathy for my side of the story, which meant I had no choice but to bend over and take it like a man.

The truth is that no matter how badly Juanita screwed me in court, the exorbitant settlement I had to fork over was well worth the price, just to end our mutual misery and put her and her parents in my past forever. That woman had the nerve to accuse me of physical and emotional abandonment, a laughable claim I could have fought. But sucking it up and paying her off was the easiest way to close that sorry chapter and move on with my life. It was only money, and I had plenty more stashed away in multiple Swiss bank accounts. I hope Juanita and Jones live happily ever after in holy matrimony till death do them part, or until their marriage falls apart and collapses in a cloud of disgusting, disreputable dust.

Let's see. What else should I tell you about?

The other day, I was meditating on the crapper, trying to compose some poignant poetry while flipping through a dog-eared copy of *Washingtonian* magazine, when I came across a profile of none other than Muffy Huffington, the world-renowned reality TV star, porn star and international celebrity. As she had predicted, she did indeed make it big with *PolitiPorn* and had two hugely hyped spin-offs in production, *BizPorn* and *Porn'O'Porn*. I assume she knows she has me to thank, because my well-publicized troubles during that week from hell definitely jumpstarted her career. I am grateful I got to have sex with her before she was famous. No one can ever take the thrill of that conquest away from me.

And the Pavlovs? As soon as I went down, those Russian gangsters dumped me like yesterday's garbage. The last I heard, they had hired 20 different lobbying firms in D.C. to do the dirty work I did singlehandedly for them. I'm not sure how close they are to completing their brazen purchase of Congress, but I would never in a million years bet against them.

Oh, yes, Slice & Dice. In an unselfish act of loyalty, Big Al tried to keep the firm going without me. "I'll hold things together until you get out of jail," he told me. Sadly, his noble effort lasted all of two months before our wounded firm was clientless, leaving Big Al virtually broke. He emailed me recently to say that after much reflection, he had moved to Vermont, where he works as a cow-milker at a small, organic dairy. "I miss the action, but I couldn't stand the pricks in politics any longer," he wrote.

Speaking of pricks, I still have no idea who was behind that brazen ambush shooting of me in the parking lot of Thongs R Us after that White House dinner. As usual, the D.C. police investigation was a colossal waste of my time and taxpayer money and yielded zippo. Not even a halfway legitimate lead. Even worse, I got the distinct feeling that Detective Ganges and his incompetent cohorts found any and all acts of violence against me to be more humorous than anything else, which I found extremely disconcerting, given the singular importance of my safety and well-being. If I were a betting man, I'd say that that specific attack was orchestrated by one or more of the following suspects: my ex-father-in-law Jorge, one of my former wives or girlfriends, or any one of my countless political enemies. May they die a painful death, whomever they are.

When I look at my life and pretend to be introspective, which on many levels is a waste of my time, I wonder how I've changed through the years. Am I essentially the same person I was growing up in New Rotica? Of course not. I had accumulated vast amounts of money and fame and power and respect since then. Maybe I lost it all, but at one time, I did have it. Therefore, I believe I have changed over the years. Substantially, and in every dimension. Except one.

My mother, in all her wretched glory, continues to be the bane of my existence. And I am that of hers. Now more than ever.

You see, after I got sent to the slammer, the D.C. police woke from their deep slumber and miraculously busted those vicious villains who'd kidnapped me, Justice Adams and the late Max Morrison, may he rest in peace. Twelve self-described revolutionaries, faculty members and grad students from the University of Maryland political-science program were arrested after blogging unrepentantly about their illegal exploits. During their trial, the culprits testified that they had kidnapped me because they had a patriotic duty to do so and were only following their moral and religious convictions.

"We felt a profound sense of duty to protect our country by confronting King and trying valiantly to preserve what little remained of our democracy," declared that bitch who carjacked me. Their self-proclaimed leader, one Adjunct Professor Melvin Horwitz, even had the audacity to justify his cold-blooded killing of Morrison as "tragically accidental," on the grounds of temporary insanity due to excessive consumption of tofu and hemp milk. "I was high and suffering severe gastric distress," he declared.

Not surprisingly, in such a toxic political climate, the jurors bought into this bullshit, and those criminals were freed after pleading guilty to some misdemeanor charges and agreeing to take an online anger-management course. This mockery of justice, this reprehensible slap-on-the-wrist, sparked a new wave of politically motivated assaults and kidnappings in D.C., as every nutcase salivated at the thought of eradicating their enemies with impunity. Which motivated my mother to enter the fray by posting a series of YouTube rants offering $50,000 to anyone who would flat-out kill me, thereby ending her ignominy of being my mother once and for all. Which resulted in me pressing charges. To make matters worse, after my mother was arrested for issuing her fatwa against me, investigators discovered that she had cunningly arranged to take out a $5 million life-insurance policy on her only child. Another massive violation of the law, which led to another round of indictments. How fucked up is that? A pathological Oedipal monstrosity of epic proportions, if you ask me or any mildly competent shrink.

Long ago, before I mellowed, I would have wished for my mother to be sentenced to death. I would have enjoyed seeing her executed. But after her trial ended in a multiple felony conviction, I took the high road, sucked up my anger and recorded a videotaped appeal for leniency at her sentencing hearing. And wouldn't you know it, against all odds, the judge cut her some slack and sent her to jail – as fate would have it, at RitzJustice in New Rotica, which means I have the pleasure of seeing her here in the hood almost every day. Sure, it's weird living with her again under the same roof – it's certainly not my first choice – but at least this time around, there are more than enough armed guards nearby to keep us from killing each other.

I have no illusions about the depth of my mother's contempt for me, and vice-versa. It is what it is. But I can tell she's a tad grateful that I fibbed under oath on her behalf, urging the judge to go easy on her because I swore she wasn't as evil as the jury unanimously agreed she was. Cold-blooded? Yes. Cold-blooded killer? Nah.

Ah, mothers. As hard as they can be to live with, I suppose they deserve a little credit, because we never would have been born without them.

"I always knew you'd end up in jail," she blurted out the other day when I saw her eating her usual egg-white and spinach frittata in the cafeteria.

"Looks like I finally lived up to your expectations," I said, unsure whether to scream or cry. I chose to do neither, simply grinning, turning around and walking away, head held high, proud of everything I'd done and will do again when I ultimately get out of this place.

After all, I am Burt King, still the king of Washington.

THE END

Made in the USA
Charleston, SC
25 August 2012